A DEADLY BETROTHAL

An Ursula Blanchard Mystery

Fiona Buckley

CRÈME de la CRIME

This first world edition published 2017
in Great Britain and the USA by
Crème de la Crime, an imprint of
SEVERN HOUSE PUBLISHERS LTD of
Eardley House, 4 Uxbridge Street, London, W8 7SY.
Trade paperback edition first published
in Great Britain and the USA 2018 by
SEVERN HOUSE PUBLISHERS LTD.

British Library Cataloguing in Publication Data
A CIP catalogue record for this title is available from the British Library.

ISBN-13: 978-1-78029-097-3 (cased)
ISBN-13: 978-1-78029-580-0 (trade paper)
ISBN-13: 978-1-78010-881-0 (e-book)

Typeset by Palimpsest Book Production Ltd.,
Falkirk, Stirlingshire, Scotland.

This book is for Anne and Alan, the best and kindest of friends

ONE

Looking Up

I have never greatly liked fir woods. They're too dark. In this one, except at one end, where some felling had been done and young saplings had been planted, there were only a few scattered gleams of light from the sky and there was no undergrowth to speak of, just a carpet of fallen needles. They were quiet to walk on, too quiet. The stillness and the heavy shadows were intimidating.

There was a woodland of the ordinary kind at my Surrey home, Hawkswood, where the trees, beech and oak and chestnut, arched over the paths and in summer the canopy of leaves gave a green, underwater tinge to the light beneath, and here and there the ground was strewn with golden dapples because in places the sunlight could shine through. In that woodland, the leaves rustled in the wind and birds sang and in spring, there were bluebells. One would not come to this fir plantation to look for bluebells.

The fir wood measured just over a quarter of a mile each way and was valuable to its owners, the Harrison family. They harvested the straight pine trunks for making ships' masts and furniture and tapped the silver firs for scented oils. It was their best source of income. The rest of the property consisted only of the house, which was just across the lane and was appropriately named Firtrees, three fields where wheat was grown and a few cows pastured, and a small parcel of land in Cornwall, which was looked after by a resident steward, and wasn't very productive.

I knew the family quite well but on that day, late in the summer of 1579, I was here without their knowledge or permission, trespassing, in fact. With me were my reliable manservant Roger Brockley, and one of our grooms, a taciturn but helpful young man called Joseph. We had come in a cart because

Firtrees was several miles from Hawkswood and also we needed to bring a ladder and some rope and a small handcart which could be carried on board.

It was not the first time the wood had been searched, but the idea for this extra, unofficial visit had been suggested to me by my friend Christopher Spelton.

'Have you,' he said, 'thought of looking *up*?'

At the time, Christopher, Brockley and I were in the study at West Leys, the married home of my former ward, Kate Ferguson, and her husband, Eric Lake. It was a small, dull, workaday room, not a likely setting for discussions about the lurid or the dramatic. Christopher, however, was watching our faces seriously, his pleasant brown eyes asking for our reply. I was nonplussed at first, but Brockley was less so. He said: 'No. Come to think of it, we haven't.'

I demurred, saying that the wood had already been searched through and through. Brockley and I had helped on two occasions.

'You *can't* conceal anything much in that kind of wood; there aren't any thickets to hide things in,' I said. 'As for looking up – think how difficult it would be, hiding a body that way! I think he must have been taken away. If the poor lad is really dead . . .'

'Do you truly think that he might not be?' Brockley's voice was gentle but his grey-blue eyes were grave. There were wrinkles in his high forehead with its dusting of gold freckles. He was an intelligent man.

'No,' I said. 'I think he probably is. But hidden *that* way? Surely not.'

'There aren't many alternatives,' said Brockley, and standing there in that commonplace study, he explained why.

'Madam, you know that Firtrees isn't isolated. There's farmland beyond the wood and to either side of it, and when the boy disappeared there were men in the fields. There are two hamlets, one to the east and one to the west, and a well-used lane that passes through both, and no one, *no one*, labourer or villager, reported seeing a boy, dead or alive, in company or alone, along the road or across the fields, at the time in question. Some lone horsemen passed along the road but no carts that could have transported a body. At the back of the house, it's open heath and there's nowhere there to hide anything. Animals graze it; there are only a few scattered bushes, which were all examined. There were people about, too; someone was fetching a donkey in and someone else was milking goats. No one in the village on the far side saw anything, either. The wood is the only place.'

'I am strongly inclined to agree,' Master Spelton said.

'But if your idea is right, whoever did it would have needed a ladder!' I protested.

'That,' said Brockley grimly, 'could have been put in place in advance. At night, possibly. This was planned, I fancy.'

'I see,' I said.

It seemed almost ludicrous, to be discussing murder, and the ways in which bodies might be hidden, in that ordinary room with its desk and shelves, and the window with its pleasant view of low hills. We could hear sheep bleating somewhere.

But then, such incongruous occasions had been happening to me for most of my life. I continually longed for domestic peace, the normal life of a country lady, and I was continually being wrenched away from it, into unlikely and uncomfortable circumstances, where I had unlikely, uncomfortable and usually unfeminine duties to perform.

My name was – and is – Ursula Stannard. I was the widow of Hugh Stannard, my third husband, whom I had greatly loved. I had a married daughter, Meg, the child of Gerald Blanchard, my first husband. In addition, I had a son, Harry, a little boy of seven, who was the offspring of my second spouse, Matthew de la Roche. Also, I was half-sister to her majesty, Queen Elizabeth, since her father, King Henry the Eighth, had not been faithful to his queen Anne Boleyn but had had a brief liaison with one of her ladies in waiting, who became my mother.

Years after, I too went to court as a lady in waiting, to Queen Elizabeth. After Gerald's death from smallpox, I needed work, for I needed money. But my stipend was none too generous and when I had the opportunity of adding to it by undertaking a secret task, I seized the chance and so my unusual occupation began. Later, after I had learned of my relationship to the queen, I became trapped in that occupation, because a bond formed between us and when she called on me, as she and her councillors did now and then, to undertake tasks, sometimes even dangerous tasks, to help her, I could not refuse.

But this time, I was not acting under orders. Neither Queen Elizabeth, nor her Secretary of State, Sir Francis Walsingham, nor her Lord Treasurer, Sir William Cecil, Lord Burghley, had sent me to look for the body of a missing young boy. That had arisen quite differently. But somehow it seemed quite as necessary.

Or that is how I put it to myself. Others, perhaps more perceptive, have told me that I am a natural adventuress, that I respond to the call of mysterious and secretive tasks as wild geese take wing in response to each other's haunting calls.

At any rate, after being urged by both Brockley and Spelton, I agreed to put the matter to the test. 'Not that I believe it,' I said to them. 'I don't. I *can't*. Would anyone really dispose of a body in such a way? It would be so awkward. But all right, let us make sure.'

So here we were. I had dressed for prowling in fir woods, by borrowing a pair of breeches and a shirt and jacket from Brockley. I had boots on my feet. I had a gown with me so that if we did find anything I could look respectable when we reported it but for the moment I had left it on the handcart. Only, what could we do this time that hadn't been done before?

Well, we could do what Christopher had suggested. We could look upwards.

It was the one thing no one had thought of trying. We and the searchers who were here before us had examined that wood one tree at a time, but had we ever raised our eyes? No, we had not. Yet, above us, the silver firs in particular had thick, dark foliage, layers of it, shutting out the sky.

'We must be methodical,' said Brockley. 'The previous searches weren't methodical enough, in my opinion. Nothing could be hidden among the new saplings; we must concentrate on the mature wood. We could do it as though we were ploughing a field. We should work in a row, moving forward in a straight line from one end of the wood to the other, searching a swathe, as it were, and then we turn round, move along to start a new swathe, and work back along that.'

It made sense. We left our horse and cart, with the ladder and rope and the handcart still aboard, at the edge of the trees, positioned ourselves at one end of the wood and began, the three of us walking abreast and looking constantly upwards. I at once bumped into a tree trunk because I was staring upwards instead of looking where I was going. I muttered a curse, and at the same moment, Brockley also growled something under his breath because the same thing had happened to him. Joseph, for once, had something to say.

'It's as well there isn't any undergrowth,' he remarked. 'We'd all be catching our feet in it and tripping over!'

'We'd best take care,' said Brockley. 'Even if it slows us down.'

It did. An hour later, I had become thoroughly disgruntled. In fact, I was on the verge of suggesting that we forgot the whole absurd business and went home, when Joseph suddenly stopped short, pointed upwards and once more, broke his habitual silence. 'Up there,' he said. 'Look.'

Brockley and I came to his side and gazed up to where he was pointing. He was right. Amid the thick fir branches above us, there was a darker, denser patch. 'And there's fallen twigs and cones hereabout,' said Joseph, pointing. 'Not new ones. But summat's broken bits off the branches up there at some time or other.'

We moved about, seeking a clearer view. 'There's *something* up there,' Brockley said.

I stayed where I was, to act as a marker while the two of them fetched the ladder and the rope. For a while, I was alone among the trees. It made me feel obscurely afraid, not of any definite danger, but in a vague, amorphous way, as though the trees themselves were aware of me and watching me inimically. Now and then I looked uneasily up at the branches above me, wondering if the darker patch really meant anything. After all, stowing it up a tree was a most improbable way to dispose of a body. Two particularly thick branches, one above the

other, could create an illusion of something solid. Or it might
be the nest of some large bird, a kite or a goshawk.

But if it were not . . .

I was so nervous that I wanted to shout to Brockley and
Joseph, to summon them back, but they were probably out of
earshot and the silence of the wood was so solemn, so mysteriously powerful that I hesitated to break it.

At last I heard their voices, calling to me. I called back to
give them my direction and soon they appeared, carrying the
ladder between them. Brockley had the rope over his shoulder.
They stopped beneath the dark patch, and Brockley, craning
his neck, said that it was a long way up. 'We'll need the full
length of the ladder.'

It was a double ladder, which could be extended at need to
twice its original length. Joseph saw to it, firmly securing the
bolts that held the join in the middle. Then he and Brockley
heaved it into position and Brockley said: 'You're lighter than
me and younger, Joseph. Will you go up? Have your belt knife
ready. I hope it's really sharp. If not, take mine.'

'My knife's keen enough, Master Brockley,' Joseph assured
him. Brockley gave him the rope, and he started up the ladder.

He had to push his way past a good many boughs, causing
more twigs and fir cones to shower around us. Presently, he
all but disappeared from view. We waited. Then his voice,
slightly muffled by distance and fir foliage, came down to us.

'It's here! Or summat is – all wrapped in sacking and tied
up with twine, like a parcel. Rammed into a fork. Can't get
the rope round it. Need both hands for that. Only got one to
spare! Daren't let go my handhold! Can use my knife, just
about! I'll cut it loose and let it fall. Sorry!'

'If it's what we think, you're not to see it,' Brockley said
to me. 'Madam, please move away.'

Manservants don't usually give orders to their employers
but I had no quarrel with Brockley over this. I withdrew to a
distance. High above, Joseph used his knife and freed what
he had found. I heard it crashing and bumping down through
the branches and then saw a dark mass tumble to the ground,
to land with a thud at Brockley's feet.

We waited while Joseph came down the ladder and then he

and Brockley, placing themselves between me and the thing on the ground, stooped to investigate it.

There were exclamations. Brockley said: 'There's more than one sack; there's four layers at least.' He and Joseph both worked together for a moment, and then Joseph stumbled aside and was sick.

'Brockley!' I shouted.

'Wait, madam! Just a moment!' He had risen to his feet with a sack in his hands. He was fumbling with something that seemed to be caught in the fabric. Then he came towards me.

'Brockley?' I said again.

'It was as we feared, madam. Poor lad. Well, he can have a decent burial now. I found this caught in one of the sacks.'

He held out his right hand and I looked at what lay in the palm. And then looked again, and after that, raised my eyes to Brockley's. 'So now we know,' he said.

I nodded, bleakly. 'We only suspected it before but now we're sure. What a vile business.'

To tell the truth, the matter wasn't only vile; it was also, in the end, embarrassing. Even Lord Burghley, who is an honest statesman and knows that I did nothing wrong, wishes I hadn't done anything at all. As for Sir Francis Walsingham, although he too knows perfectly well that I am innocent of any misdoing, was nevertheless so infuriated by the outcome of my meddling that he declared he wished never to see or hear of me again.

Only the queen is untroubled, and they're none too pleased with her!

TWO

Interconnectness

On the face of it, I became entangled in the unsavoury events of 1579 through a series of coincidences, but they aren't as random as they appear. Surrey, like most counties, has a society of its own. Some of its principal families have been there since the Conquest (or even before) and through the centuries they have become very interconnected.

Oh, there are changes sometimes, of course there are. Families move out of the county and new ones move in. There are marriages which take young people – daughters mostly – elsewhere, or bring in brides from other places. County society isn't closed. But it is still cohesive enough to make it wise, when in the company of people one doesn't know very well, to guard one's tongue.

For instance, when dining out and encountering new faces, don't ask your neighbour who the fierce-looking lady at the far end of the table is, yes, the one in purple, with the vast open ruff and the high-bridged nose and the pursed mouth. She may well turn out to be the mother-in-law of your neighbour's sister. And when watching a tennis match at a gathering where, again, there are people you don't know well, or at all, don't enquire of a chance-met acquaintance if he knows who the noisy man over there is. Your new acquaintance is all too likely to say, oh yes, that's my second cousin.

That being so, there was nothing very strange in the fact that Eric Lake, who owned a small manor near Guildford and had married my ward Kate Ferguson, was the half-brother of a man called George Harrison, whose wife Marjorie had from girlhood been a friend of my Aunt Tabitha. Aunt Tabitha was an example of a girl who had left the county as a bride, for though she had married my Uncle Herbert and gone to live with him in Sussex, she had been born and brought up in Surrey.

I knew that Eric Lake had a relative called Marjorie Harrison but I didn't know of her link to my Aunt Tabitha until the grim business of that year began. There was nothing odd about that, either. Nor was there anything odd in the fact that a man who lived in Sheffield and whose business was buying fur pelts and turning them into cloaks and coverlets and the like should from time to time make the long journey to Penzance in Cornwall. Rare furs from the New World arrived at Penzance regularly. The only real coincidences in the affair were that two women, respectively called Catherine Parker and Alice Devine, chanced to die that spring – and that just then, Aunt Tabitha finally lost patience with Uncle Herbert's increasingly irritable temper.

She wrote to me, asking me to visit her at their Sussex home, Faldene, and I decided to go.

My relationship with Uncle Herbert and Aunt Tabitha had never been easy. When my mother was sent away from court, pregnant by a man she would not name, her brother Herbert and his wife took her in. Their parents were dead and there was no one else to help her. My uncle and aunt did give her a home, and when I was born, they gave me a home as well, yes, and an education too, for I was allowed to share my cousins' tutors. But in other ways, they were not very kind either to my mother or to me. They took satisfaction in reminding us that we were dependent on their charity (which might be withdrawn if we offended them), and I was beaten for the smallest misdoings. Unhappiness wore my mother down and she died when I was sixteen. However, I suppose I can claim that I avenged her, for when I was twenty, I eloped with my cousin Mary's betrothed, Gerald Blanchard, and married him.

Uncle Herbert and Aunt Tabitha were understandably furious, and even more furious when, later on, as a result of one of my early ventures as a secret agent, my uncle was arrested and spent some time in the Tower of London. Yet the breach was mended to some extent in the end, because they called on me for help in a crisis, involving their son, my cousin Edward. After that, we had an up-and-down relationship. They held by the old religion, and thought themselves very virtuous and were appalled when I gave birth to Harry. Oh, I had once

been married to his father, Matthew de la Roche, but the
marriage was annulled and I then became the wife of Hugh
Stannard, my dear Hugh. After he was gone, I met Matthew
again, and we came together briefly, with Harry as a result.

As I pointed out, in a letter to my scandalized relatives,
Matthew was a Papist, I had married him according to
Catholic rites and in their view had surely still been married
when we met again, so why were they complaining? There
was silence after that, but although I sometimes visited my
second home, Withysham, which was in Sussex and not far
from Faldene, I didn't go to see them. Until Aunt Tabitha's
cry for help arrived.

*. . . I fear that your Uncle Herbert is grown very irascible,
for he still suffers from gout and now he has the joint evil,
which pains him greatly. I pity him most sincerely. But I would
be glad of your company for a while, if you can spare a little
time. Believe me, I need distraction sometimes . . .*

'Well, ma'am,' said my tirewoman, Frances Dale, 'you
haven't visited Withysham for a long while now. This would
be an opportunity. I like Withysham. It has such a calm
atmosphere.'

'Probably because it was once an abbey, before the monas-
teries were disbanded,' I said. I looked at the letter in my
hand. 'I feel sorry for my uncle and aunt. They're growing
old and my uncle is ailing and it's true that they did give me
and my mother a roof over our heads and enough to eat, even
though . . .'

I didn't go on. Even now, when I was a woman of property
and experience and status and was myself nearing middle age,
the memory of Aunt Tabitha's birch was still bitter.

'It would be a kindness to them,' Dale ventured.

I smiled at her. Dale was her maiden name and out of habit
I still called her that, but in my service she had met and married
Roger Brockley and no one ever had more trustworthy and
careful servants than those two. Though, for Dale, being my
tirewoman had sometimes been a demanding post. I had on
several occasions led her into danger and Dale didn't like
danger. She had pockmarks from a childhood attack of
smallpox and when she was frightened they always seemed

more noticeable. I had caused them to be noticeable rather too often and I regretted it.

However, they were not much in evidence now, and her slightly protuberant blue eyes were smiling back to me. I knew that she liked Withysham, and she approved of acts of kindness.

We were in the small parlour at Hawkswood House and looking together at the letter when Sybil Jester, my gentle-woman companion, came into the room. I held the letter up. 'This is from my Aunt Tabitha at Faldene. She wants me to visit her.'

'I saw the courier arrive,' said Sybil. 'I wondered who had sent him. Is your aunt in some kind of difficulty?'

'It would be very unlike my Aunt Tabitha to send for me unless she was in trouble!' I agreed with some asperity. 'My uncle is unwell and I think she's finding life wearisome. Admittedly, it doesn't sound too serious.'

'Shall you go?' asked Sybil.

I hesitated and then made up my mind. 'Yes,' I said. 'I'll go. Is the courier still here?'

'In the kitchen, taking refreshment,' said Sybil.

'Ask Wilder to tell him to wait. I'll write an answer for him to take back to Faldene. We'll set off . . . let me see, I need a day to prepare. The day after tomorrow, I think.'

The next day was taken up by the preparations for a journey, with deciding what to take and who to take, as well. I had instantly accepted Dale's hint that we might stay at Withysham, rather than with my uncle and aunt at Faldene. Withysham was only three miles from Faldene and if I based myself there, I could have Harry with me. I couldn't very well take him to Faldene, since my uncle and aunt disapproved of his existence.

Sybil had met Uncle Herbert and Aunt Tabitha and didn't care for them. Therefore, I left Sybil in charge at Hawkswood, along with my tall, calm steward, Adam Wilder. Adam was the son of one of Hugh's tenant farmers and had been at Hawkswood all his life. He had worked his way up from odd-job boy to steward, had married one of the maids, been widowed and had four children who were all out in service elsewhere. Hawkswood was his life and I could trust him completely.

Taking Harry of course meant taking his nursemaid, Tessie. A timid little thing when she first came to the house, Tessie had grown into a sensible and pretty young woman. Harry loved her, and I had lately noticed that the young groom Joseph was paying attention to her. It would be a suitable match and I wished to encourage it. I decided that Joseph should come, to help with the horses and continue courting Tessie.

I travelled, therefore, with Tessie, Harry, Dale and Brockley. Brockley rode his cob Mealy and I rode my black mare, Jewel, while the rest of the party went in our coach, with its team of four, and my elderly coachman, Arthur Watts, did the driving. I no longer used Arthur for long journeys because he was getting old and tired easily, but he knew the road to Withysham well, and if we set off early, we could get there by mid-afternoon.

We did this, and on arrival, we found that the Withysham steward, a competent middle-aged man called Robert Hanley, was well prepared for us.

'I didn't know if you would dine on the road, madam, and I have made preparations in case you did not. The squab pie only needs to be heated, and I have mutton chops ready to be fried. Hot water is ready so that you can all wash when you choose. I have had towels and facecloths placed in all your rooms in readiness, and a tray of wine in yours, madam.' Hanley was an excellent man.

Hawkswood was my preferred home, but Withysham had been a gift from the queen, for my services as an agent, and I treasured it for that reason. Besides, although it was in some ways a shadowy place, with narrow windows and low ceilings and a feeling of austerity which probably came from its history as a women's abbey, Dale was right about its tranquil atmosphere. It was restful.

However, I had little time to enjoy its atmosphere. Next morning, leaving Harry in Tessie's charge, I took Dale and Brockley and with Dale perched behind Brockley on the cob, we set out for Faldene on horseback.

Faldene was an old house. Indeed, mine was an old family. My ancestors had lived there since before the Conquest and Faldene was not only the name of our home; it was also our surname. The house had undergone many changes through the years; indeed, through the centuries. It was still thatched, as it had always been, and its hall had the narrow, lance-headed windows of bygone days, but at some point, before I was born, it had acquired a gatehouse and a modern wing, with mullioned windows. The house had a beautiful position, on the side of a hill, with its fields spreading down the hillside into the valley below and a view of the downs to the south. I never saw it without thinking: *I could have been so happy here as a girl. If only . . .*

If only my uncle and aunt had been more gentle. They still kept the household sternly in order. As soon as we were through the gatehouse, grooms appeared at a run, and within moments, we were out of our saddles and the horses were being led away, while a butler – a new man that I hadn't seen before – was leading us inside. He took us straight to the great hall, where we found my uncle and aunt playing cards.

The hall was as I remembered it; the rushes underfoot fresh and mixed with rosemary, the walnut panelling polished. I had never liked the one tapestry, which depicted the assassination of Julius Caesar in gruesome detail. I glanced at it once and then glanced away, repelled as always by the graphic portrayal of blood. My aunt and uncle presumably admired it.

My uncle stood up as the butler announced us, reaching for a walking stick that had been propped against the card table. Then he swore and sat down again. Aunt Tabitha left her seat and came to meet us. It was a long time since I had last seen her and she had aged. Her face was wrinkled now and her plain black gown hung loosely on a shrunken frame. Her hair, which had once been brown, was coiled into a net at the back and topped by a white cap but as far I could see, it was now entirely grey.

'Aunt Tabitha. Uncle Herbert,' I said formally, bobbing respectfully. So did Dale, while Brockley made a bow.

'Sorry I can't stand up for long,' said my uncle gruffly. 'Gout and bad joints.' Unlike his wife, Uncle Herbert had put on weight. He always had been fleshy; now he was gross, with sagging, red-veined cheeks. His brown doublet looked as though his breakfast had splashed something on to it. There had once been a vague family resemblance between us, since his hair was black like mine and we had the same greenish hazel eyes, but little of that resemblance was now noticeable.

'I'm so sorry,' I said.

'Refreshments, Alderton,' Aunt Tabitha said sharply to the butler and I noticed that her dark, snapping eyes at least were unchanged. The butler vanished as if by magic and I knew that a maidservant with a tray would appear in his stead within a minute or two. My aunt looked at the Brockleys and said: 'I see that you have your usual entourage, Ursula, and have brought them into my presence as if they were your kin, instead of sending them to the kitchens. You never did have a proper sense of what was fitting. Well, be seated, all of you, since that's what I suppose you expect, niece.'

I had come in answer to an appeal from her, but she never could resist prodding me. I made no reply. Brockley and Dale tactfully took unassuming stools. I placed myself on a settle and said the appropriate things, asking after the health of my uncle and aunt, sympathizing with Uncle Herbert about his swollen joints, enquiring after my cousins. The firstborn, Francis, was in Norway, attached to the embassy there. 'It's a permanent position; he works with whoever is the ambassador,' Aunt Tabitha said. He had a wife and a family but none of them had been back to England for years.

The second boy, Edward, had died long since and his widow had married again and gone to Gloucestershire, taking her two little girls with her. 'We hear from them now and then. They are all well,' said my aunt. Her own two daughters were also married and both lived some distance away. I learned that they too were in touch on occasion but rarely visited Faldene.

While all this was going on, the expected refreshments arrived, but Uncle Herbert picked up a cake, bit it, and then glared at the maidservant who brought them and barked: 'These saffron cakes are yesterday's. I know there was a fresh baking this morning; I smelt it. Take these away! Bring us something that's still warm!' The maidservant went pink and scuttled away. 'What's the matter with this house today?' Uncle Herbert demanded, of the air.

It was actually a reasonable question, for as I sat there, making suitable conversation, I had noticed that after all, the house was *not* quite as orderly as usual. There was a sideboard in the hall, where there was a display of silver, but today there was a half-unrolled scroll of paper there as well, held open by a misplaced flagon, creating an oddly untidy effect. Somewhere, I could hear hurrying footsteps and a woman's voice chivvying someone, and on a low table I had observed a big hamper, its lid thrown back, and what looked like clothes inside. Also, as the maidservant opened the door to leave, I saw a man hurry past with a second hamper in his arms.

'Are you expecting to travel somewhere soon?' I asked my aunt.

'I'm not,' said Uncle Herbert. 'But *she* is, yes. A lot of women's nonsense, that's what I say.'

Aunt Tabitha took no notice of him. 'I had a letter yesterday,' she said. 'From Marjorie Harrison. Is the name familiar to you?'

'Well, yes, in a distant way,' I said. 'She's connected to Master Lake – the man my ward, Kate Ferguson, has married.'

'That's right. Your ward has married Eric, has she? I didn't know you knew him,' said Aunt Tabitha. 'Marjorie married one of Master Lake's half-brothers. They're much older than Eric is. His mother married twice and had Eric when she wasn't far off fifty. I wonder it didn't kill her,' said my aunt with a sniff. 'But to keep to the point, Marjorie is actually a very old friend of mine. I've known her since I was a girl. My parents followed the custom of sending their children to other households to learn social graces from people who wouldn't indulge them as parents are apt to do. Not that I ever did. I was always firm with you children, as no doubt you recall.'

She had been much firmer with me than with her own offspring. Once more, however, I held my tongue.

'When I was about twelve,' said my aunt, 'I was sent to a family called Dacre, near Leatherhead. You know Leatherhead, I suppose – it's a small town in north Surrey.' I nodded. 'The Dacres had two little girls of their own,' said Aunt Tabitha.

'Marjorie and Catherine, both younger than I, but we made
friends and have remained so. Catherine was the younger one
and she was a good girl. Her parents arranged for her to wed
a Hampshire gentleman, well off and with land, and she did
as she was bid and it was a happy marriage, though there were
no children. But Marjorie!'

Aunt Tabitha's voice was full of exasperation. 'Young people
should be guided by their elders!' This was an intentional dig
at my outrageous theft of my cousin Mary's betrothed. Yet
again, I replied with silence. Disappointed of a reaction, Aunt
Tabitha continued.

'Marjorie fell in love – *love*! Sentimental nonsense! The
man she fell in love with was George Harrison, one of your
Master Lake's half-brothers. He didn't come from a family of
any standing – they were smallholders and poor ones at that
– the kind of people whose corn gets wheat rust and their
poultry and pigs are forever getting diseases too. George didn't
choose to stay there once he was grown up. He said his younger
brother Edmund was welcome to the family holding and with
that, George went out into the world to make his way, which
one could respect, except that instead of seeking a post in a
worthy house, where he might hope to earn well and acquire
savings or even gifts of land in due course, he went and
apprenticed himself to the furrier's trade!'

Aunt Tabitha paused here to draw breath and also to snort
in disapproval. 'Still, it might have turned out well,' she said
grudgingly. 'But when his apprenticeship was finished, instead
of allying himself to a successful business and hoping for a
partnership one day, he must needs strike out on his own.
Foolishness! He started a business in Guildford, buying pelts
and fashioning them into cloaks and coverlets and rugs! But
he had no capital, so he couldn't buy the best pelts and he
didn't do well.'

Again, a pause, this time to make *tch* noises. To encourage
the narrative further, I said: 'But Marjorie married him?'

'He was good-looking and had a way with him,' said my
aunt. 'Yes, Marjorie was quite wild for him. And her three
years older than him; not the thing at all, to my mind. Her
parents forbade the match but she ran away to him and they

were so outraged that they refused to give her a dowry. Perhaps if there had been some money in the bargain, it might have made a difference. Marjorie had a son the following year, and two years after that, George Harrison found another woman and then *he* ran off. He did it for money. The other woman was a childless widow who had inherited a healthy fortune. He abandoned his wife and child, took most of what savings he had and went off – to Sheffield, I think. Thirty-four years ago, that was. He did leave Marjorie the business, and she sold it for what it was worth – which wasn't that much – and found herself a cottage not far from her parents. They helped her a little after that, I believe, but not over-generously. Well, she deserved no better.'

She said that with a raised chin, visibly expecting me to argue. I had run off with Gerald, after all. I smiled. And waited.

'Well,' said my aunt, taking up the tale again, 'her parents died, within a few months of each other, and just after that, Marjorie's sister Catherine was widowed and Catherine came to live with her. Catherine had money, and property too, something to bring in rents, so they were comfortable enough. They moved into a bigger house and I think had quite a contented life together. But now Catherine too has died, and . . . well, see for yourself.'

She went to the sideboard and fetched the scroll, which she handed to me. 'This is a letter from Marjorie.'

I took it. Aunt Tabitha's letter to me had been a plea for help, but it was nothing more than a mild grumble compared to this. Marjorie Harrison's writing was wild, the wording disjointed, with sentences that ran into each other. She was desperate; she did not know what to do; she implored her old friend to come to her, to help her, advise her. She was sending for her brother-in-law Edmund as well. Catherine had died ten days previously and . . .

I was going to write soon anyway; we haven't been in touch as often as we should but of course I would have written to tell you, only there was so much to do, to arrange, the funeral was so distressing, it rained all day, though many people came, which was a compliment to

*dear Catherine, and some of the guests stayed the night
but they all went the next day and only a few days after
that, I hardly know how to write it, I can hardly believe
it myself, dearest Tabitha, I beg you to come to me. I
don't know what to do . . .* **George has come back . . .!**

'I wanted you to see this,' said Aunt Tabitha, 'and not just
because it explains why, when you arrive after being sent for,
you find me preparing to rush away to somewhere else. I . . .'

'Women are all fools!' That was Uncle Herbert again. 'Just
hysterics, making something out of nothing. All this fuss
because her husband's come back to the home he shouldn't
have left in the first place. *Alderton!*' His shout brought the
butler, not exactly running, but close to it. 'Get Verney! My
valet! Bring him. I want him to help me to my room. I can't
stand all this female fussing! Hurry up, man!'

But the valet was already there, and had probably been
hovering nearby in case he was needed. Like the butler, he was
new since I had last been to Faldene, a brisk, strong fellow who
took no notice of the rest of us, but supplied a powerful shoulder
for Uncle Herbert to lean on. The two of them left the hall.

'Your uncle,' said Aunt Tabitha bitterly, 'is like an angry
bear, all the time. It's the pain, and not being able to move
about freely, and I can understand that, but he behaves as though
it were my fault, which it isn't, and sometimes I don't know
where to turn! I won't be sorry to get away, even to another
crisis! It will give me a rest from him and the crisis won't be
mine, after all. And Ursula, I want you to come with me.'

'But . . . will Mistress Harrison want to accommodate me
and my servants? She doesn't know us and perhaps she hasn't
room . . .'

'There's an inn nearby where you can stay. It's called the
Running Horse; it's a comfortable place. That's not a difficulty.
Ursula, you have a certain reputation – for . . . for dealing
with situations. You know the world. You may be able to help.'

THREE

A Glossy Black Pelt

J ust what Aunt Tabitha expected me to do wasn't clear. Was I supposed to persuade George Harrison to go away again? If so, she must think I had magical powers of some kind! I couldn't imagine how I would set about it.

But I had long ago sensed that Aunt Tabitha's hardness wasn't the whole truth of her. When I read the pleading letter that had brought me to Sussex now, and on that occasion years ago, when she called on me for help, I had glimpsed another Aunt Tabitha, who needed aid and kindness from others. Life with Uncle Herbert had probably never been easy. The hardness was perhaps a suit of armour that she had donned in self-defence. Faced with Marjorie's desperation, my aunt, like me, had wondered what on earth she was supposed to do about it. What she wanted from me now was probably just support. Aunt Tabitha, who had been so harsh with Ursula the little girl, who still couldn't stop herself from pinpricking me, nevertheless needed the adult Ursula to lean on, and it was not the first time.

'Very well,' I said.

Aunt Tabitha despatched a groom with a note giving Mistress Harrison notice of our arrival and I sent Brockley and Dale back to Withysham to fetch some luggage for the three of us, and to let the household there know that I would be away for a few days. I didn't worry about Harry. When he was very young, he had always cried if I went away but Tessie had always been there for him, reliable as the Pole Star. Now, he had become quite easy about it, while I disliked being parted him. He looked like his father, which meant a good deal to me.

I sometimes wondered about that. With Matthew de la Roche, I had known great passion, but also much unhappiness, for he supported the dispossessed Scottish queen, Mary Stuart, and her spurious claim to Elizabeth's throne. Physically, we struck such sparks from each other that I sometimes wondered why our beds didn't burst into flame, but he was Elizabeth's enemy, and in the end, he was mine too. He was dead now. But I would never forget him, never quite be done with him, because of Harry.

The Brockleys came back with bulging saddlebags and reported that Harry had taken the news with equanimity and gone happily off for a riding lesson with Joseph. No doubt Tessie would be on hand, I thought, smiling inwardly, and she and Joseph would seize the chance to do some more courting. I and the Brockleys spent the night at Faldene and set off with Aunt Tabitha the next morning.

My aunt and uncle rarely travelled and didn't keep a coach. Aunt Tabitha and her tall, stern maid Annette therefore made the journey to Marjorie Harrison's home in a small cart, with a leather canopy that could be put up if it rained. They both dressed elegantly, however, Annette in dark blue, Aunt Tabitha in green and blue brocade. Their ruffs were pristine, their hats fashionable, and although they were surrounded by baggage and the cart was drawn by one of Faldene's hairy-heeled plough horses, the two of them sat stiffly upright all the way, exuding as much dignity as they would in a ceremonial coach.

The groom who had been sent to warn Mistress Harrison that we were coming had returned, only to find that he was to go straight back again, this time driving the cart. He was elderly and looked annoyed but of course he dared not say so. Faldene servants were always respectful. Those who weren't, didn't stay at Faldene long. Dale, who was not fond of riding, even pillion, shared the cart, sitting at the back, while Brockley and I were on horseback as before.

We were there before noon. I had vaguely supposed that Marjorie Harrison's home would be a country cottage of some kind, suitable as a residence for two husbandless sisters. It proved, however, to be a tall, narrow house on the north side of the little town of Leatherhead. There was a mews at the back, to which the groom took the horses and the cart while the rest of us walked through a small front garden, where hollyhocks and foxgloves and larkspur were in bloom, and climbed the steps to the front door, which opened before anyone could knock. A plump woman with greying brown hair and a lined, worried face appeared and instantly flung herself into Aunt Tabitha's arms, crying: 'Oh, I am so glad to see you, Tabby! It's been so dreadful! Dreadful! What am I to do? It's a nightmare!'

I marvelled that there was anyone in the world who could call my formidable aunt *Tabby*, and she herself said: 'Come, Marjorie, let's all get inside and talk about it, shall we?' in her usual no-nonsense voice, but when she disengaged herself, I noticed that she did it gently, and kept an arm round Marjorie as they led the way indoors.

Brockley and Dale brought the luggage in and put it down in the entrance hall, and then followed us into a parlour. It looked dusty and untidy, as though the distraction in the house had infected its contents. There were no rushes on the floor and the thick and probably costly rug of glossy black fur in front of the empty hearth was sadly in need of brushing, for there were crumbs strewn on it. The beautifully embroidered cushions on the two settles were all askew.

The room was already occupied, by a small, sweet-faced woman, fair, with bright blue eyes, and two young people, a boy and a girl who looked as though they were in their mid-teens. The boy was thickset and ginger, with features in the process of maturing, and already including a beak of a nose. The girl, however, closely resembled the woman and was obviously her daughter. They stood up as we entered.

'My sister-in-law, Lisa,' said Marjorie. 'Wife of George's brother Edmund. And her twins, Jane and Thomas. They're fifteen years old. Lisa, this is my old friend Mistress Tabitha Faldene, and her niece, Mistress Ursula Stannard, and here . . .'

Her voice checked uncertainly. I expected that. I often met this situation. Dale and Brockley were to me much more than just servants. I had long since come to see them as close friends, almost relatives, and I expected other people to accept them as such and not try to banish them to the kitchen quarters. I didn't say so, however. Once again, I held my peace in Aunt

Tabitha's presence though this time, I did so with just a trace of malice, leaving the explanations to her.

She obliged, primly. 'These are Roger Brockley, my niece's manservant, and Frances, who is his wife and also Mistress Stannard's tirewoman. She regards them as family members rather than servants.' Her voice expressed her low opinion of this attitude but she didn't enlarge. 'My maid Annette you already know, of course.'

Annette showed signs of wishing to leave us, but Marjorie shook her head and said: 'No, no, Annette, stay, like the others,' and the fair woman said she was pleased to meet us.

She had a lisp, I noticed. The word *pleased* actually sounded more like *pleathed.* Suddenly, a memory surfaced. Surely she had been among Eric Lake's relatives when he and Kate were married! The boy and girl respectively made a bow and a curtsey.

We were all invited to seat ourselves and as we did so, a maid hurried in with a tray bearing a flagon of wine, some glasses and a platter of pasties of various kinds, hastily assembled, by the look of them. The maid's cap was lopsided and there were stains on her apron. Marjorie didn't appear to notice. She said, 'Thank you, Mary,' dismissing her with a wave of the hand, and it was Annette, in response to a nod from my aunt, who distributed the wine and pasties. Marjorie took a long drink from her glass and then put it down with a bang and tumbled out her story.

'I'm thankful to have you here! I'm sorry I had to call on you, Tabby, but I need . . . I need help, support, *something!* It was bad enough that my sister – my dear Catherine – should die. It was just a cold or so it seemed, but it went to her chest and . . . oh, I don't want to describe it all. I watched her die. Poor, poor Cat. And then there was the funeral to arrange, and I had to see a lawyer about Cat's will; she left everything she had to me. She has looked after me, darling, darling Cat! I thought: I must be glad and grateful and try to be brave. I must find some other friend to share my home . . . but I didn't expect to be saddled with the companion I've got! One morning – only a few days after the funeral– there was a bang on the door and I opened it myself as Mary was busy and . . .

I didn't recognize him at first! I asked him who he was and what his business was and he said, *Don't you know me, my dear Marjorie? I'm George, your long-lost husband. I've come home.*

'I couldn't believe it! It's thirty-something years since he went and I'd never set eyes on him in all that time. He ran off with a red-headed whore called Alice Devine. Not much divinity about that one! A widow, sitting smugly on what her husband had left her and on the lookout for another man. She wasn't even pretty! I saw her a few times, before she went away with George. She had a house near us in Guildford – that's where we were living. Plump, plain, practical, that was Alice. Well, off they went to Sheffield – she was born there. George told me; he did write to me once or twice. He started a new furrier's business there, using her money mostly. With *her* money, he could afford good pelts and an assistant and smart premises to work in, and he could build his business up properly. You have to have something behind you to get a business going – he said that to me, many times, while we were together. I should have guessed what would happen!'

There were tears in her eyes as an ancient wound began once more to throb. 'We were so poor when we were together,' she said. 'It was hard for George; I did understand that. He tried to build up a business but he just couldn't . . . *couldn't* . . . get the foundations laid, so to speak. Some of his customers would buy furs elsewhere and bring them to be made into cloaks and hats and so forth, but George wanted to be able to offer them furs himself, a choice of good ones, to provide a complete service. Customers would like that. But it would only work if he could lay in a supply of quality furs and that was the difficulty. He needed capital for that and he didn't have it. He tried and tried. I'll give him that. He *tried.*'

'It must have been hard indeed,' I said sympathetically.

'It was awful! First of all, he wasn't known, so work came in slowly, and when he did get it, he would try to give a prompt service, and he used to curse the winter, the grey days and the dark evenings, because it was so hard to work well in such bad light and we couldn't afford enough candles. He used to get angry with me for using candles in the house but of course

I had to use *some*! And on top of that, to buy furs, he needed to travel and that cost money as well as the pelts themselves, and he couldn't buy the quality he wanted or the quantity and anyway, buying meant going away and while he was doing that, he couldn't make things at the same time . . . he needed an assistant but we couldn't afford that either. I tried to learn to make things but skins aren't like fabrics; stitching them is quite different. I never acquired much skill and that made him angry too. He always seemed to be angry. He sometimes talked in his sleep – cursed in his sleep, cursed not having enough money. I came to feel afraid of him. He resented it that other men were able to make money while he couldn't. All the time, there was this undercurrent of rage . . . I lived with it, day in and day out!'

She broke off for a moment, wiping her eyes, before adding: 'I tried not to mind. I loved him! I'd chosen to run away to him and I was ready to stand by that choice. But it was so hard, so hard. He wasn't afraid of work but no matter how he toiled, we couldn't seem to drag ourselves out of that . . . that *morass* of poverty. Sometimes we didn't have enough to eat.'

'I'm so sorry,' I said inadequately.

'And then,' said Marjorie bitterly, 'he met Alice Devine. She had plenty of money. Buckets of it! And she fell for him, hard! He boasted that she would do anything for him. He left me for her. I sold the Guildford business; he told me I could, but he only did that for our son's sake; he said as much! Not that it was worth much, anyway. My parents wouldn't take me back though they did give me a small allowance. I moved into a little cottage with a low rent. I could just about survive. I brought up Robert, my little boy, as best I could. But when Robert was fifteen, he left home to go into service and then my parents died and Catherine was widowed and everything changed. She joined me and together we found this house and we made a life together.'

She sighed, a sigh heavy with nostalgia. 'We were happy! Cat and I used to enjoy music and embroidery, and we would go to church and walk round markets together, and entertain our neighbours . . . all trivial things, you might say, but it was a life that suited us. But now! George comes back!

'He said: *Alice has died and I'm on my own and I don't like it. I'm nigh on fifty-seven years old now and I can't work as hard as I did and without her behind me, well, the business has failed. I've sold what stock I had – I didn't get much for it – and I'm prone to catching cold and my colds often settle on my chest; I need a woman to look after me. I've got a horse and a pack mule. I believe you've got room for them. I've kept my eye on you, all these years, you know. There's always those will send news if they're paid for it.*

'And I can guess what he meant by *that*,' said Marjorie viciously. 'Cat and I had a gardener, a man I never liked much. He used to work for my parents but after they were gone, and Cat joined me, he asked us to take him on. When Cat came, we could afford it. George knew him slightly. George *told* him to try and work for me! I questioned him and got him to admit it. He'd been taking money from George to pass on news of me! I've dismissed him now!'

Distracted she might be, but Marjorie was clearly still capable of wielding authority. 'A spy, that's all he was! But what am I to do about George? I tried to say I wouldn't let him in, but he just laughed at me and said he was still my husband in the eyes of the law and the church and what was mine was his. He said that in law, this is *his* house. How can I get rid of him?' She paused for breath and I said: 'Where is he now?'

'Upstairs, in my back bedroom. Having a rest, he says, not that he needs one. He may be prone to colds but he hasn't got one now! He's not in *my* room. I wouldn't go that far, husband or no!' said Marjorie. 'But he's eating three meals a day . . . wanting his clothes looked after; his hateful *smart* clothes; dear God, before his business failed, he obviously had the chance to buy fine clothes and how he enjoyed it! He disrupts the whole house . . . I could kill him! *I could kill him!*'

'Marjorie sent for us, for me and Edmund,' said Lisa. 'We arrived two hours ago and Edmund went straight up to see him. Edmund said it was a chance for a fraternal reunion. They're both upstairs now. Neither of us have seen George since our wedding day and that was nearly a quarter of a century ago. He was invited, in spite of what he'd done, and he came, but I only saw him that once.'

Aunt Tabitha cocked her head. 'I think I hear someone coming down the stairs. Perhaps it's them.'

The door opened. 'Yes, here they are,' said Thomas as he and his sister once more came respectfully to their feet.

Marjorie, in a strangled voice, introduced the brothers. They were a striking pair. Edmund was a big, square fellow with pale brown eyes and a high colour. He had a prominent, aquiline nose, a thick curled mouth and a tangle of curls, greying from their original sandy. He reminded me of a statue I had once seen, of some Roman emperor or other. Edmund wore a fine wool doublet and matching hose in a violet shade but he would have looked at home in a toga. If he had spent his boyhood on an unproductive smallholding, he had clearly prospered in adult life. I glanced at his hair and its sandy traces and then looked at Thomas and thought that one day, the boy would closely resemble his father. He already had the aquiline nose and he was even developing the same shape of mouth.

The errant George, who was visibly the elder of the two, was taller and thinner than his brother, with jutting cheekbones, though he had the same sensual mouth and the same light brown eyes. His clothes were certainly good but they were well-worn. The pale green doublet and the puffed breeches were of lightweight velvet, suitable for summer, rippling softly and gleaming like water in the light, but there were signs of scuffing on the elbows and a small darn on the left hip of the breeches. His knitted stockings and the satin slashings on his sleeves were deep blue but again, there was a darn on one stocking. Yet his big shoe buckles were silver and he wore a handsome pendant. Amethyst, I thought, in a silver setting. Yes, this was a man who had once prospered but had lately fallen on hard times.

After Marjorie's stiff introductions, greetings were exchanged. An uneasy silence fell.

With George in the room, his wife could hardly ask advice on how to rid herself of him. Aunt Tabitha, however, always a stickler for the proprieties, broke the hush by enquiring after George's health, learned that he had lately suffered from a cough, and began to recommend remedies. 'Horehound is one of the best, I find, and the most effective way to prepare the linctus is . . .'

The recipe was fully described and then Lisa gallantly added a contribution. 'Mullein is a useful remedy too. You can make an infusion of it, or an ointment to rub into the chest. The way to do it . . .'

The words *useful* and *chest* came out as *utheful* and *chetht*, and as she spoke, I saw George's glance light on her with a curious intensity. It was noticeable, enough to make her stop speaking and return his glance with a puzzled look.

He answered the unspoken question. 'Sister-in-law, I have only seen you once before as far as I know, at your wedding – when you were a slender lass in a blue dress rather too big for you – but I could almost swear that I saw you once in Cornwall, though I didn't realize who you were. It was some years ago, in Penzance, at an auction of rare furs from the New World. I have long been in the habit of travelling there from time to time to bid when consignments come in. There are a couple of ships plying out of Penzance that bring skins in regularly. I have an arrangement with a friend there, to let me know when auctions are to be. It's well worth the trouble of journeying to Cornwall.'

'I'm thure it is,' said Lisa. For some reason, she sounded nervous.

'Indeed,' George said, still studying her in that oddly intense fashion. 'It's amazing, the kind of furs those ships bring in. There are glorious skins from some creature rather like a leopard, only the pelts are bigger and the spots are differently patterned. They come from the central part of the New World, where there are jungles. And there are tawny skins from some animal like a small lion, and skins from bears and a multitude of sleek, glossy little animals . . . oh, it was a good many years ago, but I am sure I saw you at one of those sales. You were interested in one very beautiful black bear pelt. I am sure I heard you say that it would make a fine rug for a hearth, perhaps as a gift for someone. You had a man with you who bid on your behalf, successfully, I believe.'

Lisa turned slightly pink and looked uncomfortable. 'You are mistaken, I think, George.' Her lisp made her stumble over the word *mistaken*, which sounded more like *mithtaken*. 'I have indeed been to Cornwall on occasion. We have a small property there, Rosmorwen. But I can't recall that I ever attended an auction of furs. In fact, I can't recall that I ever went to Penzance. Rosmorwen is some distance from it. You saw someone who resembled me, perhaps.'

'Perhaps I am wrong,' said George. He stared thoughtfully at the crumb-strewn rug in front of the hearth and then turned to his wife. 'But my dear Marjorie, that rug was surely made from a bearskin.'

Lisa glanced at Marjorie and I could have sworn that it was a look of appeal. At any rate, Marjorie said smoothly: 'So it is, but Cat and I bought it together, in London. It was imported from somewhere in the heart of Europe.'

'Ah,' said George. And then remarked that the room was cold. 'This spring weather is so treacherous. Marjorie, my dear, could we not have a fire in here?'

That was the beginning. Admittedly, it was sheer chance that caused me to be there at that significant moment, although of course I didn't know of its significance. But yes, that was when it started, when the deadly seed was sown. Which ultimately flowered into murder.

FOUR

Love in the Air

Neither my aunt nor I were of much if any help to Marjorie during our short stay, for there was nothing that we could suggest. The same applied to Lisa and Edmund. Edmund, indeed, was blunt about it. The law was all on George's side, he said roundly. Marjorie would be wise to make the best of things. George, after all, was her husband. 'No one can order a man to leave his own house!' he said.

Afterwards, when Aunt Tabitha and I talked privately to Marjorie, in her room, Marjorie sobbed out her resentment of this advice.

'It's like the end of everything. How dare Edmund say that this is George's house? He hasn't been near me for years and years. Whatever the lawyers may say, it's *my* house. Cat left it to *me*. I miss Cat so and now I have to endure this instead! George expects me to look after him. Well, I don't want to! What has he been to me, all this time? Cat and I were so happy together! Have you seen our garden at the back of the house? We made it so pretty. And Cat brought a spinet with her. We used to make music together in the evenings. If only she were here!'

'It may not be so bad,' said my aunt bracingly. 'After all, George may not be much trouble . . .'

'He's trouble already! Meals on time – *he* says when. *His* choice of dishes! Shirts to wash and press, *his* shirts! He goes away and then comes back after all this time and thinks he has a right to demand my services! Robert's as bad. I haven't heard from him for years, either – he's in France, that's all I know, working for a vineyard owner, I think, but *George* is in touch with him and it seems when his red-headed whore died, he wrote to tell Robert and whine that he'd been left all alone with no one to cook his meals or wash his linen, and it was apparently Robert who wrote back advising him to come home and batten on me!'

I said: 'Oh, dear,' and my aunt tut-tutted, neither of which was very helpful. Marjorie raged on.

'They're selfish, both of them, they seem to think a woman is just there for them to use when it suits them and ignore the rest of the time, as if she were something put away in a cupboard when not wanted and do you know, I *said* that to George, when he first walked in, and he laughed, yes he did, he just *laughed* and said, yes, that's it exactly, that's what women are for! When I said I could kill him, I meant it!'

I hoped that George wouldn't fall ill and die in the near future. I would never feel quite sure that Marjorie hadn't helped him to it.

'But there it is. He *is* still your husband, Marjorie.' Aunt Tabitha was not unsympathetic but spoke an air of simple realism. And indeed, she spoke the truth.

I was sorry for Marjorie, though. Even during the short time since our arrival, her plumpness seemed to have fallen in, as though she were shrinking inside her skin. She struck me as a woman made by nature for a placid domestic life, of caring for a home, doing fine sewing – I now knew that the pretty cushions in the parlour had been embroidered by Marjorie and Cat – playing the spinet, entertaining friends and shopping. From now on, Marjorie would be a servant to a man whose demands threatened to wipe these calm pleasures from her world. And there was no help for it.

My aunt and I and our companions did stay for a few days. We spent the nights in the Running Horse inn, a pleasant gabled black-and-white hostelry by the river Mole. Here we hired bedchambers, but we spent the daytimes with Marjorie, I think in the hope of somehow encouraging her, steadying her against the demands of her altered future.

Lisa and Edmund and the twins, who had been staying in the house, left after two days, a little to my regret, because I liked the twins. They were very quiet in the presence of their parents but otherwise they were lively enough. Jane was a feminine girl, fond of pretty dresses and particular about having clean white ruffs; Thomas, boylike, was interested in horses and helped their groom to care for the horses and the pack pony they had brought with them from their home.

The house seemed oddly quiet after they had gone, and three days after that, realizing that we were of no more use, Aunt Tabitha and I also made our farewells. Once back in Sussex, I took the Brockleys back to Withysham and we stayed there for two weeks, visiting Faldene often, but Aunt Tabitha was as far beyond the reach of help as Marjorie. My company gave her, I think, a little relief; I was someone to talk to, a distraction when Uncle Herbert was particularly grumpy, and that I had come to her at all perhaps gave her a feeling of family support. But at the end of the fortnight, having accomplished nothing much, I took my party back to Hawkswood.

Once there, other things arose to occupy me. Most were to do with the house and the stud of trotting horses that I was building up, to be Harry's inheritance. To accommodate it, I had rented some land from a farmer whose fields marched with ours (he was getting old and was glad to make money out of his land without having to work it), and I'd had stabling built there. The work of the stud was getting beyond my own grooms and I needed to find a couple more, whose duties could be exclusively with the stud. In addition, Joseph's courtship of Tessie had ripened. There was a wedding to plan.

But in early July, a friend of mine from court, Christopher Spelton, arrived, bringing news which would take me away from home once more. Christopher was officially a Queen's Messenger but also acted as a secret agent, as I sometimes did. This time, though, he was simply a Messenger. He had a letter for me, from Lord Burghley, Sir William Cecil, the queen's Lord Treasurer and her most loved and trusted adviser.

He gave me the letter in the larger Hawkswood parlour, usually known as the east room because it received the morning sun. It was also quiet, being well away from the kitchen end of the house. If anyone in the east room wanted to call for service, they had to step out through the adjoining music room and the overflow linen store beyond, and shout.

After some conventional enquiries about my health and

well-being, Cecil's letter asked me, in the near future, to come
to court and stay for a while.

*The old idea of a marriage between her majesty and a member
of the French royalty has been revived. This would be a means
of strengthening a treaty we hope to make with France, under
which the two countries would come to each other's aid if
threatened. The most likely source of a threat, of course, is
Spain, and that will be so, I fear, as long as Mary Stuart of
Scotland is here in England and yearning to find support for
putting her back on the Scottish throne. Her majesty's marriage
might also, God willing, bring the country an heir. There is
still time. Her majesty's physicians have confirmed this.*

*But her majesty is ill at ease with the plan and I confess
that along with some other Council members, I too have doubts.
The suggested bridegroom is Francis, Duke of Anjou, though
the queen is still apt to speak of him by his former title, the
Duke of Alençon. He is said to be not handsome, and at twenty-
three, he is of course much younger than her majesty. However,
he is also said to be cultured and witty, which may well appeal
to her. Like the queen, he needs an heir, since his brother King
Henry III of France seems unlikely to get one. Francis of
Alençon is the heir at the moment and needs a posterity.*

*The final decision must be hers, but for the moment she is
not decisive. She blows hot and cold. I think she feels she
should – even must – consent to this marriage, but she has
always seemed to fear the thought of matrimony. Her ladies
try to encourage her, but you are her sister and have an
understanding of her that is bred in you, and she both loves
and trusts you.*

*I am writing, in fact, at the behest of her majesty, to ask
you to come to court as soon as you may find convenient and
do what you can to advise her majesty wisely. She may well
require you simply to keep her spirits up and her resolution
steady, until Alençon can come to England to speak for himself.
He is expected next month. She will agree to nothing anyway
until she has seen him. His servant Jean de Simier has been
to England with gifts, to start the courtship, but it can go no
further until the principals have met . . .*

'You know what is in this?' I asked Spelton.

'The gist of it, yes. It's an order, disguised as a request, I fancy.' Christopher was a stocky man with a balding head and nice brown eyes, which now smiled at me with full understanding. He knew all about my secret activities. 'But at least, as an assignment, it's fairly safe!' he said.

'For me,' I said. 'But in other ways, it's alarming! What is the Council thinking of? The queen is in her mid-forties! And she *has* always feared marriage, for good reasons! Yet, if she asks it, I am – at least, I think I am – expected to encourage her? That's what this letter *seems* to be suggesting! And I think the whole idea is madness!'

'I understand,' said Christopher, 'that the queen feels the marriage may be necessary. Does the letter say that she is seeking your help herself? Because I believe that that is the case.'

'Yes, it does. Though what form that help is to take . . . well, really, it isn't clear. Well, I had better go. Am I needed instantly, do you think? The letter does say *as soon as you may find convenient.* I have things to do here. Two of my servants – my groom Joseph and Harry's nurse, Tessie – are to marry in four days' time. I want to be here for that.'

'I think that would be all right. I intend to ride on to pay a brief call on the Lakes before going back to court. I can come through Hawkswood again on my way back and escort you to Hampton Court. That's where the court is just now.'

'Have you any special business with Eric and Kate?'

Christopher looked abashed. 'Not really. It would be a social call. Eric is my cousin, after all. I helped to arrange for him to be introduced to Kate! God, if only I'd known! I'd hardly noticed her before, though I'd travelled with you both, for days. It wasn't till I saw her on the day they were introduced to each other, dressed so beautifully, the centre of attention, as though a strong light were playing on her, that I saw . . . and by then, I knew how brave she'd been when you were both in danger. What I've missed! I can't help myself. I just want to see her, to make sure all is well with her. I'll do no harm. I just want, now and then, to be in Kate's presence. I think of myself' – his eyes were rueful – 'as a knight in one of those old romances, worshipping his lady from afar, but ready to serve her if at any time she has need of me.'

'Is that wise?'

'No,' said Christopher candidly. 'But as I said, I can't help myself.'

'Between the queen, and my Joseph and Tessie, and now you, love seems to be in the air,' I said. 'Though not all of it in the happiest way.' I looked at him with kindness. Once, he had proposed marriage to me and I had declined. It had been a somewhat practical proposal; we liked each other, but he hadn't pretended to be in love. Later, I began to think that nevertheless it could have been a good marriage for me. Only by then he had fallen genuinely in love with Kate. Who was married to Eric Lake and had no idea of the longings in the breast of a stocky, balding Queen's Messenger with friendly brown eyes.

'I will come with you to see Eric and Kate,' I said. 'As long as your visit really is short. I've seen nothing of Kate for months; I'd like to call on her. We can be back here in good time for the wedding, and directly after that, I'll come to court and you shall be part of my escort, along with the Brockleys.'

FIVE

Catastrophe

Eric Lake was of yeoman stock and West Leys, his home on the other side of Guildford, although we often referred to it as a manor, only just qualified for the title. It was a pleasant half-timbered dwelling on a hillside, facing west, as its name implied, with the higher part of the hill sloping gently above it towards a saddleback. A path from the back of the house ran up to the saddleback and Kate had told me that it was a walk that she and Eric liked to take on summer mornings.

'The rising sun hovers over the dip as though it were there to greet us as we reach the top,' she said. 'We love it.'

The farmland that went with the house spread in front of it, down the hill and into a valley with a river running through. When I arrived, escorted by Spelton, on a warm July afternoon, I thought that the land looked in good heart, and I noticed that the cows grazing there were glossy and healthy.

My former ward Kate looked well, too, when she welcomed us at the house. Very well, in fact. I looked at the sheen on her dark hair and the liquid sparkle in her dark eyes and said: 'You didn't let me know! When is it due?'

'We think in January,' said Kate, smiling. She was a good-looking girl altogether and she had a serenity now that she had never had before her marriage, when she was in a constant state of rebellion against her father, who was forever trying to marry her off to older men because he considered that she needed to be controlled. She had reacted to that with a most ill-judged elopement. I had helped to rescue her from it, and it was after that, that her father committed her to my care. I had seen her settled with Eric Lake, and with him, it seemed that she had found contentment.

Eric was a spectacularly handsome young man in a bronzed,

blond, blue-eyed fashion. To look at, in fact, he resembled a
young pagan god, perhaps the splendid Balder, whom the
Vikings had once worshipped. He appeared to be just what
Kate desired, though my own impression of him was that
however much he might look like a Viking deity, he was actually a trifle dull, with no skill at witty conversation. If one
made a joke in his presence, he often failed to see the point.
However, Kate didn't seem to mind, or even notice. I was glad
that she was happy.

Eric was out on the farm when we arrived, but Kate sent
for him and we settled down in the big kitchen, which was
spacious, with a long pinewood dining table at one end, well
away from the worktable where eggs were beaten and pastry
was rolled and meat cut up. There were seats here and there
with colourful cushions on them. Although it was July, the
fire was alight for cooking, with a stockpot simmering on a
trivet and a spit ready for use, but the back door was open to
let the heat out, and let in the scent of newly mown hay. 'We
hardly ever use the parlour,' Kate said. 'It faces north, so it's
never very bright. The kitchen's more cheerful. We don't go
in for formality.'

The two women who were working there went on with what
they were doing, while Spelton and Kate and I sat talking of
this and that – and particularly of Kate's prospective baby. It
was all very pleasant, and yet, after a while, I began to think
that something was not quite right. The two maidservants were
minding their own business a little too noticeably while Kate
and Eric, though they appeared to be in excellent health,
seemed a little distracted, even worried. They looked at each
other meaningly from time to time and when, somewhere in
the distance, we heard a woman's voice calling, and youthful
voices answering, both of the Lakes turned sharply to look
out of the back door and were so obviously uneasy that I said:
'Kate, is something amiss?'

She glanced at Eric and then said: 'Well, you didn't warn
us that you were coming, or we might have put you off for a
little while. You see . . .'

Her voice trailed off and I said: 'But we are only here for
a few hours. We'll go home before nightfall. Is there a problem

about us dining with you? But there are only the two of us. Surely . . .'

One of the maidservants uttered an amused snort at this point and Kate said: 'No, of course not! We always have good stores of food. You're both welcome to dine! But the fact is, we have unexpected guests here already and . . . oh, dear . . .'

Her voice trailed off again and Eric, stepping in, said: 'I believe you know them, Mistress Stannard. Indeed, they have mentioned meeting you, at the house, I understand, of my sister-in-law, Mistress Marjorie Harrison. One of them is my other sister-in-law, Mistress Lisa Harrison, and with her are her twins, Thomas and Jane. Lisa is in serious trouble and she and her twins are here because – they have had to leave their home, Firtrees House, for the time being . . .'

His voice too dwindled away. Kate took up the tale again. 'Lisa keeps crying, and doesn't want to show herself. She saw you approaching and she took the twins out for a walk to avoid you. Hoping you wouldn't stay long, I fancy. They arrived here yesterday, distraught, all three of them.'

Spelton and I gazed at our hosts in consternation, not sure what to say, and then there were footsteps crossing the farm-yard and the light from the back door dimmed briefly as Lisa Harrison and her twins came through it. They stopped short when they saw us. Lisa had indeed been crying. Her reddened eyes and drawn face told their own tale. Jane had been crying, too. Thomas' young face simply looked pale and grim.

'I'm thorry,' said Lisa. 'We are dithturbing you. But Jane is tired and couldn't walk any further and I thought perhapth you had gone . . .'

Her lisp was very pronounced; I thought with nervousness. There was a fraught silence until, feeling that someone ought to say something – we couldn't stay as we were for ever, as though we had been suddenly turned to stone – I ventured: 'Mistress Harrison! We didn't know you were here. We . . . er . . .'

I found myself tongue-tied, and stopped.

Christopher Spelton said: 'This is impossible. What has happened? Or would it be best if I and Mistress Stannard simply left and went home? We don't want to intrude on anything private.'

Lisa found a stool and sank onto it. 'You'll find out in the end. The whole county will know! Edmund will cry his outrage to the skies and anyway he'll have to explain what he's done, to all our friends, his and mine!'

Her voice was bitter and most of her sibilants came out as *th*. She was trying to control herself and master the letter s, though with variable success. It would be tedious to record all the times when she failed and I will not do so. She dissolved into miserable weeping and Jane, who had also found a stool and sunk wearily onto it, let out a sob as well. Thomas moved closer to his mother, not seeking protection but offering it. He looked at us challengingly, as though daring us to condemn her, though I didn't know for what.

Christopher said mildly: 'Mistress Stannard and I are both well versed in the ways of the world. We are not easily shocked. May we know what has happened?'

Lisa said: 'Edmund is a good man. But he can be – hard. Harsh, even. Even to the children. That was why . . . well, I think it was . . .'

'I know. I remember. I saw your face, that time, the way you looked at Father afterwards.' Thomas sounded older than fifteen. His voice, his tone, were those of a man. 'You were just trying to protect me. I was only twelve.' He looked round at the rest of us. 'I'd done something wrong – not attended to my books or something – and Father beat me. It had happened before and Mother often protested but he never would heed her.' He turned back to her. 'Only *that* time, it went on so long and I was screaming so much that you caught hold of his arm to stop him and he threw you off and hit you and you fell onto the floor, and when you got up your nose was bleeding and yes, as I say, I saw your face. I remember promising myself that one day, I would protect *you*.'

Lisa looked wretched. 'If it hadn't been for that – that particular time – I think I might not have, would never have . . .' She stopped and swallowed. At length, she said: 'I have never been really happy with Edmund though I've tried to be a good wife and as I said, he is a good man, in his way. He's honest, always does his duty. But . . . Our marriage was arranged by my parents. My family and Edmund's lived near each other; we all knew each other. Edmund's family had a smallholding, not a good one, but after his father died, Edmund worked to improve it. He sold it for a reasonable price and bought a better place; he was a promising man, my father told me, and I didn't have a big dowry. When he asked for me, my parents thought he would do. I did what they told me but Edmund made me nervous, from the beginning. He was so quick to anger, often over little things. I never knew what would offend him. He used to hit me. But just after that time when I tried to stop him from beating Thomas, and he threw me off and made my nose bleed – and I had a black eye, too – well, just after that, the time came for us to go to Rosmorwen – that's the piece of land in Cornwall, that Edmund bought not long after our marriage. He could barely afford it, though it was cheap, but he said it was always worth having land and he raised the money somehow . . . we go – went – there once every year to stay for a while . . .'

She became confused and broke off. Thomas took over. 'It's small,' he said knowledgeably. 'A few fields and a little stock. It's about four miles from Penzance. There's a hamlet close by where the farm workers come from – Black Rock, it's called, because of a funny lump of dark rock on the moor just beside it. Rosmorwen isn't rented out. Tenants don't stay; the earth is so unproductive. So there's a steward in charge of it and he sees that the fields grow what they can and sells the produce and sends us the money from that, less his and the labourers' wages and the upkeep of the place. It doesn't amount to much.'

'Well,' said Lisa, regaining confidence as our faces showed only interest, 'it was time for our annual visit but there were business things that my husband wanted to deal with, and he sent me to represent him. He'd done that before. There's never much to do and I am quite equal to it on my own. I have only to hear a report from the steward and look around for myself. I am capable of seeing when a fence wants repairing or cows aren't thriving. Edmund gives . . . gave . . . me credit for that. So I went. The name of the steward then was John Merrow. I'd met him the year before, when he was new there, and we liked each other then. So I went to Rosmorwen that time – three years ago now – without Edmund and . . . well . . .'

She stopped. Her eyes became huge and scared. I helped her out. 'You had an affair?' I said. 'It's all right. My own past hasn't been one of total virtue. I am not likely to throw stones at anyone.'

'Nor am I,' said Kate. She looked at me. 'Lisa knows of my foolish elopement. That was why she felt safe in coming here for help.'

'We had an affair. We were careful,' said Lisa. 'There were no . . . results.' The word came out as rethults and it imparted an oddly childish air to her tale, although it was no childish story in itself. 'One day,' she said, 'wanting for once to be alone together, to enjoy each other's company in broad daylight, we went to Penzance, to attend an auction of rare furs from the New World.'

I suddenly realized what was coming. 'Was that the sale that George Harrison mentioned, when we met him in Marjorie's house? He'd travelled to Cornwall from Sheffield to attend it?'

'Yes. I bid for something when we were there,' said Lisa. 'I bought that bear pelt you saw at Marjorie's home. John did the bidding for me. I had it made up into a rug as a Christmas gift for Marjorie. George spoke of it – do you remember?' She had overcome her tears now but her blue eyes were huge and wet. 'Marjorie doesn't – well, no doubt she soon will – know about my . . . my indiscretion but I know I gave her a *help me* look and she was quick-witted enough to pretend she'd got the rug in London. Dear Marjorie. In fact, I never have told her where I bought the fur; I've never told anyone about that auction. Only – George attended it. I had no idea. He didn't know me by sight and I didn't know him, either. He'd only seen me once, at my wedding, nearly drowned in the great big farthingale and the huge ruff my mother put me into for the great day. But at the auction, it seems George was standing near enough to overhear some of the talk between me and John. Loving talk. He heard John call me Lisa. And he heard my lisp. When we met at Marjorie's house – the time you were there – he remembered it. And then he realized who I was.'

'I see,' I said. 'And what he overheard was enough to tell him how things were between you and John Merrow?'

'Yes. It was a brief affair,' said Lisa. 'Only for those two weeks when I was at Rosmorwen without Edmund. It was a comfort to me.' She was crying again now. 'John was kind, tender. I still had traces of that black eye. He saw them and he was angry on my behalf. He got me to tell him what had happened and I cried in his arms and . . . one thing led to another. Can you understand?'

'I think so,' Christopher said. 'Go on.'

'John left Rosmorwen the next year; he's gone from my life but I'm grateful to him,' Lisa said, with sudden passion. 'I'll never forget him! His gentleness was like . . . balm on a wound. Like a warm hearth and a warm drink when you come in from a snowstorm. But for some reason, George has told Edmund! And now I have been ordered out of my home and made to take my children with me because Edmund won't believe they're his. We were married for a good seven years – nearly eight – before I had the twins and I've had no more children and he says maybe I needed a different man if I was to have children . . . he says the twins *can't* be his, only they *are!*'

She turned fiercely to her children. 'You *are* his! You were born long before I met John Merrow. And that was the only time I strayed. I had been so unhappy, and frightened too. That time when I tried to make him stop beating you . . . he *wouldn't* stop and it was as though he couldn't! You were in a terrible state. And then he knocked *me* down. He terrified me. John comforted me. I needed that comfort. But you, my children, are Edmund's son and daughter. Only he won't believe it and he's cast us all off. I brought us all here because we can't go to Marjorie; *he's* there – George.'

Her desperate gaze fastened on me. 'Edmund says he will disinherit my children! He calls them bastards, fathered by God knows who. He'll leave all his property to somebody else. I and Thomas and Jane can be a charge on the parish, for all he cares!' wailed Lisa.

Good, moral people should no doubt have been scandalized by Lisa's admission. But as I said, most of us were in no position to throw stones. I, and I think all the others, felt sincerely sorry for her.

SIX

A Marriage of Great Value

'But why,' I said to Lisa, 'did your brother-in-law want to tell your husband what he knew – or guessed – about John Merrow? Does he dislike you?'

'He doesn't know me! Before George came back and Marjorie sent for us, we had only seen each other once, knowingly, at my wedding. I suppose it was just moral outrage,' said Lisa miserably.

'After he had walked out on his wife and lived with his mistress for years and years?' I said.

'It's different for men,' said Christopher heavily. 'Men like to know that they really are the fathers of their children.'

'But Thomas is obviously his father's son!' I exclaimed.

Thomas really was strikingly like his stocky, sandy father and as he matured, would probably become more so. He had the hair, the nose and the mouth and later, his head might well acquire Edmund's Roman emperor bone structure. Jane resembled Lisa, but as she was Thomas's twin she had presumably been sired at the same time. I shook my head in puzzlement.

'I think,' said Eric sadly, 'that to George, what he did doesn't matter, but if Lisa strayed . . . he would feel that was different.'

'I suppose so,' I said, also sadly.

Once again, there was nothing that any of us could do to help. We could not suppose that calling on Edmund and trying to persuade him into taking his wife and children back would have the slightest effect. If he was so blinded by rage that Thomas's obvious resemblance to him made no difference, then nothing that any of us said was likely to change his mind.

So, as with Marjorie, it was a case of soothing platitudes. Eric and Kate were willing to take Lisa and the twins in. They were his own kinfolk, Eric said, and as such, couldn't possibly be thrown on the parish. Kate could do with the company of another woman, especially just now, and Thomas could help on the farm.

'We can find a tutor for them, to finish their education,' said Eric. 'I'll just count them as stepchildren. Thousands of men look after stepchildren.'

Lisa and the twins were safe, at least. Kate and Eric would take care of them. Christopher Spelton congratulated Eric and Kate on their generous decision and kissed Kate goodbye with perhaps a little more fervour than was quite correct, but no one else seemed to notice that. Then Christopher and I set off for home and the wedding of Tessie and Joseph.

This, in contrast to our visit to West Leys, was a jolly occasion. My chief cook, John Hawthorn, always seized any chance of showing off and the feast would have done justice to a royal wedding. I virtually forgot about Lisa and her troubles. The day after that, accompanied by Christopher and the Brockleys, I started for Hampton Court.

I did visit court occasionally, and had established a routine about it. Sybil usually stayed at Hawkswood, once more looking after it in partnership with Adam Wilder. I had never taken Harry to court, although this time I did consider it and mentioned the idea to Christopher.

'If some of the Council are trying to persuade the queen that she should have an heir, and she really does want me to encourage the idea – I can't say I think it's a good idea because I don't but the queen must know her own mind – well, perhaps seeing a small child might . . . might make her really, strongly, want one of her own. I suppose that could be what she wants to feel. What do you think?'

'It's been tried,' said Christopher. 'Some of the Council – the Earl of Sussex was much to the fore – have been telling her of the joy that would come to her on beholding an imp of her own, and someone did have the happy thought of bringing a woman with a small baby to see her. The baby was put into her arms, but I suppose the people crowding round and the queen's stiff brocade dress and her huge ruff were too much for it. It was frightened, screamed at the top of its lungs and then peed on the brocade. The queen was revolted.'

We were talking in the small parlour, in the company of Dale, Sybil and an aged Welshwoman, Gladys Morgan, who was a hanger-on of mine. As with the Brockleys and Sybil, I treated her as though she were a relative, but this was largely because Gladys regarded herself as part of my family and it was impossible to quell her. I often longed to do just that!

I had acquired her by accident, years ago, in Wales, when Brockley and I had rescued her from a charge of witchcraft. Thereafter, she had attached herself to me and I think was devoted to me in her cross-grained way. She was not only very elderly, but had become lame and was always ill-tempered, with a deplorable habit of cursing people she disliked, a trait which had got her arrested for witchcraft all over again after joining my household. Once again, she had barely escaped being hanged.

She was however skilled in making medicinal potions and ointments and for this I valued her. She could be disconcerting, though. She now responded to Christopher's rueful account of the queen's first meeting with an 'imp' by throwing back her head and emitting a screech of laughter, expelling spittle through the gaps in her brown and unlovely teeth.

'Gladys, please!' I said. 'Harry's seven! He wouldn't do that! I've taken care over teaching him his manners.'

'No,' said Christopher, 'but he's lively and noisy, and the court and the queen would be very strange to him. He's quite capable of being scared, or rude, or forgetting to bow, or . . . better not, Ursula.'

'I'd say not,' said Gladys irrepressibly. 'No point looking for trouble. This looks like being just one time when that man Burghley's asked you to do a job for him that won't lead you into danger. Don't spoil it all! Don't go provoking the queen.'

I glared at her, mostly because she was right. Gladys had a maddening habit of being right. Nearly all of the past assignments on which Lord Burghley, otherwise Sir William Cecil, had sent me, had led me into danger. And a wayward child might indeed annoy the queen. Gladys was no fool.

She hadn't finished, either. Undeterred by my scowl, she added: 'Let's hope this request don't have a sting in the tail after all. Just like scorpions, that man's ideas are.'

'What do you know about scorpions?' I snapped.

So, except that Spelton was riding with us, the party that set off for court was the usual one. I rode Jewel, and was accompanied by Brockley on Mealy, with Dale seated behind him, and a pack pony on a leading rein. Stabling accommodation at court was often crowded, and if the Duke of Alençon was expected soon, he would no doubt have an entourage. This way, I would only need stalls for three horses: Jewel, Mealy and the pony, and Brockley would look after them. Spelton had his own arrangements.

We arrived at Hampton Court in sunshine, in the early afternoon, having dined on the way. I had always thought Hampton Court one of Elizabeth's most beautiful palaces. Its warm rose-coloured bricks glowed in the bright air and were pleasingly contrasted by the grey ornamental edging to walls and doors while its tall chimneys with their bricks laid in patterns were a delight to the eye. The place had gracious proportions; an air of space and lightness and dignity, all combined.

But it had known tragedy. There was a gallery which the servants didn't like, especially at dusk, for King Henry's young fifth wife, Catherine Howard, had fled along it in terror when the guards came to arrest her for treason, after she had been caught in infidelity. She had glimpsed Henry himself in the distance and she ran towards him, screaming his name, begging him for help. He turned his back and the guards seized her and dragged her away. Not long after that, she was beheaded. It was said that sometimes, especially at dusk, an echo of her screams could still be heard in that gallery.

I had never heard them myself, but I did not like that gallery either. I had been there at twilight, and to me its shadowy air did seem to hold a memory of fear and despair. The fact that it was my own father who had closed his ears to the mortal terror of a young girl probably made those feelings worse. I know they made me feel ashamed.

I never set eyes on my royal father but everyone knew what he had become; it was common knowledge. He had been a monstrous, diseased hulk when Catherine Howard, hauled by an old man's lust and thrust at him by her ambitious family, was married to him. He had been no husband for a beautiful young lass. She had not been an innocent maiden; that was true. But because my own life had not been wholly innocent either, I was sorry for her, as I had been for Lisa.

And now I was sorry for the queen, who was also being dragged towards a fate that she feared and that indeed held serious danger for her. I wanted to rescue her but knew I might be asked instead to take her hand and coax her to sacrifice herself. Hampton Court was beautiful but I wished with all my heart that I were somewhere else.

Christopher Spelton left the party just before we reached the palace, and rode to his own home, which was not far off. I and the Brockleys were expected and a suite of three rooms in the Base Court, the first courtyard after the gatehouse, had been made ready for us, with an array of flagons and glassware and a pile of platters, and there was service. We could dine in private if we wished, though we could also eat in the big dining chamber.

The outlook wasn't particularly good; there was no view of the river but only of a rear entrance where goods were delivered for the kitchen. Brockley caught sight of a vintner's cart there and raced out to buy a keg of wine for us. Wine was served in the common dining chamber, but in private, you had to supply your own.

Dale and I unpacked together. We had hardly finished before I had visitors, in the shape of two Frenchmen. The usher who brought them to my rooms introduced us to them, and presented them to us as Jean de Simier, personal servant to Francis, Duke of Alençon, and his clerk, Antoine de Lacey. The usher then bowed and withdrew, leaving us all to contemplate each other. Behind me, I sensed Brockley and Dale taking stock as I myself was doing. In Dale's case, it would be with suspicion. Dale did not like the French. In my service, she had once had a terrifying experience in France.

De Simier was a brisk-looking man, not young but not yet middle-aged either, well-made, with dark, intelligent eyes. The restrained colour of his dark-blue doublet and hose declared his position as a greater man's emissary but I sensed at once that he had a forceful character. The clerk, de Lacey, was somewhat younger, and was different, being nondescript in appearance, dressed plainly in buff, with ink stains on his fingers. He had a bland face but his grey eyes were cold. I didn't take to him.

'As you heard,' I told them, 'I am Mistress Ursula Stannard, of Hawkswood in Surrey. What the usher didn't say was that I am a blood relative of the queen, though perhaps you already know about that. May I know what I can do for you? Would you rather speak French?' I added. 'I am quite at home with it.'

'Thank you, but here in England, we will use your own tongue,' Simier said. 'We both speak it well.' He had an accent, but his English seemed fluent.

He came straight to the point. 'I understand that the queen has asked you to be with her as she considers the merits of marriage to my master. I have come to request your support. I am told that she trusts your judgement. Mistress Stannard, this marriage means a great deal to the Duke of Alençon. He not only seeks it for political and expedient reasons. All he has heard of the queen, and seeing a miniature portrait of her that has come into his hands, has made him fall in love – yes, fall in love, at a distance! He has written to her to declare his love. I saw the letter and indeed persuaded him to moderate his sentiments somewhat because I understand that . . . forgive me; I mean no impertinence . . . that she is a maiden queen and I felt that certain passionate phrases were almost unseemly in the circumstances. Believe me, Mistress Stannard, some of his sentiments could set fire to water! De Lacey and I came on ahead of my master, to do his courting by proxy, until he can come himself. He will soon be here. He is eager. But . . . the queen seems hesitant. I don't know why . . .'

He stopped, apparently wanting me to say something, to explain the queen to him. I, however, said nothing at all. For one thing, I didn't believe a single word of this wild talk about falling in love at a distance. The Duke of Alençon wanted a marriage fit for a king's heir and he wanted an heir of his own, and he wanted to confirm a very useful treaty. Those facts were obvious. Also obvious were the facts that he was twenty-three, whereas Elizabeth, no matter how pretty her miniature portrait might have made her, was forty-five, and young men in their early twenties rarely fall in love with middle-aged women they have never even met. I waited.

'This marriage could be of the greatest value to England and France alike,' said de Simier. 'The treaty it would ratify would protect both countries from Spanish aggression. Treaties on parchment can be tossed into the fire, but when the parties are married to each other and, God willing, have children, the bond is strengthened a thousandfold. And both realms need a new royal generation.'

He paused, and de Lacey said quietly: 'It isn't only that the queen seems uncertain. There are factions in her Council that are not in favour of the Duke's suit.' He was not putting himself forward in any impertinent manner, for I had seen de Simier give him a nod. He was speaking up with permission, and restrained though his tone was, it also held a ring of real feeling.

Privately, I was only too glad to hear that there was resistance somewhere in the royal council. 'Which factions?' I asked.

'Sir Robert Dudley, Earl of Leicester,' said de Simier. He sounded as though the name tasted bad. 'And Sir Francis Walsingham – who seems to think that such a union would provoke Spain rather than intimidate her – and Lord Burghley is doubtful, for several reasons, we think. If you can stiffen the queen's resolve, I pray that you will do so.'

He smiled at me, most engagingly, as a trustful child might smile at an adult whose goodwill might bring forth treats, such as sweetmeats or a new pony. I inclined a gracious head.

'I will always do my best for the queen and for England. I always have,' I said, in the most regal voice I could manage. I was aware of Dale and Brockley behind me, and I thought I heard, though very faintly, a snort of amusement from Dale. She and Brockley had recognized the ambiguity. The Frenchmen had recognized it too. De Simier's face hardened and Antoine de Lacey's chilly eyes gave me a piercing stare. I said: 'I must go to the queen.'

It was dismissal and they took their leave but as de Simier went out, Antoine lingered momentarily. In a low voice, he said: 'I fear that you may be among the doubters, Mistress Stannard. I sense it. Am I right?'

'There are – several sides to the matter,' I said diplomatically.

'We would agree there. But that his suit should succeed truly does mean a great deal to my master and to the duke. It could be of immense value to both France and England. I believe this marriage would be right for all concerned.'

Not so nondescript, then. De Simier probably used him regularly as a mouthpiece, just as he was himself the Duke's mouthpiece. 'I will think carefully,' I said, and Brockley, who was already holding the door open, held it wider. De Lacey went out.

'Well!' I said as Brockley closed the door after him. 'What did you think of that?'

'They're both admirable servants to their masters,' said Brockley. 'But whether they are the best of friends to her majesty is another matter.

'I think that too,' I said.

SEVEN
The Frightened Queen

Half an hour later, I was summoned to the queen. I had been expecting this, but I was surprised when the message was brought not by a page, as was usual, but by a young woman who announced herself as Lady Margaret Mollinder, the queen's newest lady in waiting.

She was a pretty thing, with striking looks, since she had ash-fair hair and brown eyes. She was small and slender and she was so very young that I would have taken her for a maid of honour, except that as she led me to my appointment she chatted artlessly and I learned that she was married and very much in love with her husband, although he was at the moment part of an ambassador's suite in Austria. Her pretty mouth turned down as she told me, sadly, that she did not know when she would be with him again.

'I couldn't go with him because I was expecting and not very well. But two weeks after he had left, well, it all came to nothing – oh, it was such a wretched business; so painful and frightening. *Awful.* I cried for days.' She tried to brighten her tone. 'My family and my husband's family both have influence and to help me get over it all, to give me an interest, they arranged for me to come to court as a queen's lady. My mother-in-law looks after things at home.'

She probably wasn't aware of it but her tone was revealing. I sensed the existence of a mother-in-law who hadn't wanted to see the household rule pass into the hands of a lass barely out of the schoolroom, and had been only too willing to help Lady Margaret choose gowns for the royal court.

As we were climbing the final staircase towards the queen's apartments, Lady Margaret said: 'I am glad you have come, Mistress Stannard. The queen has mentioned you at times. Some of the other ladies are puzzled because just now she seems to want you rather than them, but I understand that you and she are closely related. I can see that it's natural.'

'Do you like being at court?' I asked her.

'No,' said Lady Margaret frankly. 'At least, I like the dancing and the masques, and things of that sort. But sometimes . . . it's uncomfortable.'

'How do you mean?'

'It's so tense, like a thunderstorm brewing. The queen is nervous. It scares me. *She* scares me,' said Lady Margaret unhappily. 'She slapped me once. But I think it's because she's worried and upset – she doesn't like to talk about marriage, even though she is getting ready to welcome the Duke of Alençon.'

Young, but not, I thought, dim-witted; ingenuous but observant as well. Lady Margaret Mollinder would one day grow into a wise, even a formidable woman.

'I will help her if I can,' I said.

We reached the royal apartments. Lady Margaret led me through the crowded first anteroom, full of courtiers and the lesser ladies in waiting, and here we came across someone who was clearly anxious to relieve any storminess in the atmosphere, if it really existed. Antoine de Lacey was there, entertaining those present with, surprisingly, a display of juggling, with wooden balls, green and blue and red. I had already realized that he might not be as nondescript as he looked, but I would never have associated him with the talents of an entertainer.

He saw me staring at him, and walked towards me, still deftly tossing his colourful balls. For the first time, I saw him smile and how it lightened his face. 'Mistress Stannard! Good day to you! You find me employing a humble skill for the enjoyment of the court.'

He let the balls fall into a heap on a nearby settle, leant towards me, still smiling, and said: 'Mistress Stannard, it is really most unwise to put seashells right into your ears. They may be hung from your lobes as earrings but to push them right inside . . . tut . . .' His right hand rose, flicked round my left ear and withdrew with a sizeable seashell on his palm. Lady Margaret gave a delighted giggle and from the rest of the gathering there was laughter and applause.

I laughed too and said: 'Next time, try to find a gold angel or two in one of my ears!'

'But I'd have to let you keep them,' said Antoine, replacing his smile with a woebegone look. 'After all, they would have come from *your* ear!'

Still laughing, I nodded to Lady Margaret to continue on, and leaving Antoine behind, we proceeded through a second anteroom, to which only the queen's ladies of the bedchamber and the more illustrious guests had been admitted. I smiled politely at the ladies, for I knew most of them. Some smiled back and some did not. They would be the ones who were jealous of me and the fact that I was in their eyes privileged, since the queen seemed to need me more than she needed them.

Privileged! I thought cynically, as Lady Margaret, having announced me, turned back and left me alone with my royal sister. This was no privilege. My feet were dragging.

I had dressed with care, but the queen was casually clad in a loose robe, with slippers on her feet. She was seated at a desk, reading. She put a marker in the book as I entered, and turned towards me. 'Ursula! There you are! I have been anxious to see you. I have been passing the time with a little Roman history – the *Annals* of Tacitus, in his original Latin. There is nothing like the study of history for giving one a sense of proportion.'

I had sunk into the correct curtsey but now she rose and came to me, holding out her hand to raise me. 'Come. No formality, sister. You know why you are here?'

'Yes, ma'am. But . . .'

'Here in private, you may call me sister. But . . .?'

I said: 'I'm not sure what you want of me. Lord Burghley wrote to me, saying that you are considering marriage to the French prince, Francis, Duke of Alençon, and that he will shortly come to England. Lord Burghley seemed to think you wished to . . . to consult me. I have briefly met the duke's emissary, Jean de Simier. He sought me out this morning.'

'I dare say. He wanted your support, no doubt.'

'Yes.'

There was a silence. Elizabeth turned back to her desk, sat

down again and stared at Tacitus. She sighed, a deep sigh, coming from some lonely, unhappy place inside her. I looked at her, this great lady who was sovereign of all England, and saw a tired woman, beset by fear. I knew what it was she feared, but it was not something I could mention before she did. I waited.

At last she spoke. 'I am forty-five and I have not married and you know well enough why. You know that I have seen how marriage puts the woman into the power of the man, and how that prospect horrifies me, because I have also seen what can happen when a man abuses that power. I am among those who have heard the echo of my stepmother Catherine Howard's screams in the haunted gallery. Oh yes, those tales are true!'

'I remember her whenever I am in that gallery,' I said carefully. 'But whether there's more in it than that . . .'

'There is,' said Elizabeth, cutting me short. 'I have only heard them once – on a winter evening, when the light was fading. But I *did* hear them. It is not just a matter of remembering and imagining, though I do recall her, very well. Her youth. Her passionate nature. Her terror. She was not well brought up. No one had ever taught her discretion, or . . . the nature, the duties, of a queen. She was no more than a child, at the mercy of instincts she didn't know how to control. She didn't even understand that she ought to control them. But my father didn't recognize any of that. She was in his power and he used that power, and he killed her. It was his second such killing.'

Briefly, she was silent. As usual, she had avoided mentioning her mother's name, but I suspected that she thought of her mother often.

She said: 'I am saying this, Ursula, so that you fully understand my present doubts. You must also understand that I need you to help me deal with those doubts. I don't ask you to dispel them; they can't be dispelled. I need you to brace me, so that I can face them. Marriage in itself is dangerous. And so, of course, is childbirth. For a woman of my years to bear a child for the first time is extra dangerous. I know well enough that I would be gambling with my life.'

I couldn't think of anything to say in answer, and therefore remained silent.

Elizabeth said: 'The stakes are high. But if I do marry and I bear a child – especially a son – think of the advantages! England would have a direct heir. And not only would the treaty with France be strengthened immensely just by my marriage, but the birth of an heir to me and Alençon would mean that one day the crowns of England and France would be united.'

I still said nothing. Elizabeth looked at me and I at her, though I could not read her face. It always had reminded me of a shield. It never expressed her feelings. But her golden-brown eyes sometimes did. At the moment, they were pleading with me. She wanted me not only to understand what she was saying, but to agree.

'Long ago,' said Elizabeth, 'before Christianity ever came to these shores, before Christ was even born, ancient peoples existed who sometimes made human sacrifices of their kings. Did you know?'

'Yes. When I was a child, I shared my cousins' tutor. He was knowledgeable about ancient beliefs and legends, and sometimes told us tales of such things. My aunt and uncle didn't approve of that, but they didn't always know!'

I had never been close to my cousins; my aunt and uncle had made it too clear that as an illegitimate child, I was an object of charity and socially below them. But in concealing our tutor's forays into the pagan world, we had for once co-operated. His tales and legends were so interesting. None of us wanted them to be forbidden.

'Some of those ancient tribes,' said Elizabeth, 'sacrificed their kings annually. The old king, dying, would represent the death of the old year. The new king would represent the spring of the new one. For twelve months he would have everything a man could wish – wealth, women, rich clothes and food – but at the end of those months, he had to die in his turn. In other tribes, the custom was different. Their kings sometimes reigned for years. But if trouble came, famine, plague, or a threat from a dangerous enemy, then it was the king's duty to placate the gods who decided the fate of the tribe. He had to surrender his life.'

Once again, I was not sure what to say, and yet again, said nothing at all.

'If I marry,' said Elizabeth, 'I shall have to face what I hate the very thought of; the duty of lying beneath a man and letting him invade me. Ugh! When the physicians examined me to see if I were still fertile, they hurt me. I cried with the pain of it! That prospect is bad enough, but if I should conceive, I would have to face – the possibility of death. Yet the possible gains are so tremendous that I cannot refuse the risk. That is what royalty means, Ursula. That is one reason why we have palaces and adulation; it's why I have gowns sewn with pearls and magnificent horses to ride and a thousand people to serve my needs. Oh, part of it is so that England can make a show in the eyes of foreign powers. But part of it is . . . compensation, if you like, for the fact that one day my death may be demanded. I think that now . . . it is required of me to gamble with my life and yes, perhaps, to lose it. Help me!'

I listened to this with horror and then, looking once more into those golden-brown eyes, I saw, with pity, that their owner was more than just afraid. She was terrified.

And with that, I blurted out the truth of what was in my mind.

'Sister, I don't think you *do* need to endanger your life in this way. You ask me to help you face it, because you say it is in England's best interests, but I can't agree about that. If it did . . . go wrong . . . England could be left with no queen and perhaps with no heir either. If there should be a baby and it lived but you did not, well, what kind of sovereign is an infant in a cradle? And if it should be a daughter, she couldn't unite the crowns of England and France. The French have a law against it.'

'I was a daughter,' said Elizabeth. 'And laws can be changed. An honest Protector could be found to see England through while a child matured; I am sure of that.' She sighed again. 'In fact, there is a possible heir, though he too is still young – only thirteen as yet. He has been reared as a good Protestant. I mean James, the son of Mary of Scotland, who is, after all, a cousin of mine. He is descended from King Henry the Seventh, as I am. And,' said Elizabeth, 'if he were on the throne of England, Mary might stop trying to start a Catholic rising in her favour. Oh, she still tries, even though I keep her as close as I can. Walsingham says that if she could find someone willing to assassinate me, she would, and he may well be right. But she might balk at trying to assassinate her son. Whatever happens, England will still have an heir. But a direct heir, and a firm treaty with France, would be far better. *Far* better. And as England's queen, I must try to achieve the best possible future, the greatest possible safety, for my country. Unless Alençon is as repulsive as a snake – or even if he *is* as repulsive as a snake – I must marry him. The possible gains are immeasurable.'

There just wasn't an answer to this. Once more, I sat speechless.

'I need you to steady my nerve,' said Elizabeth. 'You have been married, you have borne children. You survived. I need you to warm my heart and quiet my fears. To see me through. Ursula,' said the queen, 'give me your courage.'

I could do nothing but bow my head and agree, but I was full of sorrow for her. She was the queen. She did indeed have ropes of pearls and a string of palaces; she was surrounded by hundreds of people, all concerned for her well-being. Yet at the heart of it all was this dark pit, this yawning abyss of terror. I was thankful in that moment that my mother had not been one of King Henry's lawful wives.

EIGHT
Seeing Double

I returned to my quarters, heavy of heart. I knew now what was asked of me. I was to encourage the queen and thrust her towards a peril that appalled her, and for good reason, for her fears were justified. I too was appalled.

Deep in unhappy thought, I entered the room which we were using as a parlour, and then halted, because Sir William Cecil was there, evidently awaiting me, being entertained by the Brockleys and sipping the wine that Brockley had purchased.

'Lord Burghley!' I said, formally.

'Good afternoon, Ursula. You have been with the queen?'

'I . . . yes.' I made my curtsey and sat down. Dale at once poured a glass of wine for me and I took it absent-mindedly. 'What brings you here, my lord?' I asked.

'A natural wish to welcome you to court. And I want to ask you how you found the queen and what you think of this new marriage ploy, and also to ask you to undertake a small – and quite harmless – task for me – for us, that is, the queen, myself, Sir Francis Walsingham.'

I might have known. *I might have known.* Somehow, whenever Cecil came over my horizon, he had a task for me. It was always small, it was always allegedly harmless, and it usually turned out to be neither. No, let me correct that. It *always* turned out to be neither.

'But first,' said Cecil, who knew perfectly well what I was thinking though he didn't comment on it, 'the queen. Ursula, what is your opinion of this latest development? The treaty with France is obviously a good thing, but is the marriage equally worthwhile?'

'I don't like it,' I said candidly. 'I think it's dangerous.'

'For the queen or for England?'

'Both. We risk losing the queen, and there really is a risk. The queen is in her forties. If the worst happened, we would be left either with an heir who is an infant in a cradle or a boy in his teens, who has never set foot in England before.'

Cecil nodded. He was always a pensive man. Today, he was dressed, as he so often was, not in doublet and hose, but in a long, formal gown of blue and grey, and the worried line that was always there between his light eyes, was deeper even than usual. He kept on uneasily stroking his fair, forked beard.

'My feelings exactly, Ursula. Walsingham thinks the same and he also says that although the treaty would mean that France would help England if Spain attacked us, and vice versa, the Spanish might be so incensed by such an agreement that it could cause a war rather than discourage one. And the Earl of Leicester heartily agrees with both of us, although he is being rather careful at the moment.'

'For any particular reason?'

'There is indeed a particular reason. You had better know, if I can rely on your discretion. Can I?'

'Of course.'

He looked at the Brockleys, who were trying not to appear agog.

'And theirs,' I said.

'They would hear soon enough, anyway,' said Cecil. 'All the Council knows. Only the queen, the one who matters most, does not. The Earl of Leicester, the queen's Sweet Robin, got himself married last year. You will find that he has since then found excuses to leave court for prolonged periods now and then, and that's why. He goes home to his wife. You know her.'

He paused, while I looked enquiring, and then smiled. Cecil had a knack of – just now and then – saying something totally unexpected. He was a professional lawyer and therefore discreet. But now, just for once, he spoke with a wicked glint in his eyes and a touch of malice in his voice.

'Leicester has married that sloeberry-eyed charmer, Lettice Knollys. Her mother was the queen's first cousin – a niece of Anne Boleyn.'

I did indeed know Lettice and hadn't taken to her. Nor had Cecil, by the sound of it. The queen would be furious when she heard of this. Her Sweet Robin had never been her lover, of that I was certain. But she assuredly regarded him as her possession. 'No wonder Leicester is being cautious,' I said.

'Jean de Simier hates him,' said Cecil, 'because he knows that Leicester is against the French marriage and he also knows that Leicester has great influence with the queen. De Simier doesn't know about Lettice as far as we are aware and we hope he doesn't find out, but he may do. He has an enquiring nature, and that clerk of his, Antoine de Lacey, is worse. He looks harmless, but I have talked with him and believe me, he has the sort of mind that pokes into every crack like a chisel and tries to pry secrets loose. If de Simier doesn't find out about Lettice, then de Lacey very well may. Thomas Radcliffe of Sussex, of course, has always wanted the queen to marry and have children and he is in favour of the match. So are a good many other members of the Council, though by no means all. Some share our doubts. It's an awkward situation – fraught, even. What did the queen say to you?'

I repeated the gist of it as well as I could and Dale couldn't stop herself from exclaiming: 'Oh, the poor woman!'

Cecil sighed. 'At heart, I hope that when Alençon gets here, she doesn't like him, or he doesn't like her so that the whole enterprise falls quietly through. And yet – England really does need that treaty with France, and could certainly do with an heir.'

Into the silence that followed, I said: 'And the little, harmless task you have in mind for me?'

'Ah. Yes, you remind me. On the Continent just now,' said Cecil, 'is an agent of ours. I won't tell you his real name but his code-name is Janus.'

'The Roman god of the threshold, who had two faces and looked both inwards and outwards?'

'Yes. And our Janus is indeed two-faced. In the eyes of the world, he is an ardent Catholic and an enthusiastic supporter of Mary Stuart's claim to our queen's throne, who has exiled himself to France for his own safety. He often gets himself involved in various schemes intended for Mary's benefit – mostly they concern encouraging other supporters and raising money . . .'

'I know all about that sort of thing,' I said. 'I learned much when I was married to de la Roche.'

'Quite. But to continue. Janus not only learns what he can of plots in the making and passes on to us what he has discovered; he also scuppers the said plots where possible. He seeks out those who have promised men or money, arranges vital meetings where they can get together and then makes sure that the meetings somehow fall through, and the parties blame each other. He finds people willing to sell land or valuables to raise money for Mary but somehow the land or goods are declared worthless, or the vendor's right of ownership is mysteriously challenged. Or the donation is made but goes astray. Our Janus has all manner of ploys and a wide knowledge of useful people who can be bribed or blackmailed into helping him. He is a most gifted agent. And a brave one. He travels to Spain sometimes, which is risky. He is also ruthless.'

Cecil's eyes became thoughtful. 'To my knowledge, he has arranged the deaths of two men who had become suspicious of him. I have myself asked him to avoid this sort of thing and that is partly why I am about to make a certain request of you.'

'I don't understand,' I said.

'You will in a moment. Janus occasionally visits England to call upon relatives. He is here now and somewhat worried. He has been accustomed to send letters and reports to me and to Sir Francis Walsingham through an intermediary, someone purporting to be a cousin in England, with whom he corresponds. This man has died. As far as Janus knows, he is not at the moment under suspicion but he soon would be if he took to writing direct to any influential person in England. He needs a replacement for his so-called cousin. We have been thinking, Janus and Walsingham and I, that while he is in England, why should he not happily make contact with a sister that he lost touch with, perhaps many years ago? There need be nothing remarkable about that.'

I was ahead of him. 'But now he is to pretend that on this latest visit to England, he has met and renewed acquaintance with a sister from whom he was separated, perhaps in childhood, and they wish to write to each other?'

'Yes. He will return to France and he will receive a letter from this imaginary sister, full of family affection and solidarity and delight in having met her estranged brother and made friends with him. He will talk about the letter and about his sister, to his associates. He will be very touched by her wish to keep in contact with him. He will reply to her. The correspondence will flourish,' said Cecil.

'What about his own real relatives? He obviously has some! You have just said that he visits them.'

'They're ordinary folk, and we – Walsingham and I – prefer not to involve such people in secret work,' Cecil said. 'It can be unsafe. Some would be bewildered or even repelled; some excited and liable to talk. It's better to keep secret matters in the hands of those who are used to them.'

'Like me, you mean? I take it,' I said, 'that you want me to be Janus' long-lost sister.'

'Exactly. To receive his letters and pass them on to me or to Walsingham. To Walsingham, I think would be best. Will you do it? There's no danger,' said Cecil persuasively. 'This time, Ursula, you are not being asked to do anything that can possibly bring you into danger. When you return home, regular messengers will call at Hawkswood to collect any letters you may receive, so you need not worry about how to get letters to us. They will be addressed to you under your maiden name of Faldene, and that way, you will always know that they come from Janus. Also, of course, the name of Stannard may be more widely known than we would wish, but Faldene should be safe enough. Few people now remember what you were called as a girl.'

I had been so often assured that my assignments wouldn't bring me into danger, but this time it looked as though it must be true. I couldn't, surely, come to harm just by receiving letters and passing them on. Once again, as so often before, I agreed to do as I was told.

NINE

A Wooer and a Will

I asked if I could meet Janus, but apparently he had left the court to visit the relatives who were, alas, so unsuitable as a means of transmitting information back to England. On thinking it over, I found that I didn't truly want to meet him; I had enough to do already. Like Janus himself, I felt as though I were facing in two directions at the same time, one towards the queen, one towards the mysterious letters I would soon start to receive, from my pretend brother.

My services were to be paid for, of course. The first instalment was paid at once, a purse of six gold angels. There would be four such payments during the year. Twenty pounds annually, just for receiving letters and passing them on. Twenty pounds would keep an ordinary yeoman household for nearly a month. Janus, it seemed, did work of importance.

For the time being, however, I must concentrate on the queen. She called me to her several times during the next few days. On these occasions, I was conducted as before to the private room where she read and studied, received favoured guests and practised her music, but now I was led there by way of a privy stair. This avoided the public performance of passing through successive rooms with guards at the doors and crowds of people. Few others knew of our meetings and there, alone together, she and I would talk, mainly on the subject of marriage.

Because it was what she wanted, I tried to reassure her, to convince her that lovemaking was not alarming and remind her that she was, after all, the reigning queen; she would not be in the power of her husband as her mother and stepmothers had been. She herself said that she did not intend to share power with her husband, if she married.

'The wedding vows may have to be adapted for us,' she

said, using the royal plural. 'We cannot promise obedience to any, even a husband. We are England's sole monarch.'

I wondered what Alençon would think of that and privately hoped it would turn him away from the marriage. However, I didn't say so. I was also reticent on the subject of childbirth and Elizabeth didn't ask me to elaborate. No words could smooth those risks away.

July passed. Not only did I have those meetings with the queen, but I was also approached, almost courted, occasionally by de Simier but more often by de Lacey, who more and more seemed to me to be an enigma. He tried to appear unobtrusive, and in his dress and general manner he mostly was, but repeatedly, there were flickers of something quite different. The juggling and conjuring with which he sometimes amused the court did not fit with his usual nondescript appearance, and sometimes, he made unexpected remarks. But I didn't think about this too much, because I was fretting, wanting to be at home, wanting to be with Harry, but knowing that the queen would not let me go, at least not yet. If all went well when Alençon arrived, then perhaps I would be released, but not before.

Christopher Spelton, in his capacity as a Queen's Messenger, was often at court and was regularly sent to carry letters to a gentleman in Kent, the tenant of a manor owned by Walsingham. When he was with the court, we often met and talked. I learned from him that since his route to Kent always took him close to West Leys, he usually seized the opportunity of calling on his cousin Eric and – though he didn't actually say so – gazing at the face of his forbidden love. Early in August, on returning to court from one of these journeys, he came to see me, with news of Lisa Harrison.

'Things have altered considerably, Ursula. The fact is – Edmund Harrison has died.'

'Died?'

'In the last week of July. He had a seizure. Eric says that it was very likely brought on by rage and distress. Well, he's gone. He was buried two days ago. The servants sent to inform Lisa, of course and she went back to Firtrees House with the twins and since then has stayed there. There is no one now to say her nay. The servants there are fond of her – much fonder than they ever were of Edmund. Lisa is trying to grieve but in truth, I think she's relieved!'

'Well, at least she can stay in her own home,' I said. 'If it *is* hers, that is. How was the property left?'

'Edmund originally left everything to Lisa but just before he died, he made a new will. Eric says he thinks that doing that helped to bring on the seizure; that at heart he really did care for Lisa and really did know that the twins were his and it all built up inside him and killed him. He was a hard man – so hard that he actually did go through with changing his will and cutting out Lisa and the twins – but under the surface, he still had feelings. Under the new will, Firtrees House and the land that goes with it – the fields and the fir plantation – have all been left to Edmund's brother George and after him to Robert, George's son.

'George says that Lisa is welcome to live there; he prefers to live in Leatherhead with Marjorie. Lisa can be his tenant and pay him rent for Firtrees, he says. I strongly suspect that he's having pangs of conscience. After all, it was his fault that Edmund cast her out! He has actually told her that though he disapproves of her behaviour, he doesn't think the twins should have been disinherited. Thomas can inherit the tenancy and George says he'll give Jane a dowry. Whatever Lisa has done, he says, is not their fault. Also, I understand that he sees Lisa as a good housewife, the kind that never runs out of flour or candles or lamp oil. She will run Firtrees properly. He won't admit it,' said Christopher, the man of the world, 'he won't admit it – few men would – but at heart he does realize that he's hardly in a position to throw stones.'

He grinned. 'Edmund didn't consider that when he changed his will! As for the little property in Cornwall, which I believe isn't worth very much, that has been left to Eric. He hopes to visit it soon. Though for some reason, it's a limited bequest. It's only for Eric's lifetime. After his death, the Cornish property reverts to George or his heirs. Kate isn't pleased. It may not be very valuable, but every little is useful.'

Christopher never talked for long without bringing Kate's name into it. I asked after her, as I knew he wanted me to do. 'She is well,' he said. 'Blooming, in fact.'

'I'm glad,' I said sincerely. 'And glad for Lisa, too. She has her home back now.'

'Eric says he has advised Lisa to go to law and challenge the will, because Thomas looks just like Edmund and so the reason for cutting the twins out can't stand. But Lisa is too overset as yet to make plans and is afraid of the expense.'

'She may well be,' I said. 'The law's a slow and costly business!'

On the 17th of August, a page came to my apartment, bidding me to attend on the queen at a reception. Francis, Duke of Alençon, had arrived.

Unexpectedly, he had arrived without attendants, and his presence was a semi-secret. He and the queen had met briefly in private before most of the Council even knew he was in the country. He must now meet them and this reception had therefore been planned. Dress would be formal. I chose an outfit in my favourite tawny and cream: tawny for the overgown and its sleeves, and a kirtle and sleeve slashings of cream silk, with little tawny flowers embroidered on it. With it went amber jewellery and gold kid slippers, and gold edgings for my ruff.

In my capacity as an enquiry agent, I regularly wore gowns open in front, so that a pouch, hidden but quickly accessible, could be stitched inside the skirt, and in that pouch I often carried such useful things as a little extra money, a small dagger in a sheath and a set of picklocks. But on this occasion, my skirt had no secret pouch. I was not on duty now, or not in that sense.

It was horrible weather. Outside, in the grounds, it was raining hard, and a sharp wind was tearing leaves from the trees and the rose bushes in the gardens. Passageways and galleries were shadowy, though there were cressets in holders here and there. Nevertheless, as I hastened along, I sensed a busyness in the air, a feeling of lively expectation. Here and there, knots of people stood talking quietly but excitedly; and servants were scurrying about, valets and tirewomen with garments over their arms, serving men and maids bearing trays loaded with wine and platters of all kinds of food from small pies to a complete cold roast goose.

At one point, I had to stop while two men carrying a massive table between them emerged from a side passage and then put the table down in my path and stood there massaging their arm muscles and grumbling about the weight. A few yards further on, we were overtaken by a harassed man pushing a handcart piled high with boxes of candles. Hampton Court, in fact, was humming. If the duke's arrival had been a secret, it was clearly not so now.

Eventually, I mounted the staircase to the lofty state apartments, which, unlike the gloomy galleries and passageways I had traversed to get there, were brilliantly lit, by banks of candles and numerous stands bearing multiple candlesticks. At Elizabeth's court, candles were used with such abandon that I felt sure there must be several chandlers whose sole customer was Queen Elizabeth, and who were busy all day long, keeping up with her requirements. The smell of melting wax mingled with the scent from the rushes underfoot, which had been mixed with mint and rosemary.

Guards in scarlet tunics stood outside every door in the series, clashing halberds to the floor as they admitted the guests, who were then handed over to the ushers, one of whom led me through to the Presence Chamber.

Here, I paused to take in the scene. A further door, slightly open, gave a glimpse of a room where tables were being positioned and refreshments set out, and in the room immediately before me, the guests were gathered. To one side, the queen's ladies formed a smiling cluster along with some of the foremost male guests. Sir Francis Walsingham, tall, dark, hollow-cheeked and clad in black, was among them, as was the queen's vice-chamberlain, Sir Christopher Hatton, who was one of her close associates, and also Jean de Simier.

De Simier, who I supposed was present as the friend of the guest of honour, was dressed with propriety, in a light brown suit that had a soldierly air about it. Hatton on the other hand was in a rust-red doublet and hose which went with his dark beard and hair and his strong, good-looking features. Hatton was the best dancer in the court and was possessed of dramatic eyebrows that went up at the outer corners. At the moment, although he seemed to be talking pleasantly to his companions, the inner corners of those brows were drawn together. He did not look happy.

Nor did the Earl of Leicester, who was standing alone. His smile looked as though it had been painted on to his tanned features. His crimson doublet was tight, probably to show off his wide shoulders and his flat stomach. Cecil, wearing his formal robes, was on the other side of the room, talking to Thomas Radcliffe, the Earl of Sussex. Cecil's face was watchful but Sussex was beaming. And in the centre, in white and silver and three ropes of glimmering pearls, was Queen Elizabeth, deep in conversation with the Duke of Alençon.

I looked at him, and stood motionless, at gaze.

Francis, Duke of Alençon, certainly wasn't handsome. He was straightbacked enough but he was barely over five feet tall and his face, which was partly turned towards me, was sadly pitted with the marks of bygone smallpox. But his dark eyes sparkled with intelligence and merriment, and from where I stood, I could hear him speaking, in fluent English, and I have never heard a more melodious voice. It was as though his lack of inches and his scarred face were irrelevant, and not just because of the bright eyes and the beautiful voice, either. He had that indefinable thing called Presence. Simply by being in the room, he made every other man dwindle. It was as though, wherever he stood or walked, a brilliant shaft of light followed him, a light that had nothing to do with the innumerable candles.

Listening to that pleasant voice, I realized that he was quoting a piece of English poetry. I gathered that he was completing a quotation which the queen had begun. He finished, and Elizabeth said: 'You know that poem by heart! Have you memorized much verse, my lord? You speak it so well.'

'I have always had a liking for poetry, ma'am.' His smile was as delightful as his voice. 'I take pleasure in committing it to memory. Such interests balance the martial skills that all men should learn. They complete a man, make him into a rounded being.'

He was assuredly that. All the ladies were glancing towards him with visible admiration and the queen's shield-shaped face, usually so pale, was softly flushed, like the face of a girl who has just been paid her first compliment. I looked again at Hatton and Leicester, and saw that Hatton's dramatic eyebrows had almost met and that Leicester was holding himself rigidly, as though he were encased in an invisible suit of armour. The queen was pleased with Alençon, but they were not.

At that moment, there was a mild disturbance behind me. Turning, I saw that close to the door was a bank of lights that must have been lit before the others, for some of the candles were burning low. Someone must have noticed and asked for replacements, for servants were just hurrying in with boxes of fresh candles. As they set about replacing the old with the new, one of them dropped a box lid. It fell with a clatter, whereupon Leicester, suddenly glowering, strode over and in a low but savage voice, ordered them to stop making a noise, to finish quickly and go.

He then swung round and went to join de Simier and Hatton and I witnessed the way he put his painted smile back on to his face, assuming a sociable mien. I also saw something knowing in de Simier's manner as he replied to something Leicester said, and I knew that he was perfectly aware that Leicester and Hatton were furious and that Leicester had taken out his rage on the hapless servants.

The queen caught sight of me and smiled, a lovely smile, and for once, she was not concealing her thoughts. She gave me a little nod.

It was all right. Leicester and Hatton might seethe, Walsingham and Cecil might doubt, but Elizabeth had taken to her suitor. She was going to let him woo her. She looked as though she had forgotten all her fears.

My responsibility was over. The Duke of Alençon would assuredly finish the work of reassurance. Fearing for the queen as I did, I was sorry for it, but if it was what she herself wanted, then I – and Cecil and Walsingham, Leicester and Hatton – would have to put our worries aside and pray for her. I could go home.

TEN

The Breaking Storm

B efore the queen released me, she called me to one more private meeting. She welcomed me with a smile and handed me a fan. The chilly wet weather had gone, to be followed by two hot days and then a windless, sultriness with a hazy sky. My stiff ruff pricked my neck and under my expensive green brocade gown I was sweating. Sweat also gleamed on Elizabeth's skin, beneath her open ruff. I was glad of the fan.

It was the start, though no one could have known it, of a stormy season, which would affect the events that followed, as though Fate itself were guiding them.

Without wasting words on preamble, Elizabeth said: 'All goes well, my Ursula. You have no doubt wondered. Francis of Alençon is a most remarkable young man. I never expected to take to him as I have, to feel as much at home with him as I do.'

'I am happy to hear it, ma'am,' I said dutifully. 'When I saw him at the reception, I must say he impressed me.'

'Yes. He has a keen mind, and a vigour, an aura, even though he lacks inches and there are the marks of the pox – well, I have a few of those too . . .'

'They aren't noticeable, ma'am.'

Elizabeth put up a hand to touch the little marks on her forehead and under her left cheekbone. They were very faint, even when she wasn't wearing powder and today she was. 'Mine are nothing,' she said. 'But his are nothing, also, because after a few moments in his company, one can't see them any longer. Ursula, he can talk of *anything*, and in knowledgeable fashion. He can talk of music, poetry, history, of exotic food-stuffs from other lands, of the management of horses and how to cultivate quinces and the latest scientific theories about the stars. And he can make puns. Even in English! We are never dull.'

'That is an accolade indeed,' I said. The queen laughed and her golden-brown eyes danced in a way I had rarely seen before.

'Dear sister. It is going to be all right. And so – I love to have you by me, but it would make my other ladies jealous if I kept you here too long, and besides, I know you want to be at home with your little boy. You have my leave to go when you wish. But there is one more thing that you can do for me.' Her eyes became serious. 'You can pray for me, pray that I too may soon have a little boy, to rule after me, to guard and guide this green realm when I am gone. Will you do that?'

'Of course I will.' I would also, most ardently, pray for her safety in the perilous seas of childbirth. 'Though even if your child should be a little girl,' I ventured, 'why should she not be a worthy successor to you? As worthy as you are yourself, my sister.'

'I wouldn't wish such a fate on a girl,' said Elizabeth unexpectedly. 'A crown is a heavy burden. I have done – I intend to do – my duty, but it is harder for a woman than for a man, harder to be in command, harder to be responsible for the succession . . .'

Just for a moment, the old uncertainty was there again. She said: 'It seems that the treaty which my marriage to Alençon is supposed to clinch may actually be dependent on the marriage. I mean, that the French won't sign until we have exchanged our vows. It's just as well,' said Elizabeth lightly, 'that he and I have agreed together as we have.'

I kissed her hand and wished her joy, as I knew she wanted me to do, and then I went away to tell Dale that we could pack.

We started for home the following day. There was no straight road between Hampton Court and Hawkswood, just a choice of serpentine ones, but the one I preferred took a route that passed through the market town of Epsom and on through the villages of Ashtead and Leatherhead, until, to reach Hawkswood, one turned off from the road between Leatherhead and Guildford, and took a track leading westward. This, eventually, led to Hawkswood.

It was a day's ride at our pace though a man in a hurry could do it in less. We were not in a hurry and we didn't expect to be home before suppertime.

We had passed through Ashtead when we noticed that the hazy sunshine was dimming further and that in the southwest, the sky looked very dark. 'I think rain's on the way,' I said, pointing.

'Yes. It looks as though it might be heavy,' said Dale uneasily.

'In that case,' Brockley said, 'we'd better seek shelter somewhere.' He looked about him. There were no habitations to be seen, only fields and commons and patches of woodland.

'We're getting near Leatherhead,' I said. 'What about the Running Horse inn?'

They both murmured agreement. We had all liked the Running Horse, liked its clean white plastered walls, its eye-catching gables and its comfortable rooms from which one could hear the purling of the nearby river Mole. Brockley had approved of the inn's airy stables and competent ostler.

'The Running Horse it is,' I said.

We shook the horses into a trot. Dale bounced uncomfortably but gallantly held on to Brockley. We were near the first houses of Leatherhead when, all in a moment, the darkening sky became very dark indeed, a wind sprang up and the rain began to spatter.

'Cloaks!' said Brockley. 'It's going to pour!'

Since we had set off in warm weather, our cloaks had been stuffed into our saddlebags. It was easier to put them on when not sitting on a horse, so we all dismounted. We had just got our cloaks on when the spattering rain turned into a deluge. It fell out of the sky as though from a waterfall. We were soaked in a moment, cloaks and all. 'We'll never make the inn in this!' I gasped. 'It's at the far end of the town! But Marjorie Harrison's house is near. Look, it's that one! Let's try there!'

We blundered forward, pulling our horses after us. They were drenched as well, their coats shining with water. At Marjorie's gate, I threw my reins to Brockley, ran through the garden and up the steps and pounded on the door. Dale came after me, panting. The maidservant Mary opened it, and stared at us in amazement.

'I'm Mistress Stannard!' I said. 'I've visited Mistress Harrison before.' I was cold all through and Dale was shivering. 'We've been caught in the downpour – we were nearby so we came here to ask shelter.'

'Who is it, Mary?' Marjorie had appeared behind the maid. She stared for a moment, and no doubt, in my saturated cloak and hat, with water streaming down my face and a strand of soaking hair plastered to one cheek, I was scarcely recognizable. I started to repeat my introduction. Halfway through, Marjorie's face cleared.

'Of course, of course! Mistress Stannard . . . Oh, you poor things, come in, come in! Is that your man out there? Call to him to go round to the stables; he'll remember the way, won't he?'

We were made welcome at astonishing speed. Brockley vanished with the horses to see them stabled; I knew that within minutes he and Marjorie's own groom would be wiping them down with handfuls of hay and straw and finding cloths to put over their backs. Marjorie looked tired and harried, but she was brisk about leading us indoors. She had apparently been working with Mary in the kitchen when we arrived, for she had an apron on, over a dun-coloured working dress, and wasn't wearing a ruff.

Dale and I were taken straight to the kitchen, where there was a fire, the only one in the house. Our wet cloaks and hats were taken away and towels were found so that we could dry our faces. Marjorie herself set about preparing mulled wine and at her orders, Mary took a pot of hot water off the trivet over the fire. 'We heated that to boil a cabbage, but I expect your man will want it now,' Marjorie said.

She was quite right. As we thankfully sipped the wine, Brockley came to the back door. He had a horse blanket thrown over his head and was carrying his own wet cloak and hat. 'Can I leave these here to dry? Is there any hot water? The horses need bran mash!'

'Water's ready,' said Marjorie, presenting him with the pot, along with a cloth to protect his hands from scorching. 'Blessed forethought,' said Brockley, and departed, carrying it. Outside, the rain continued to pour down and there was a rumble of thunder.

'What terrible weather,' Marjorie said. 'Well, you're in time for dinner as it happens; I have a meat pie in my oven and some beans ready to fry, and there will be sweet pancakes with quince preserves to follow. Mary, put on more water for the cabbage and then prepare some extra beans.'

The kitchen door opened, to admit George with another, younger man. 'We heard someone arriving.' George said, glancing at me and Dale without apparently recognizing us. 'They'll be dining, I suppose,' he said to Marjorie. 'They can't ride on in this. Why isn't the table being set in the dining room? Surely we're not going to eat in here? It's hardly the proper thing when we have visitors.'

George had very much the air of the master of the house and I saw Marjorie bristle. He sat down on one of the stools that encircled the kitchen table. His companion patted his shoulder and said: 'Well, we eat here quite happily when it's just family. Our guests probably find the fire welcome. We heard you ask for shelter,' he added, speaking to me directly. 'You must have been drenched.'

'We were,' I said. 'And yes, we're glad of warmth. We don't mind eating here.'

'Just who *are* our guests?' George enquired.

'This is Mistress Ursula Stannard and her woman, Frances Brockley,' said Marjorie over her shoulder, while she busied herself with cutting up a cabbage and Mary shook white beans into a pan of hot fat. 'You have met Mistress Stannard before. That'll be enough, Mary. Put some salt with them. Their groom, Brockley, is out in the stable now; he'll want some food as well. And my dear, I really do think we should eat here in the kitchen where it's warm. It's amazing, how cold that storm has made the air, all of a sudden.'

'Mistress Stannard. Of course. I didn't know you at first. You look so bedraggled,' said George with tactless candour. He turned to his companion. 'Mistress Stannard is related to your mother's friend Mistress Tabitha Faldene. And a former ward of hers is now married to your Uncle Eric. The society of Surrey resembles knitting.'

'After a kitten has played with the wool?' said the younger man dryly. He wasn't so very young; I estimated his age as the mid-thirties. 'I am happy to meet you, Mistress Stannard. I am Robert, the son of the house. I live in France normally but I came over when I heard of my Uncle Edmund's death. I've stayed on for a while, as there has been much to do.'

'The news was sent to me and George the day it happened,' said Marjorie. 'George sent off a messenger to France at once and Robert was here in time for the funeral.'

'Both the messenger and I were lucky with getting passages across the Channel,' said Robert. 'Such a sad business, Uncle Edmund's death.'

He offered his hand and I shook it. I looked at him with interest. So this was Robert, the son who had been so long out of touch with his mother and had helped to saddle her with his father. He didn't look much like either of his parents except that he had the light brown eyes and sensual mouth that seemed to be characteristic of the Harrison males. The person he resembled most, I thought, was his now deceased uncle, Edmund. He had the same thickset build and his hair, which curled as Edmund's had done, was sandy.

Like his father and his uncle, he clearly had a taste for good clothes, and his were quite new. George was in the same smart, if not new, outfit that he had worn the first time we met but there were no repairs or scuffings to be seen on Robert's lightweight summer doublet. It was of a rich blue with silvery slashes on its sleeves and looked as though it had silk in its weave. Its big buttons were surely lapis set in silver. Each glowing blue stone had a little motif carved into it. His hose was blue and silver and his leather shoes had been dyed to match the doublet. I glanced at Marjorie in her dull dun gown, and wondered at the contrast.

Dale was still shivering, however, and I myself mulled some more wine for her. It seemed that the maid Mary was Marjorie's only servant. I began to dislike the male Harrisons. They were anxious enough to wear showy clothes but neither had thought to provide Marjorie with more help in the house now that she had two men to look after.

Brockley reappeared before long, accompanied by Marjorie's

groom, both of them swathed in horse blankets, which they removed and hung round the fire to dry. It seemed that the whole household normally ate together. Both Marjorie and Mary were constantly up and down, handing dishes round. The dinner was good, though, and blessedly warming. To make polite conversation, I asked Robert about his work abroad and gathered that he served as an assistant to a successful wine grower.

'A Huguenot. They weren't all killed in the Massacre of St Bartholomew and there is more tolerance now in France. I seek out customers and help with the grape harvest too,' he said, and smiled at my obvious surprise. 'Yes, I know, I am something of a dandy, am I not? But I can roll up my sleeves and go out to the vineyards with a wooden pail and scratch my hands on tough vines with the best of them. I hope this storm isn't raging in France as well and afflicting our grapes!' The downpour was still heavy and he had to raise his voice to be heard above the sound of thunder. 'I enjoy winemaking,' he said. 'It's an intriguing process.'

'I believe there is a great deal to it,' I said politely. 'More perhaps than most people realize.'

'Yes, indeed. Since I have been obliged to come to England, I shall take the opportunity of calling on some of our English customers, hoping that they will renew their orders. Then I must go back for this year's harvest, though it won't begin till well into September. Meanwhile, of course, I must help as much as I can with the aftermath of my uncle's death.'

'There is much to do,' said George. 'The property in Cornwall has to be handed over to Master Lake, there are decisions to be taken and documents to be signed and personal belongings to distribute or dispose of. Though I have no doubt,' he added dryly, 'that you *will,* as you say, go wandering off to see your employer's English customers, Robert.'

'My employer would be annoyed if I didn't,' said Robert. 'It's important to him to run a profitable business. I agree with him.' He grinned. 'You could say that we are always on the side of the angels, whether winged or golden.'

He had a curiously feral grin; presenting one with a fine display of teeth, right back to the molars. He made me uneasy in a way I couldn't quite explain. It was an atmosphere, an aura. I recognized it, because Walsingham had a similar one. It suggested an underlying harshness, even ruthlessness. I laughed at his jest, however, and the grin softened into a smile, this time without exposing his back teeth. Whereupon, I unexpectedly became even more uneasy. I tried to push the feeling away but then I met his eyes, and was startled to read in them something I certainly did not want to see. I hoped I was imagining things.

A moment later, he confirmed that I was not. Turning to Marjorie, he said: 'Mother, I find it a great pleasure to be with you again after so long, but I am doubly happy to find you have such a charming and beautiful acquaintance.'

He then turned back to me and said: 'I hope you will not mind the compliment, Mistress Stannard? Mother has talked of you and told me how kind you are, and what pleasant company. What she has said, has impressed me very much. I am delighted to have met you myself and had speech with you.'

And now the timbre of his voice echoed the expression in his eyes. I had heard and seen them both in the past, in other voices, in other eyes, and I could not mistake them. I was, after all, a widow, still (just) of childbearing years and with property. I lived in a practical world and since Hugh's death, I had had to fend off several unwanted advances. Here, I foresaw the danger of another. The man was younger than me, but that would be no hindrance, not with the example currently being set by the queen. Silently, I cursed.

'I thank you, sir,' I said, aware that Dale was now gazing out of the window at the front garden with its hollyhocks and foxgloves and its faded larkspur as fixedly as though a camelopard were straying there, while Brockley's face had frozen. I said: 'The thunder is passing.'

It was still raining, though. I longed to get away but Dale had sneezed three times and I didn't want to drag her back into the wet. We would have to wait.

And wait we did, all through the afternoon, passing the time with games of backgammon and listening as Marjorie played a spinet, probably the one that her sister had left her. The groom went back to the stables but Brockley stayed with us and I was glad to have him as a partner at the backgammon board, since it kept me away from Robert Harrison, who partnered his father. I gathered anyway that they were both skilled players, which I was not. I found backgammon a complicated game and Brockley seemed to feel the same.

Eventually, the sky cleared but Dale sneezed again and looked exhausted and Brockley said: 'I think Fran shouldn't have to ride on too far today, madam. I don't think we should try to reach Hawkswood tonight.'

'Oh, dear.' Marjorie looked worried. 'I would give you beds, only, with Robert staying . . .'

And with George presumably still occupying one of the spare rooms – somehow, because there were nuances in the way they spoke to each other, I was fairly sure that Marjorie had kept to her original decision and not let him into hers – there wouldn't be enough space for us. Thank goodness for that. I need not spend any longer under the same roof as Robert. 'We'll go to the Running Horse,' I said.

The Running Horse, fortunately, had rooms for us, and the stables had stalls for our animals. We had a late supper there and retired thankfully to comfortable beds. But in the morning, I answered a knock on my bedchamber door and found Brockley there, looking anxious.

'Madam, it's Fran. She's not at all well. I fear she got a chill yesterday when we were caught in the rain. She has a bad throat and I think she's feverish. I recommend that we go no further today.'

'Let me see her,' I said.

One look was enough. 'Stay in bed, Dale,' I told her. 'We'll stay here till you're better.'

Poor Dale was somewhat prone to illnesses of this kind. I had seen it all before, but I always felt concerned about her. The innkeeper and his wife were helpful, supplying hot herbal drinks and mulled wine and soft foods like porridge, and bread soaked in milk and honey, which an invalid with a bad sore throat could swallow easily.

The next day, mercifully, the cold broke. The bad throat got better, although Dale continued to sneeze violently and had to blow her nose so much that I had to go out into Leatherhead to buy extra handkerchiefs. It was three days before her fever abated and five altogether before she could leave her bed. It was nearly a week before she was able once more to mount behind Brockley and ride on to Hawkswood.

We were all thankful to be home. As soon as we were off our horses, I told Dale to go to her bed.

'I've been dressing myself for days,' I said when she protested. 'I can go on doing it.' At the Running Horse, one of the maids had helped me with difficult fastenings and here at home there was no shortage of maidservants. Dale departed, looking relieved, the groom Joseph and Simon, another of my grooms, came to see to our horses, and Brockley, having heaved the saddlebags off, carried them indoors. I followed, going in through the door that led directly to the great hall. In the doorway, I came face to face with my steward Adam Wilder, looking harassed.

'Madam! My apologies – I was occupied and didn't realize you had ridden in, or I would have come out to you at once . . .'

'What is it, Wilder? Is something wrong?'

'Well, yes, madam, in a way. Oh, not something wrong *here* but . . . well . . .'

'Wilder, what are you havering about? Tell me!'

'Master Lake, Mistress Kate's husband, is here and . . .'

But I had already seen him, for Eric had appeared behind him. He still looked like a pagan god, but now he was a worried god, with a creased brow and unhappy eyes. 'I came to tell you – Kate sent me to tell you—'

'Is Kate all right?' I jumped to the wrong conclusion. 'Is it the baby? Has something gone amiss?'

'No, no, Kate is perfectly well. But Mistress Lisa Harrison has been to see us . . . she is frantic. It's her son, Thomas. It seems,' said Eric in a bewildered tone, 'that Thomas has . . . has . . . well, he's disappeared.'

ELEVEN
The Only Possible Place

'We can't discuss this in the doorway,' I said and steered us all into the hall, where I found Sybil and Gladys both with anxious faces. Brockley joined us and I gathered us all round.

'Now,' I said, 'what is all this?'

'Lisa came to West Leys to see us yesterday,' said Eric. 'Distraught! It happened two days before, it seems. It . . .'

'Is Lisa still at West Leys?'

'No, she has gone home again. She didn't want to be away for long, in case Thomas was found, or came home, or . . . only she wanted to let us know and ask for help. I couldn't offer much. There has already been a thorough search. But I thought of you and she agreed. You have a reputation, you know. Kate said yes, surely you would try to help, and sent me here to find you. To find that you were not at home! You have arrived at just the right moment, thank heaven.'

'I see.'

We had all sat down by this time, except for Eric, who kept pacing about. 'Just what happened?' I asked.

'Lisa said it was just an ordinary day,' Eric said. 'You know she is living at Firtrees again – she went back after Edmund died. George is the owner now but he is letting her stay, to look after the place. It's convenient, he says, whatever may have happened in the past.'

'Yes, I know about that. Let him who is without sin, cast the first stone. Go on.'

Eric, typically, failed to grasp the oblique reference to the misdemeanours of George and looked puzzled. However, he didn't pursue the matter. 'Have you ever been to Firtrees?'

'No, I haven't. Go on! And Eric, please sit down.'

Reluctantly, he did. 'It's a bit to the south of here,' he said.

'It's a quiet place. The nearest farmhouse, Badgers, is about a mile away. Their fields and the Firtrees ones are in between. Firtrees also has a wood of pines and silver firs that provide timber and oils. The house is about the same size as ours at West Leys. There are gardens, flower and kitchen, at the back and a stable yard alongside, a gate at the rear and a small courtyard in the front, and a wall that encloses it all. There's a little gatehouse but no porter. Lisa keeps the front gate open all day though it's bolted at night. There's an apple tree in the courtyard.'

'Yes? And?'

'I'm sorry, but I'm trying to give you all the details, as Lisa gave them to me. I know the place, so I can picture it all, but you can't do that. It was in the morning. Thomas went out to look at the apple tree, to see what kind of crop it was likely to produce this year. Lisa was in her parlour and could see him from the window. She saw him looking at the tree and then he turned towards the gatehouse as though he had heard something – someone calling him, perhaps, because he suddenly ran outside into the lane. Lisa couldn't see who might be calling, but he's friendly with the two boys from Badgers and she thought they might have come to see him. She thought no more of it for an hour or so – she had this and that to do and was busy – but when the twins' tutor arrived to start their lessons for the day, Thomas couldn't be found.'

My senior maid, Phoebe, came in just then, bringing wine and ale. I poured for everyone and Eric gulped half a beaker of ale straightaway, as though he were in desperate need of a stimulant.

'It seems that Jane was already in the schoolroom with her books,' he explained. 'Jane likes her studies. But Thomas doesn't and as there was no sign of him, Lisa thought he was just playing some boyish game. He's been known to hide when it's time for lessons. She thought he might have come back into the grounds and gone to the stables – he's often there – but he hadn't. She asked the grooms to help find him. They searched the tack room, the hayloft, the grain store and a garden shed that Thomas finds interesting – it's where shears and spades and ladders are kept, and a wheelbarrow and trugs and other oddments. But there was still no trace of him.'

'There were men in the Badgers fields, it seems,' said Sybil. 'But they hadn't seen anyone crossing the farmland.'

'No. And the boys at Badgers were with their own tutor. They hadn't called on Thomas.' Eric ran his fingers through his hair. 'The lane past the Firtrees gatehouse passes various cottages and small hamlets, in both directions. One way, it eventually leads to Leatherhead and it goes to Woking in the other. No one, anywhere, had seen the lad go by. The track winds a lot; it isn't a major route and there isn't much traffic on it. A few riders were seen going by but none of them matched the description of Thomas. He had vanished, just vanished!'

I said: 'What's at the back of the house? More farmland?'

Eric gulped his ale again. 'No – common land. A heath. Sheep graze there, and some goats and donkeys. It's about half a mile each way and beyond it there's a village called Priors Ford . . .'

'Yes, I know Priors Ford,' I said.

'There was no trace of Thomas there either,' Eric said. 'He hadn't passed through the village. Someone would have seen him; many of the villagers know him by sight. There is no one, no one at all, in any direction, who that morning saw, or even glimpsed in the distance, a boy who even *might* have been Thomas. The search has been careful. The Badgers' people all left their work and joined in. They had to call off the hunt when night fell, but it began again the next morning, and folk from the villages joined in. The fir wood opposite the house was gone through then, inch by inch, Lisa says. Not a trace was found anywhere! Nothing! But he must be somewhere. Well, Mistress Stannard, Lisa thinks that perhaps you might have ideas . . . would you go to her? Would you help?'

People were for ever asking me to help, I thought. Aunt Tabitha called on me when Uncle Herbert was being difficult; she and Marjorie seemed to think I could help when George walked back out of the past and put Marjorie out so badly; the queen thought I could soothe away her doubts about marriage. Now it was Lisa Harrison and the Lakes, wanting me to do something about the disappearance of Thomas, even though by the sound of it, everything that could be done, had been, was being, done already.

But how could one refuse a plea like this? I sighed in sympathy and then felt privately exasperated. I had only just come home and I wanted to take up the reins of my household, to play with Harry and supervise his education. I had taught him to read and write and I had started him on Latin, and begun teaching him to play the spinet. But I couldn't devote all my time to that, so I was planning to find a tutor who would educate him properly, though I intended to continue with the music lessons. I wanted, so much, to be left alone to attend to these things. But instead . . .

'Tomorrow,' I said. 'I'll go to Firtrees tomorrow. Today I must catch my breath.'

'I don't know what we're doing here,' I complained. 'I couldn't say no to Mistress Harrison, considering the state she's in, but I can't see the point of searching the wood all over again.'

We were standing in front of the wood, which began on the opposite side of the lane that ran past Firtrees House. There was only a bank between the lane and the first dark line of trees.

'I think we're just obliging Mistress Harrison,' said Brockley. 'I can't see much use in it, either. If the boy wanted to run away, and to me that is the most likely explanation, he could have slipped off through the wood and out to the farmland beyond. It's nonsense to say he must have been seen. A boy would know well enough how to keep out of sight, alongside hedgerows, or using ditches. He could have got away unseen, right enough. But this search is what Mistress Lisa asked of us and we are right to humour her. It's the only thing that will calm her.'

'I too feel that he must have run off,' said Eric Lake. 'Who would want to attack a harmless young lad who was just standing in a courtyard and looking at an apple tree?'

'But why would he run away?' I said. 'What would make him leave his mother and his twin without a word? Leave them in such fear and doubt!'

'He must have been distressed by losing his father, and

before that, being rejected by Edmund. Those things might have overset him badly,' Eric suggested.

'But we were talking to Lisa just now,' I said, 'and according to her, he was pleased that they had been allowed to come back to Firtrees to live and he'd talked of contesting the will!' Eric became thoughtful. 'Yes, that's true. He asked me if I could set that in hand on his behalf. He said he looked enough like his father to convince any jury that he really was Edmund's son! He said there were plenty of people who would remember what his father looked like. That does sound like common sense and not at all like someone about to abandon his home and his family. You're right about that.'

'And Lisa said he was quite normal at breakfast that day,' I remembered. '*She* doesn't think he's run away. She's sure he wouldn't do such a thing.'

'Oh, well,' said Brockley, 'a second search will do no harm. We might find something, some sign. As I said, we are really here to please Mistress Lisa. That's what it amounts to,' he added ruefully.

Lisa, red-eyed, exhausted, dressed in an old gown to which pine needles were adhering and her arm round an equally tearful and untidy Jane, had begged and pleaded with us.

'He would never just run off. I think he must be . . . he must be . . .' She broke down and then, through her tears, said: 'He must be dead. There's no other explanation. And his body is in the wood. It's the only possible place. The wood is so difficult to search, to search thoroughly, I mean. The people from Badgers went through it, and that's what they said. I went out there again myself, this morning. They were right; it's hopelessly difficult. I didn't know *how* to search. I just peered and stumbled about . . . everyone says that he would have been seen if he'd gone or been taken along the lane, whether east or west, or across the fields or over the heath to Priors Ford. *I want that fir wood searched again.*'

I started to say 'But . . .' but Lisa, standing there in her parlour, dishevelled and despairing, cut me short.

'Ursula, I beg you, I beg you, will you do it or at least get Brockley and Eric to do it? I believe Thomas is there. I believe that something happened to him – a friend called him outside and perhaps there was a dispute, or an accident and his friend is frightened and has hidden the . . . has hidden what he's done and . . . Thomas would never run away or do anything to hurt himself. He *wouldn't!* Something has *happened* to him! I know it has! I've lost my son. But I can't bear not knowing just how. Anything is better than not knowing. *Please will you search that wood!'*

Brockley and Eric said they would undertake the task but I was the one Lisa had called on, and I said that I must join them. I borrowed an old gown from Lisa, a skimpy one in thin wool, with skirts that could be kilted and narrow sleeves. Thus clad, I was fairly well fitted to go stumbling about in woodlands.

'But how do we go about this search?' I asked plaintively. 'These trees don't even have dens or caves between their roots; their trunks aren't wide enough for that.'

'We must just do what we can,' said Brockley.

'Yes, we must try,' said Eric.

We did try, and I hated it. That horrible wood was so silent. I could hear no birdsong. The scent of the pines was pleasant but muffling too; one was *aware* of the trees to an excessive extent. It felt as though they were watching us. I felt, as I moved through the shadows, that this was a place that might well hold secrets, but if so, it would keep them. I walked along, scanning the ground for signs of disturbance, scanning the tree boles for holes, for hollow trunks, for anywhere where . . . where anything . . . a body? . . . could possibly have been hidden. I saw nothing. Nor did Eric or Brockley.

It seemed to me that we spent a lifetime in that wood. At the end of it, we were all hungry and thirsty, having eaten nothing at midday, and we had only failure to report. I don't know whether I felt relieved or regretful. Finding anything wouldn't, after all, have been pleasant, but Lisa might have preferred it to this empty nothingness.

Disconsolately, we made our way back to the house. We arrived to find a man clearing up horse droppings from the courtyard and a mild air of bustle, which was explained when we went indoors and were led to the parlour to be greeted not just by Lisa but also by Robert Harrison.

Lisa looked questioningly at us and Eric shook his head. 'No, Mistress Harrison, Thomas is not in the wood. We searched it from end to end. We've been at it without a break.' 'I am not surprised,' said Robert. He was as well dressed as before, in the same blue and silver, though I noticed that the doublet was rather tight. It looked as though Marjorie had been feeding him well. 'I understand that a search has already taken place, twice, in fact, without result,' he said. 'It was good of you all to make such efforts to please Aunt Lisa. We all came at once, of course, when Thomas was first found to be missing. Aunt Lisa sent word, and we stayed here that night, but next day my father started coughing so we took him home. He's been in bed ever since, and my mother is looking after him. But we all wanted to know if there was any news, so today I rode back.'

'It was kind of you,' said Lisa. 'If only there were news. If only there were *something*.' It came out as *thomething*. Her lisp was much in evidence again.

'I shall have to go home again tonight,' said Robert. He looked harassed and tired. 'My parents will want to know whatever I can tell them, and tomorrow I must set off to see some of my employer's customers in England. Appointments have been made. I have already kept some, but several are still outstanding and between those and Uncle Edmund's affairs and now this, I wonder how to fit it all in.'

'You must all be ravenous,' Lisa said. 'You've ridden from Leatherhead, Robert, and the rest of you have been out searching. I've asked for something to be got ready – halfway between supper and dinner, as it were. Jane and I had hardly anything midday, either. Let's all eat.'

I was grimy and ill-dressed but I was too tired to do anything about it. If Dale had been there, she would have urged me to change, but Dale was still pulled down by her illness and I had left her behind. Dale didn't like seeing me go off with Brockley and without her; there had been a time, long ago, when Brockley and I had come near to being more than lady and manservant, and Dale knew it. But Eric Lake had been in the party, and that had somehow reconciled her. She had raised no objection. So here I was without her to keep me in order, and I went, still grubby, to the dinner cum supper that awaited us. Jane, who had not been in the parlour, came quietly in to join us.

'I was at my books,' she said unhappily. 'It's something to do, to think about. Is there any news, Mother?' She went to Lisa and put an arm round her shoulders and I realized that Jane, apart from being bereft of her twin brother, was also attempting to be a support to her mother. It was a heavy burden for one so young, and no wonder that she looked so wan and exhausted. 'Was . . . was anything found?' she asked.

'Nothing,' said Lisa and Eric said: 'Your cousin Robert came over to ask just that.'

'I did have another purpose,' Robert said. 'There is something I want to say – to suggest. But presently, after we have all eaten.'

Lisa, hardly listening, said: 'If only . . . if only . . . one *knew*. It's this emptiness, this silence, this nothingness! Where *is* he? Where is Thomas? How can anyone – a grown boy, active, strong, sensible – just disappear into thin air?'

There was no answer to that, but Robert, helping himself to chicken pie, said: 'My dear, I may be able to ease some of the more immediate consequences. But first, please, let us eat!'

TWELVE
Proposals

We were all rather silent during the meal. I kept wondering what Robert had meant by his cryptic remarks about easing immediate consequences, but Lisa, lost in miserable contemplation of our failure to find anything, did not pursue the matter. Jane tried to, without success. She was so very wan and as she had her mother's fair colouring, her black mourning gown made her even more waiflike. Somehow her voice was in keeping. She could barely make herself heard and after a dispirited half-sentence or two, ceased to try. Eric then attempted to question Robert, but Robert just shook his head at them and said: 'Later.' When the meal was finished, Lisa led us from her dining chamber to the parlour. There we sat about, awkwardly, until Robert cleared his throat and at last seemed ready to speak.

It was surprising, I thought, how a room could take on the mood of the people in it. The parlour had bright cushions and a tapestry wall-hanging depicting colourful flowers and a pretty cabinet with a display of silverware in it and it should have been cheerful. Instead, it was full of sorrow and shadows. Always pale, poor Lisa was now unhealthily so, and as with Jane, her black gown made things worse. I could understand that, of course. She had lost husband and son in swift succession, and the loss of Edmund must have created an intolerable emotional muddle, since he had preceded it by hurling accusations at her and disinheriting their children. I looked at Robert, questioningly.

'Aunt Lisa,' he said. 'And Cousin Jane. I want to help. And I have thought of something. I can't magically produce Thomas but I might do something for Jane, at least.' He looked gravely at her. Jane, seated beside her mother, said: 'What do you mean, cousin?'

'I thought of this when my father told me about Edmund's new will,' Robert said. 'He apparently made it in our house. He wanted to talk it over with my father, it seems, though he didn't take much notice when my father said he didn't approve of it!'

'He wrote to me about it!' said Lisa, suddenly violent. 'It was a horrible letter. Spiteful! He wanted to hurt me, as much as he could. I came to Firtrees to plead with him. My servants let me in. He was here, in this room. He tried to put me out but I clung to the doorpost and pleaded with him. More than pleaded! I wept, I howled, I begged him not to reject his children, I kept on saying that Thomas was beginning to look like him and that if Thomas was his child, then Jane must be as well, since they're twins. I wailed and begged and then I was angry and I darted past him and went to that cabinet . . .' she pointed '. . . there where I keep some of our silver and I threw it at him, all of it, every dish, every pitcher . . .'

I regarded her in astonishment, finding it difficult to visualize gentle little Lisa doing any such thing. But appearances can deceive and the meekest, most submissive people can turn savage if provoked too far.

'He wouldn't listen,' Lisa said. 'He got hold of me and dragged me through the house and put me out by force. And then, it seems, he went to George to talk the new will over with him.'

'Which didn't quite work out as he meant it to,' said Robert. 'I wasn't there, of course; I was still in France. But once I got home, I soon heard all about it. It was because of my father, Uncle Eric, that you only have the Cornish property for your lifetime, and can't hand it on to your own family. My father considered that it shouldn't be left to you at all, to tell you the truth; he wanted it all to be left to him and me. But Edmund apparently wished you to have something. Only, my father made such a to-do about it that in the end, Edmund did compromise a little.'

'I wasn't expecting anything at all,' Eric said. 'I am pleased about even this restricted bequest. I shall go and inspect it soon. I had better know what it is that I own, even if I only own it for the time being.'

'I have brought you the deeds,' Robert said. 'I have them in my saddlebag. The will you have seen; my father showed it to you and to Aunt Lisa after Edmund's funeral. It was in with the rest of Edmund's papers. Father has taken charge of all that.'

'But this idea that you have, about making anything better?' said Lisa, returning to the original point. 'Come along, Robert. What is it?'

Robert smiled, that disconcerting smile that revealed his molars. For a moment, he seemed troubled. Unexpectedly, he caught my eye and to my surprise, gave me what seemed to be an apologetic glance. He was wearing slippers and one of them seemed to be falling off. He leant down to adjust it and there was a comical moment as one of his lapis doublet buttons shot off and landed in the parlour's unlit hearth.

'My mother feeds me too well,' he said, as he stooped to pick it up. 'But I shall lose my spare flesh when I am back at the vineyard, harvesting grapes. Mother will sew the button back on for me.'

'You ought to get married,' said Eric. 'Then you would have a wife to do these little tasks for you.'

'Yes,' said Robert. 'And getting married is what I have in mind. Firtrees and its land have all passed into the ownership of my father and will eventually come to me. Thomas is not here to stand before witnesses who know how much he resembles his father. If you go to law now, Aunt Lisa, it will be harder without Thomas. You might be successful but no one can be sure. It could mean serious expense – just lining lawyers' pockets – and that if it failed, well, it's money wasted . . .'

'I can't afford it,' said Lisa shortly. In fact, both she and Jane looked alarmed at the mere thought of going to law. Robert smiled at them. 'So I offer you a simpler way! Jane, you are of marriageable age now. We are first cousins but that's no longer a bar to marriage. These days, there's no need to seek dispensations. Aunt Lisa, I do not condone what you did in the past but I can't think it right that your children should suffer for it, especially as I believe that they really are Edmund's. I suggest,' said Robert, 'that I should marry Jane, and thus restore to her in due time the inheritance that should have been Thomas's. And we may not have to wait so very long before Jane's rightful inheritance comes to us. It isn't easy to say such things, but they happen to be true. My father suffers from frequent chest infections and the cough he has now is a bad one. I have seen such cases before. I fear the lung rot.'

'And if Thomas comes back?' said Eric.

Robert looked at him gravely. 'Do you think it likely? And if he did, he could not claim his inheritance without a lawsuit. Meanwhile, we must deal with things as they are. I can at least correct the injustice as far as Jane is concerned.'

'It . . . could be a good idea.' Lisa looked at her daughter. 'We must consider it. But I hope your father isn't seriously ill, Robert.'

'He proposes to take a sea voyage soon,' said Robert. 'He says he knows a captain who will hire himself and his boat to George for a week or two of sailing up and down the south coast. He hopes the sea air will make his cough better. We may pray that it does. But whatever happens, meanwhile, marriage to me would make Jane secure. I know my father has promised her a dowry, but I frankly doubt if it would be a generous one. My offer could be better.'

Jane looked bemused. Lisa raised a hand to her brow and rubbed her palm across her forehead as though trying to clear her mind. Robert looked from one to the other.

'Jane would come back to France with me,' he said. 'But I hold a good position in my master's household. I have rooms in his house, which Jane could share. My master has a wife and a daughter of about her age; his younger brother also lives there and he has a wife as well. Jane would not be a servant, but simply one of the women of the house, engaged on ordinary homely duties just as I have no doubt she is here. Or, Lisa, if you and she would prefer it, she can go on living here, and I will visit her from time to time. By the way, do you speak French, Jane?'

'Not . . . not very well,' Jane stammered.

'If you chose to come to France, you would soon polish it,' said Robert. 'But as I said, you need not leave Firtrees yet unless you wish it and your mother agrees. You are still very young. Well, you both need time to think my proposal over. I realize that.'

'You've taken us very much by surprise,' said Lisa. 'We certainly do need time!'

Robert rose to his feet. 'There is no need to decide today. You must indeed think, and consider.' He smiled at them, molars and all. 'Meanwhile, there is my offer.'

It was too late by then to get home the same day. Lisa said that anyone who wanted to stay overnight would be welcome and Robert said that after all, he would stay, though he must leave early in the morning. I was weary but before retiring, I went out into the garden, which I hadn't seen before. The place was warm and scented in slanting evening light. The miserable and useless search in the wood, and the atmosphere of grief in the house, had left me with an abraded feeling, as though my very spirit had been harshly scraped. In the garden, in solitude, I might find a kind of healing.

The parlour had a door opening on to a terrace at the back of the house. There were three shallow steps down to a square stretch of scythed lawn, and beyond that were some parterre flowerbeds in crescent and diamond shapes, and a small shrubbery. I wandered about for some time, before returning to the terrace, where I paused. A footfall made me turn my head and I saw that Robert Harrison had stepped out to join me.

'It's a beautiful evening,' he said. 'May I walk with you for a while? You permit?'

I could see no reason to refuse him, though I didn't want his company and couldn't really see why he should want mine. Stiffly, I said: 'By all means, Master Harrison.'

'There is something I wanted to say to you,' he said.

'Oh?'

'If all this had not happened . . .' He fell in beside me and we began to stroll slowly along the terrace. He made an impatient gesture. 'I have to do what I can for my cousin Jane. I feel I must. A wrong has been done to her and since it is in my power to put it right, to some extent at least, then I must do so. I have just had a few further words with Lisa and Jane, and I think they will accept my proposal. I shall marry

Jane quite soon, and I intend to be a good husband to her. I hope to make her happy, in time, when her grief has had time to heal. I must return to France for a while, to do my duty at the grape harvest, but after that, I shall come back and the wedding can take place. Jane will have had a little time to get used to her loss, and accustom herself to the idea of marriage. But I wanted you to know . . .'

'Yes, Master Harrison?'

'I met you for the first time at my mother's house, the day of the storm. But I had already heard of you and as I think I said on that occasion, what I had heard impressed me. When I first saw you, I was even more impressed. Mistress Stannard, I want you to know that if this disaster had not overtaken my cousin, then – well, it is high time I was married – I would be making my proposal to you.'

I stopped short and looked at him. 'Really, Master Harrison . . .'

'I know. I shouldn't be speaking to you like this, not now that I am betrothed elsewhere. But I wanted you to know.'

'Thank you!' I swallowed and then strove to say the correct things. 'I have no doubt that this is a compliment for which I should indeed be grateful but I think you should know that even if you had proposed to me, I would have refused you.'

He looked taken aback. 'Would you really? But why? You must be in need of a husband. I know you have two houses and their land to look after. You must often feel burdened by your responsibilities and . . .'

'I feel nothing of the sort.' I tried to say it in a neutral tone of voice, but it came out snappishly. 'I take pleasure in caring for my son's inheritance and have no intention of letting anyone else take that task over – which a husband probably would do. Since Master Stannard's death, I have refused several offers and am prepared to refuse any further ones. Please don't concern yourself with me. I think you are doing an admirable thing in marrying Jane and I wish you every happiness with her.'

I could only hope that Jane would have every happiness with Robert Harrison, though in view of this present distasteful conversation, I had doubts about that. 'Good night,' I said, and then I walked away from him, and in at the door to the parlour. After that, I broke into a run, fleeing through the parlour and out of it to the vestibule beyond, and the staircase to the room I had been given. I had an illogical fear that he would follow me. Fortunately, he did not.

THIRTEEN
Streaks On A Wall

When Eric Lake went to look at his new property in Cornwall, I went too, and indirectly, Robert Harrison was responsible.

That embarrassing conversation on Lisa Harrison's terrace haunted me afterwards. Tired though I was, it was long before I slept that night. I kept thinking of the various proposals I had refused. I didn't recall these with regret, but with irritation, wondering how many more were to come and knowing that almost all of them, past or potential, had been, would be, inspired by the fact that I was a widow of means and still a possible source of children.

Only one had been different, and that was the offer from Christopher Spelton. But even he had not been in love with me, just concerned about me and feeling that I ought to be looked after. I had refused him just as I had refused the others, but in his case, I had later thought better of it. Only by then he had fallen into a state of hopeless love for Kate Lake and I had missed my chance.

But I had since realized that I didn't mind. Christopher would not have tried to interfere with the way I cared for Hawkswood and my Sussex house, Withysham, but even so, the law would have allowed him such a right, if he had chosen to use it. No, I was doing the right thing by myself, by my son Harry, by the houses and land, by keeping control in my hands. The stud of trotting horses that I had started was now proving profitable. The first foals had matured and been broken in, with help from Brockley, who was gifted at such work, and had been sold for healthy prices. I intended in due course to invest in a stallion, and that would bring in stud fees. I knew what I was about and I would never allow my authority to be endangered. Besides, I was tired of emotion, of love and grief and the risks of childbirth.

I still missed Hugh so much . . .

Next day, Robert took his leave, saying that he must finish helping his father with Edmund's affairs and complete the visits to his employer's English clients, before returning to France to pick grapes. I decided to go home and did so, accompanied by Eric Lake and Brockley. Eric went on home; I hugged Harry, asked after various household affairs, and retired to my room as to a sanctuary.

In privacy, I then gave way to the emotions that had been brewing up in me ever since I fled from Lisa's terrace and Robert Harrison. I lay down on my bed and buried my face in my pillow, and although it was over eight years since Hugh had died, I cried for him as desperately as though it were yesterday.

He had died with his hand in mine. I had sat with him all through those last hours when he groaned with the pain in his chest, and his eyes grew huge and dark as he struggled for air. He had fallen unconscious at last, and I had stayed there, listening to his grating breaths as they grew more and more shallow and further and further apart. There came a moment when it seemed that there would not be another, and I thought: *I am alone. He's gone.* Then he gasped again and for just one more moment, I was not alone after all; he still lived and I was still his wife.

But no other breath followed. That was truly his last. Between one moment and the next, I had become his widow.

And I still mourned him. Dale found me. She tried to raise and comfort me but I only cried harder and said: 'I want Hugh. Oh, God, I miss him so. Oh, Hugh, my love, my darling, come back to me!' Dale called Sybil and then Gladys. Gladys, predictably, fetched a soothing potion for me. I took it in wine and finally, I fell asleep.

I woke to be told that during my absence, a messenger had delivered a letter for me. Sybil brought it to me. 'It's addressed to Mistress Ursula *Faldene*,' she said, puzzled. 'That was your birth name, of course, but I wonder . . .'

'It's all right,' I said. 'I'll be receiving letters like this from time to time – it's something I'm doing for Walsingham. I shall have to give it to a Royal Messenger, and someone will no doubt call soon to see if I have one.'

It was, of course, the first letter from Janus. As it chanced, Christopher Spelton, riding into Kent once more, arrived the following day, enquired if Janus had sent me anything, and took charge of the missive.

And that letter, somehow, was the finishing touch to my unhappy and exasperated mood. I was tired, tired out with being forever called upon to help people, to do something about impossible situations. Aunt Tabitha. Marjorie. The queen. Lisa. Walsingham and his wretched letters from Janus. I had had enough of being needed, in fact, I had for the time being had more than enough of responsibility. Perversely, Robert Harrison was right about that. I did sometimes find the task of looking after my properties a heavy weight. It did mean hard work and much thinking. Once in a while, I needed a rest from it, wanted to think about something new that would interest but not burden me. I wanted to see new places, new faces, without anxiety, without being on duty.

And that was why, when Christopher left, remarking that he meant to call on Cousin Eric before riding back to court, I went with him, to ask Eric if he would allow me and a few companions to travel with him when he went to Cornwall. I was fairly sure that it would be quite soon.

Kate liked the idea. It was better, safer, she said, on a journey, to be one of many. Eric, amused, asked why.

'Footpads!' said Kate. 'And accidents.'

'Sweetheart, I can look after myself. You have too much imagination,' Eric protested.

'You haven't any!' Kate retorted, but she was laughing as she said it. 'And Mistress Stannard really wants to go with you,' she added.

'Yes, I do,' I said.

'Well, I'd enjoy company,' Eric admitted.

In fact, he seemed pleased with the idea and when we set out, we were almost a cavalcade. This time, as well as the Brockleys, I took Sybil with me, and also Tessie and Harry. They all travelled in my four-horse coach, with Tessie's new husband Joseph to drive it, while Brockley and Eric and I rode alongside. Brockley rode Mealy, I had Jewel, and Eric too had his own horse, a handsome dark-chestnut gelding. It had taken a week to prepare. On reaching West Leys, Christopher found that Eric had already sent into Kent to ask Kate's married brother and his wife to come to West Leys to be with Kate during his absence, but it took time for them to arrive. They were needed because Eric expected to be away for some weeks. Rosmorwen was about three hundred miles away and he didn't know how long he would need to stay there. Due to her condition, Kate did not want to come with us, nor would it have been wise. Even coach travel can be jolting.

Before leaving Hawkswood, I left instructions that if any letters arrived addressed to me by my maiden name, they were to be handed over to any Royal Messenger who arrived and enquired for such letters. Having thus disposed of Janus for the time being, I set out feeling so thankful to be getting away from all my responsibilities that I was hardly even inquisitive about our destination. However, that mood wore off eventually and one evening, when we were well on our way and putting up at a somewhat scruffy inn under the shadow of some bleak, wild hills apparently called Dartmoor, I asked Eric how much he knew about the Cornish property.

'I understand that it's called Rosmorwen,' I said. 'And it's said to be not very productive and it isn't rented out. But that's all I know.'

'I've never seen it myself,' Eric said. 'Mistress Lisa has told me that there's a married pair who live there as steward and housekeeper. Not John Merrow, the steward that my sister-in-law had her foolish love affair with; this is another one, with his wife. A family from the little village nearby – Black Rock – come most days to help out. They're a middle-aged couple, apparently, with a grown son and daughter. The womenfolk help in the house and the dairy; the father and son work the farm.'

'What sort of farm is it?' I asked.

'I understand that the land is rocky so the soil is thin and windswept and no use for wheat. Edmund told me once that it could grow oats and beans and there are some cows and there's poultry, of course. The place is about four miles from the port of Penzance, this side of it, but inland.'

We reached Cornwall the next day, by which I mean that we crossed a river called the Tamar, which formed the boundary between Devonshire and Cornwall. I thought that since we were now in the right county, we must be near our destination but we weren't. Cornwall occupies a long peninsula and Rosmorwen was near the far end. We were another day and a half on the road. This ran along the spine of the peninsula, passing through wild moorland, and it was badly rutted, which slowed us down. In places, we could see the sea both to left and right, which I found interesting but Sybil, who detested barren landscapes, would hardly look out of the coach windows at it.

The land round Rosmorwen, however, was more friendly, since there was cultivation to be seen and a few trees, though they were somewhat stunted. But the house wasn't very welcoming. We reached it in the afternoon of the second day. It was a grey stone building facing south-east and crouched just under the brow of a hill. It was badly proportioned. It had three gables in front which should have been attractive but were not, because they were crowded together and were too narrow and too sharp for beauty. They had a bristly look. In fact, Rosmorwen reminded me of nothing so much as a hedgehog taking shelter from the weather.

The slope below it was scrub, with grass and some gorse bushes. The fields, all smallish, were on the flat land below, with a stream across the corner of one of them. There were some black cattle, also smallish, and beans and oats were being grown.

One field, just at the foot of the hill, seemed to be empty meadow but though there were no crops or animals, there still appeared to be some activity.

'What's going on over there?' Eric said, rising in his stirrups. 'It looks as though someone's digging into the hillside.'

'The steward will know,' I said. I was tired and I knew that inside the coach, Harry and the other women were tired as well, not to mention the team in the traces. Eric looked ready to divert us all to the mysterious goings-on in the field, but I didn't agree. 'Better go to the house first,' I said. 'Whatever's happening over there won't run away.'

We had sent no word in advance and we were not expected. We passed under a gate arch into a small courtyard with a stable block to one side and the steward and his wife, who had presumably seen us coming, emerged to greet us, looking bewildered. Eric, as the new owner, presented us all. They evidently recognized his name and were aware that he was now their employer, but the arrival of such a large party obviously flustered them. They were both dark of hair and short of stature, with slate coloured eyes and anxious faces, and their names, they said, were Walter and Kerenza Meddick.

'Kerenza?' I said, not sure if I had heard aright. They both had strong Cornish accents.

'An old Cornish name,' said its owner, bobbing a placatory curtsey. 'Born here in Cornwall, we both were.'

'Kerenza,' said her husband, 'get Marge out of the dairy and get some food ready and rooms made up. If you'll all come this way . . .'

We sorted ourselves out. Joseph and Brockley saw to the horses while the rest of us followed Walter Meddick into a bleak parlour which looked unused. The plank floor was bare and there was no scent of polish, no wall decorations, no cushions on the wooden settles. Tessie sat down on one of the latter, with Harry beside her and remarked frankly that she hoped some food and drink would be forthcoming soon.

'I'm hungry,' said Harry.

'We all are,' said Dale, as candid as my son.

Eric, however, detained Meddick when the man was on the point of leaving us to fetch the required sustenance. 'We saw some digging going on in one of the fields at the foot of the hill. What's happening there?'

'What? You don't know, zur?' His soft local accent mostly turned S sounds into Z. 'And you the new owner?'

'I am indeed the new owner, and no, I don't know,' said Eric, with some irritation. 'I know little about Rosmorwen, as I never expected to inherit it.'

'But Master Harrison knew all about it, zur,' said Meddick.
'I daresay, but he died before he could tell me,' Eric said.
'It's tin, zur. There's tin been found on the land.'
'Tin?'
'They London folk – Guild of Bronzesmiths or some such
– always looking out for sources for tin, they are. Or so we
was told. Some of them have made theirselves into a . . . a
what-do-you-call-it?'
'I wouldn't know,' said Eric. 'What *do* you call it?'
'A consortium, zur, yes, that's it. And they've hired these
prospectors to go round to likely places in this here county of
Cornwall. They come here and I give them permission to look
– well, it 'ud make the place worth a lot more if they found
aught. Master Harrison wouldn't have to put money into getting
the mine producing; this consortium thing'd do that. They'd
work the mine and put money into it and claim the profits but
they'd pay for using the Rosmorwen land. I wrote to Master
Edmund Harrison about it all. I write a good letter, zur, it's one
reason why I was took on to look after this place. Well, they tried
panning in our liddle stream, and yes, there was tin there; then
they had a look at some rocks stickin' out of the hill, at the foot.
Then they got all excited, like and now they've started a tunnel.
Not got very far yet but they do zay the lodes are good.'
'Lodes?' I said.
'Marks on the rock, like. Zigns there do be tin there.'
'I see,' said Eric. 'All right, Meddick. Feed us, if you please.'
When Meddick had gone, Eric said: 'Tin! I had no idea of
that. I expect Meddick's letter is among Edmund's papers.
George didn't show them to me and I didn't think of asking
to see them! Tin would make an immense difference to the
value of this place. I know about this. With silver, landowners
don't get anything – it all goes to the crown – but with tin,
whoever owns Rosmorwen would be paid for the use of the
land and if the land were sold, it would command a very good
price. Not that I have the right to sell it,' he added moodily.
'It has to revert to George after me. Pity. I wonder if I can
negotiate with him. We might share the proceeds . . . if there
really is a worthwhile amount of tin, of course. Well, well!'

*   *   *

The food that the Meddicks produced was simple but good: mutton ham and fresh bread with butter and quince preserves and some thick yellow cream, and a choice of ale or mead, tasting of honey, to wash it all down.

After that, Sybil and I looked round the house and met the two women who helped Kerenza and were evidently the mother and daughter from the village family that Eric had mentioned. They were a bustling pair, with strong local accents, and to his amusement, they both addressed Eric as *me handsome*.

None of the rooms in the house were large and most were both dark and poky. However, they were also clean, and there seemed to be ample bedlinen. Rooms had been made ready for us and it looked as though our stay would be reasonably comfortable.

The weather was warm and the air was soft. Eric at first wanted to go out to the diggings that evening but it wasn't long before the effects of the meal – and probably the mead – had us all yawning, and at last he said he would put off visiting the mine until morning.

I slept deeply that night and I daresay we all did. In the morning, Harry begged to be allowed to see the mine and I too was curious. I put on the old dress I used for travelling, which had no farthingale and was not too generous in the skirts, and put Harry into an old shirt and breeches. Meddick recommended that though the weather was still warm, we should all take cloaks.

'Likely you'll want zummat over your mouths if you'm goin' into any old mine,' he said. 'Dusty, that's what mines are.'

Sybil, Tessie and Dale all decided against coming, but Harry and I set out with Eric. We found half a dozen men busy about the site, tough-looking local miners in leather hose and shirt-sleeves, except for two who had dispensed with any clothing at all above the waist, apart from a coating of sweat mixed with rock dust. They all had a vague resemblance to the Meddicks. They had made themselves at home in a rough and ready way, since there was a cooking fire, over which a pot of something savoury was heating, and a water barrel stood nearby, with some pewter cups on a bench alongside.

When we arrived, a cartload of broken rock, pulled by two strong horses, was just leaving the site, presumably to be smelted somewhere else. A foreman came to greet us, distinguished from the rest by a sleeveless leather jerkin over his shirt. He introduced himself as Ninian Tremaine and seemed pleased to see Eric.

'Heard you'd arrived, zur.' He had a husky, gravelly voice. 'Allus best to have the owner takin' an interest. Want to see how far we've got? All of you?' He looked doubtfully at me and Harry.

'Yes, please!' said Harry.

'Harry and I will both come,' I said. 'I should like to. Unless there's any danger. Is there?'

'No. We've shored his sides up proper.' It took me a moment to realize that *his* referred to the mine. 'My men know their business and take care of theirselves. We've not got far in, anyhow. This way.'

They had delved straight into the side of the hill. 'It's called lode mining,' Tremaine said. 'In the past, gettin' at the tin's been mostly pannin' for it in rivers, or sometimes diggin' open trenches, but in late years, there's been interest taken in traces of tin where trenches aren't any use. Like here – we found lodes on the outcrops outside at the foot of the hill and that told us that there'd likely be tin inside. No good trenchin' from above, so we're makin' a tunnel and the signs are good. Very good!'

'Where do you crush and smelt the ore?' Eric asked knowledgably.

'Not here, zur. There be a place a mile towards Penzance – it serves another mine as well as this one. No point buildin' new blowing houses as we call them when there's one so handy. Cheaper to hire time there. Now, over here . . .'

He showed us an outcrop beside the tunnel entrance and the dark marks in the rocks which were apparently the sign that tin was present. Then, after pausing to make way for a perspiring miner who was wheeling out a barrow-load of broken rock, he led the way inside.

It was a low tunnel and Eric and I had to bend our heads to get in. It was dark, but Tremaine took down a candle lantern that was hanging by the entrance and lit it from the cooking fire. He went ahead of us to light the way. Harry was excited and kept saying: 'Oooh!' I felt a little nervous, even though there were stout timber supports on either side. There were more dark lodes, long blue-black streaks in the walls of the tunnel. 'Likely, they could lead for miles,' Tremaine told us. 'But we're gettin' good ore already.' He began to talk technicalities to Eric, explaining how the smelting was done, recommending him to inspect the blowing house. 'Not a place for ladies or children, but the next cartload will be settin' off soon and you and I can go together. Three teams of horses we've got, though only two work at the same time. We're always needin' horses for this or that little errand, so each team has a rest from carting rock every third day and gets used for other things. My men are all lodged in Black Rock and some have their families with them . . .'

I lost the rest of what he was saying, on account of the sound of hammering from the far end of the tunnel, which grew louder as we came nearer. We came in sight of a rock face, where several perspiring men were working with picks. The air here was full of dust and Harry started to cough. So did I. Eric and Tremaine looked as us in concern.

'You'd better not come any further,' Eric said to me anxiously. 'I want to see the miners at work and then I'm going to the blowing house with the next cart, but I don't think this is a good place for either you or Harry.' He then coughed as well, and Tremaine said: 'Best put a fold of your cloak over your nose, zur.' Eric did so.

'I agree,' I said. 'I've seen enough. Come, Harry.'

'But I want to go to the blowing house with Master Lake! I want to see what happens to the bits of rock.'

'They're smashed to smaller bits, washed, and then what's left is heated to make the tin run out,' said Tremaine. 'Nothing very special, young master. You go with your ma, now. Blowing houses b'ain't no places for younglings, 'cept when they'm learnin' their dad's trade. Off you go.'

'Come along, Harry,' I said.

He grumbled, but obeyed. I didn't need a lantern to see our way out, for the entrance wasn't far away and beyond it was the sunlight. I got us both out into the open air and thankfully took deep breaths of it. Well, I had seen a tin mine. It was interesting but I didn't particularly want to see another one. Harry, of course, was full of questions, most of which I couldn't answer.

'Master Lake will tell you all about it when he comes back to the house,' I said, steering my son on to a path across a field of oats. 'It's no use asking me! Come *along,* Harry.'

FOURTEEN
A Shape Half Seen

I t rained that afternoon and Harry, excited after our visit to the mine, fretted at being kept indoors. When, near the end of the afternoon, the rain ceased, he evaded Tessie and slipped out of the house.

'Oh, let him go,' Eric said, when I protested that this was a strange place to him, that he didn't know his way about and might get lost. 'He'll come to no harm. I expect he's gone towards the mine, but the miners won't let him get into any trouble. I'll go out later and fetch him in.'

We were all in the parlour, which was less bleak now that it was populated. Eric and I were passing the time with a game of chess, since the rain had discouraged him from going round the farm. Sybil and Dale were working at embroidery and Tessie was patching the elbows on one of Harry's shirts.

We had already begun to talk about the journey back. Eric said that tomorrow, weather permitting, he would spend the day looking at the crops and the stock and the day after that he would devote to studying the farm's accounts, but we might start for home the day after. Presently, as he had said he would, he went out to fetch Harry and brought him in, flushed and laughing. He had been playing with a couple of lads, the sons of two of Tremaine's miners.

'They were having a contest with some home-made bows and arrows,' Eric said cheerfully. 'Shooting at a bit of a boulder. All good fun and no harm in it.' I said I hoped he hadn't made a nuisance of himself and Tessie tut-tutted, but Eric shook his head at us. 'He's a boy. Don't coddle him!'

Evening fell and we had supper. Afterwards, we dispersed for various purposes. Tessie saw Harry to bed, Joseph and Brockley went out to the stable to settle the horses for the night; Eric said something about going to the stable as well, and disappeared, while I joined Sybil and Dale in the parlour for a last cup of mead before we retired.

We gathered for breakfast the next morning, but Eric wasn't there. We were wondering why not, when Kerenza Meddick came to say that she had knocked on his bedchamber door to call him, had received no answer and had ventured to look inside, and his bed had not been slept in.

Ten minutes after that, Master Tremaine, white-faced, was at the door, to report that part of the roof and one side of the mine had fallen in, and that a foot, in a boot, was sticking out from the rubble.

Meddick, Brockley and I went with Tremaine to the mine. Tremaine looked askance at me but I said firmly: 'If Master Lake is – not here – then I am in charge of this household. I ought to come with you and I intend to,' and Brockley said: 'Madam has seen unhappy sights in her time, Master Tremaine. She is a woman of some experience. You need have no fears for her.'

Tremaine shrugged. We collected cloaks and outdoor shoes and made our way to the site of the disaster.

Tremaine had already set his men to clear the rubble. It was an ugly sight; a pile of destruction where there had so lately been order and efficiency. The pathetic boot and the two or so inches of leg sticking out from the tangle of fallen rock were stained with dried blood. I and my companions stood back and waited. Tremaine joined his miners, who had already made considerable progress. It was not very long before between them they brought the victim out. And yes, it was Eric.

He had fallen face down and his handsome features were not much marked. There were contusions on nose and forehead but no more than that; otherwise, his face was just dirty. But the back of his head had been smashed. It was a ghastly mass of blood and bits of shattered rock, and his body had been crushed and flattened under a slab which took six straining, cursing men to shift it. From what lay beneath, I turned my head away, sickened.

They laid poor Eric on the grass. Tremaine himself had

carried the mangled shoulders and supported the damaged head. Some of the men were still busy with the rockfall, where something seemed to have caught their attention. One of them called for Tremaine, who hurried back to the mine. He returned looking grim.

'They've found one of the roof supports, lyin' flat. I tell 'ee, that there support was a solid piece of seasoned oak, thick as a man's body and strong as steel, and jammed in firm. It never come down on its own! My men know what they're about. They've shored up trenches and tunnels afore this, time and again and never had an accident. He was safe, this mine was. I'd never have let anyone – certainly not you, ma'am – near him if I'd had any doubt, any doubt at all. If that there support come down, it were *made* to come down. Might be done with a rope and a horse.'

'Why did he come out to the mine on his own, without telling anyone?' Brockley asked, puzzled. 'What brought him here? It must have been quite late last evening; he was at supper.'

'He had a note,' said a youthful voice, startling us all and causing us to turn round sharply. Harry, overwhelmed by curiosity, had once more evaded Tessie and come uninvited down the hill to join us. Brockley and I instinctively stepped between him and the dreadful remains on the grass.

'What are you doing here, Harry?' I demanded. 'You know you shouldn't be.' He was getting too much for Tessie, I thought. As soon as we got home, I would arrange that tutor.

'What's all this about a note?' said Brockley.

'I saw it come. Master Lake was walking across the courtyard – he must have been to the stable, to see his horse, I suppose,' said Harry. 'Tessie had put me to bed, but I wasn't sleepy and I got up again and looked out of the window. Master Lake was coming back towards the house, when a boy came in at the gate and spoke to him and handed him a note. He read it and sent the boy away and then he came inside and I heard him come upstairs at a run, and then I heard him go down again. He came up for a cloak, I think – he was swinging it round him while he went to the gate. He went out. It must have been the note that made him go.'

'Why didn't you say so this morning when we were all wondering where he was?' I asked indignantly

'Tessie's always telling me not to bother the grown-ups, and she gets cross if I get out of bed after she's seen me into it. But I wanted to know what had happened and . . . is that Master Lake? There . . . on the grass . . .'

Despite our precautions, he had glimpsed the body. Curiosity and excitement had collided with hideous reality and suddenly his small face – the dear small face that was already so very like the face of his father, Matthew de la Roche, with whom I had known little happiness but oh, so much passion – suddenly it was contorted with shock and distress. His mouth shook and he began to cry.

'Hush,' I said, going to him. 'Hush. I'll take you back to the house. Don't look at . . . Master Lake.'

'Is he dead?' Harry whimpered.

'Yes, dear. He is. He was . . . caught in a fall of rock. It must have been very quick. I don't suppose he knew much about it.'

Harry looked at Tremaine at this point, and Tremaine nodded reassuringly. He said: 'Ma'am, we will make Master Lake decent and bring him up to the house. You had best go ahead of us. This will take a little while.'

Brockley and Meddick stayed to help the miners. I took Harry back to the house. He was pale and quiet, holding my hand as he used to do when he was younger. At the house, Tessie and Sybil both came out to meet us. Tessie was inclined to scold her nursling but I said: 'Take Harry to his room and give him something hot to drink. He has had a shock. Master Lake is dead.'

'What? How?' gasped Sybil.

'It was an accident with a collapsed mine roof. He'll be brought back soon but . . .'

Tessie understood. Harry was not to see. She took him away at once. I called Kerenza and told her to make a warm, soothing posset for Harry. I told Sybil and Dale about the note that Harry had mentioned and Sybil said: 'We should find that if we can. I wonder if it's in Master Lake's room.'

'We'd better look,' I said.

We went upstairs. The Meddicks had given the new owner

the master bedchamber, and Eric's room, at the front of the house, with a window in one of the spiky gables, was just a little larger than the others. There was a clothes press and a washstand and next to the tester bed was a small table, where a candlestick stood with a tinderbox beside it.

On the table was a piece of folded paper. Sybil pounced at once. 'This is it!'

We gathered round to read it.

Master Eric Lake, Greetings. Please come at once to the Rosmorwen mine. One of my men thinks he has found signs there of copper, which would add greatly to the value of the mine. However, I am not sure. I think I should show you and that we must discuss it, only it should not be bruited about for the moment. For this reason, I suggest that you come alone and say nothing to any as yet. I don't like to start possibly groundless rumours. I will meet you there. Best not leave this note about. I advise destroying it. Tremaine.

'He didn't do as he was told, did he, ma'am?' said Dale tremulously. 'He didn't destroy it. Do you think . . . was it . . . a trap?'

'It could be. If Tremaine really wrote this, why hasn't he said so?' In fact, it seemed to me to be a very obvious, not to say a blatant, trap. But though Eric had a fine physique and spectacular good looks, he did not have a complex mind, let alone a devious one. To him, that note probably meant simply what it said. Or had it? I might be doing him an injustice. He might have a straightforward mind but he wasn't a fool. Perhaps he had had doubts. He had perhaps assumed, as he had said to Kate, that he could look after himself, but just in case, had left the note for us to find. We would never know.

'Tremaine surely can't have wanted to injure Eric Lake,' Sybil said in bewilderment. 'He *can't* have written this!'

'I agree,' I said. 'Dear God, we shall have to take Eric home to West Leys and tell Kate! This is . . . it makes no sense!'

The three of us stood there, staring at each other in bewilderment and horror.

'I never wrote this, of course not!' Tremaine bristled with indignation. He, Brockley, Meddick and a burly miner had between them borne Eric up to the house and carried him to his room, on a makeshift bier, covered discreetly with a blanket. Once he was laid on his bed, I summoned Tremaine to the parlour and there, with Sybil and the Brockleys as witnesses, I produced the note. Tremaine read it and at once exploded.

'No one has suggested that there are signs of copper in that mine. I've not seen any. It's nonsense! And even if there were, there'd be no need for all this secrecy and carryin' on as if it's some kind of skulduggery! And that there ain't my signature. Find me a pen and I'll show you what my signature is. I can write but I don't use all them big, noble words, neither, words like *bruit*. I know its meanin' but I wouldn't *use* it.'

We gave him a pen and he demonstrated his signature. It bore not the slightest resemblance to the one on the note. I stared from one to the other for some moments, and was certain. Tremaine's signature was plain and clear. The handwriting on the note was more elaborate, shaping some letters quite differently.

'Who was the boy who brought this?' I said. 'Can we find out?'

'We could ask Harry,' said Brockley.

'But I don't want Harry having to think about . . . oh, well, I suppose he will anyway.' But we would have to be careful. At the mine, when he told us about the note, Harry had been gratified by the adult attention, but he was still just a child and might become tongue-tied if faced with direct questions. 'I'll do it,' I said.

I found Harry in his room, reading. Tessie was sitting with him, this time mending one of his jackets. Harry, a proper boy, could be hard on clothes. I sat down on his bed and said: 'Harry, you say you saw a boy bring a note for Master Lake. Did you know the boy or was he a stranger?'

Harry looked uneasy. 'It's all right,' I said. 'No one is angry with you. We've found the note but we don't know who sent it. If we knew who the boy was, that would help us to find out.'

'Tessie was cross yesterday when I went out and played with the boys whose dads work at the mine.'

'You had no permission to go,' said Tessie sternly.

'There was no harm done,' I said. 'Let it be, Tessie. Harry had a pleasant afternoon practising archery. Harry . . .'

'I don't know,' said Harry. 'I thought . . . I thought it was Jem Horne – his father's one of the miners. He was one of the boys I played with. But I don't know him well and the boy with the note was away across the courtyard from me . . .'

'That's a start,' I said, smiling at him. 'Thank you, Harry. You can go downstairs now. Go out to the stable and help Joseph.'

Having seen Harry sensibly occupied, I returned to the parlour, to report what my son had told me.

'Jem Horne?' said Tremaine. 'Aye, his da's Will Horne. He helped bring Master Lake up the hill. He's in the kitchen now, takin' some ale. I'll fetch him.'

Will Horne was the burly miner, a hard-faced, heavily built man, who came into the parlour reluctantly, staring round at us, obviously wondering why he was there and what he could have done wrong.

'Will,' said Tremaine, 'where is your son Jem? Seems it might have been him as brought a note to Master Lake, that got Master Lake down to the mine.'

'A note? My Jem? He didn't say aught to me about it!'

'Harry might be mistaken. But he glimpsed the boy who brought the note and thought he looked something like Jem,' I said. 'We feel we must ask. Could you bring him here?'

Master Horne was clearly irritated, but Tremaine looked at him sternly and he did as he was bid. It took some time, as the boy was apparently at home with his mother and sisters in their lodgings in Black Rock, but father and son eventually appeared together. Jem was about ten, I thought, an intelligent-looking lad though at the moment a sullen one. Harry, it seemed, had identified him correctly. Jem's father had already questioned him and to begin with, it was Will Horne who told us the story, with Jem nodding and saying: 'Yes, that's how it be,' every now and then, and rubbing a suspiciously reddened ear. Will Horne had evidently not approved of his son's errand or its secrecy.

It was a simple story enough. Mistress Horne, the previous day, had had a fancy for some fresh fish and the Penzance fisherman had probably gone fishing in the morning. There would be fish for sale late in the day.

'Fish straight out of the sea and fried in butter, nothing like it,' Will Horne told us. 'My wife she sets great store by it and she'm right. She allus goes to the same fisherman. Ned Shaw, that's 'un's name.'

The previous afternoon, as soon as the rain had stopped, Mistress Horne had despatched Jem to Penzance to buy from Ned's catch. 'He took one of the hosses as hadn't been working at the mine yesterday. Trotted off bareback. Wouldn't take 'un long to get to Penzance,' said Horne.

Jem had found the fisherman on the quay in conversation with a man, a stranger, who was apparently asking if Ned Shaw knew of a messenger who could go to Rosmorwen in a hurry. 'Someone had told him that Shaw knows just about everyone in Penzance,' said Horne.

Jem had arrived at that moment and Shaw had immediately recommended him. At this point, Jem spoke for himself. 'He told him my dad was working at the mine at Rosmorwen, and that we'm living in Black Rock, so couldn't I take the message – it'd hardly take me out of my way.'

The stranger had given Jem a little roll of paper, sealed, and told him to be very careful with it, because it was of serious importance. And it was also very private. He was to give it only into the hands of Master Eric Lake – did he think he could do that?'

'Aye, I've seen Master Lake, I knew what he looked like,' said Jem. 'And he give me a silver coin, worth a lot, that is . . .' Here, he glowered at his father and I surmised that Will had not only boxed his son's ears; he had snatched the silver coin as well. 'Give it me so as I'd get the letter to Master Lake and no other and not tell no one,' said Jem resentfully. 'Not even your own father, he said to me. So I did. Honest business. Then I went home with the fish.'

'At your age, you don't have business that you don't talk to your da about!' barked Horne.

'Well, I did then. So I brought the letter and as I come in through the gate here, I see Master Lake, so I give it him. That's all.'

'What did this stranger look like?' Tremaine asked.

'Dunno. Cold wind off the sea and he had a cloak on with a hood and hood were up. Couldn't see much of 'un's face, 'twere all in shadow. He were just a man in a cloak.'

'Talkin' to strangers! Takin' money for errands 'ee don't understand!' Horne fairly snarled it. 'Time you was workin' alongside me at the mine and keepin' out of mischief and earnin' proper money that I know all about. I'll see about it, if Master Tremaine here'll take on a mischievous brat like you . . .'

Tremaine and the Hornes departed presently, wrangling over Jem's future. Meddick, shaking his head in shocked bewilderment, went about his duties; Sybil and Dale, pale and distressed, went to the kitchen to help Kerenza, who was very upset. The two village women had been so badly distracted by the disaster that Kerenza had sent them home. Brockley and I stayed in the parlour. I was thinking. Many small things were sliding together in my mind and making an unpleasant picture.

Brockley said: 'Whoever gave that note to Jem could have followed him, on horseback. With a rope. Could have got Master Lake to walk ahead of him into the mine, struck him down from behind and then used the horse and the rope to bring down the support and make it look like an accident.'

But who? The unspoken question hung in the air.

At last, I said: 'I'm like someone peering through a window with very small panes, so that the view outside is all criss-crossed with the lead frames, and the glass is thick, so nothing outside is clear. There's something out there but I can only see pieces of it. But . . . I think it's a monster.'

'I know,' said Brockley. 'And I think I could put a name to it. Or them. I can glimpse two monsters. Can you?'

'Yes,' I told him. 'Yes.

FIFTEEN
The Grievous Homecoming

'I don't understand,' said Kate, sinking down on to a settle in the West Leys parlour. She had taken one bewildered look at our sombre faces when we arrived at the door, and another at the sight of Eric's dark-chestnut horse, which we had brought home hitched to the back of the coach, and had then mutely obeyed my gentle warning to go inside, yes, into the parlour, for privacy's sake, and sit down, Kate. We have unhappy news for you. She had now been told the news, but clearly couldn't take it in. 'You say that Eric is . . . is . . . *dead*! But . . .'

Her hands folded protectively over the hump that was their child. 'Our baby will be born in January. It's his son or daughter. He'd want to see his child! He *can't* be dead!' She saw by my face that he was. 'What happened? Was he ill? Eric is never ill! He . . .'

'We've brought him home,' I said. Whatever else we all had on our minds, and as far as Brockley and I were concerned, that was a good deal, we had known that to bring Eric home to West Leys was our first duty. 'He's outside, in a coffin, on a wagon. We hired it in Penzance.'

'I have told the driver and Joseph to go to your kitchen for refreshments,' said Brockley. 'They are being looked after.'

'And I have sent Tessie and Harry upstairs for the moment,' I said. 'I hope you don't object, as this is your house. But we came straight here – I didn't want to turn aside so as to leave them at Hawkswood – and now that we've got here, I wanted them out of the way while we broke this sad news to you.'

'If Eric is . . . there . . . then I want to see him,' said Kate.

'No,' I said. 'No, my dear.' She had been my ward and I was very fond of her. This was a hard task for me. 'The coffin has been nailed shut and . . . it's been nearly three weeks.' It was better, I thought, not to describe his injuries. 'We had to get the coffin made and the wagon arranged,' I said, 'and there was an inquest and then we were two weeks on the road and the weather has kept so warm . . .'

'You mean he's not fit to be seen?'

'I mean that, yes, dear Kate. I am sorry.'

'He's dead. I'll never see him again. He'll never see his baby. He . . . I . . .'

As the tears came, I went to put my arms round her. Sybil said: 'Come, Dale, let's ask in the kitchen for some wine . . . or something . . . Kate must have something.'

They went out. Brockley hovered, looking worried and helpless. Kate drew herself out of my arms, and rose and stumbled to a window. 'Look,' she said.

The window faced the back of the house and the slope of the grassy hillside that rose beyond. A few sheep were grazing there, and the path leading upwards vanished over the saddle-back at the top.

'Up there,' Kate said. 'That's where Eric and I used to walk, early on summer mornings. I think I've told you about it. Even before we broke our fast, we used to walk up to that dip in the hill, and the sun would be just high enough to be hanging over it, as if it was welcoming us. We would climb hand in hand. And now . . . now . . .'

'I know,' I said. 'Yes, you did tell me. Oh Kate, I'm so very sorry.' I steadied her back to her seat. Sybil and Dale appeared with the wine and I coaxed Kate into taking a glass and sipping it. Sybil said: 'We brought him home as quickly as we could. He can have a resting place in the parish churchyard here. You can . . . visit him there.'

'But what *happened*?' Kate demanded. 'You haven't told me! You didn't answer when I asked! What *happened*?'

Carefully, I said: 'Tin has been found on Rosmorwen land. A mine has been started, with a tunnel. Eric went alone to inspect the tunnel for some reason and there was a fall of rock. He must have been killed at once. There was an inquest, and the verdict was accidental death.'

This wasn't the moment to say so, but the inquest had infuriated me. The coroner seemed to be out of his depth. The mysterious note had not been given proper importance and in my opinion and Brockley's the coroner had sadly misled the jury. But this wasn't the right time for telling Kate that her husband, Eric Lake, that handsome, upstanding young man, who looked so much like a Viking god, had almost certainly been murdered, and that Brockley and I thought we knew by whom.

West Leys was in the parish of a church called St Peter's, which stood in the village of Brentvale, half a mile away. Kate was incapable for the moment of making any arrangements, but her brother Duncan and his wife Bessie were there, although when we arrived at West Leys, the two of them had actually been in the village, ordering stores.

On their return, the grievous news was broken to them and I was thankful to see them, because they were kindly and sensible and they at once wrapped Kate round with the right words, the right caresses, and the right kind of care. She was to rest and leave everything to them. They would see the vicar of St Peter's, they would inform Eric's parents, they would organize the funeral. Kate would in any case not attend; it was never wise for spouses to be present on such occasions; they were likely to become too upset and Kate must not be upset any more than she already was; she had the baby to think about.

Bessie, helped by Dale, put her sister-in-law to bed while Duncan sped back to the village to see the vicar. He returned to say that the ceremony could take place the next day; the gravedigger had already been set to work.

'We can leave quite soon after that,' I said to Brockley. 'I'll send Joseph to Hawkswood to let Wilder know what has happened and tell him when to expect us. Duncan and Bessie say they will stay on for a while. They have offered to take Kate back to Dover with them, but she says she would rather stay here, that the place needs a mistress, and there is the farm to look after. Harvest is near.'

'Kate's brave,' said Sybil. 'She will come through.'

It was wet on the day of the burial, with a thin, penetrating drizzle, infinitely depressing. There was no wind to speak of, just drifting veils of fine rain, obscuring the hills, as though the smooth grey skies were also weeping. It was difficult to believe that the Eric Lake I had known, that striking, healthy, good-hearted young man, was no longer part of the world, was inside the coffin that was being lowered into the wet wound of the grave, would lie in the earth for ever.

When the vicar pronounced the committal, I cried and so did Dale and Sybil, standing one on either side of me. Brockley stood apart, quiet and serious. The West Leys farm workers were there, together with acquaintances from the village, and Duncan Ferguson too. Christopher Spelton was absent, on duty, but had written a beautifully worded letter of condolence. Eric's parents were not there, either. They did not live all that far away but they were both in their seventies and had sent word that they were too stricken to face the horror of witnessing the funeral of their only child. His mother, apparently, had taken to her bed.

Kate on the other hand hadn't stayed abed for long. During the funeral, Bessie had remained in the house with her, and the two of them had busied themselves, preparing to receive the mourners after the ceremony. Food and drink would be provided. It would do honour to Eric. Now that the first shock had passed, Kate was indeed being brave. As I would have expected. I had seen in the past how courageous she was. She would certainly come through this, and – all going well– she would have Eric's child to comfort her. My heart still wept for her and the future she had lost.

When we returned to the house, at the head of a straggling procession of mourners, all on foot, we found that Joseph had returned from Hawkswood and was at the trough, watering the horse he had used. Beside him, another man was also watering a horse. 'Christopher!' I said. 'You came after all!'

Spelton turned to me and Joseph said: 'Leave your horse to me, sir. I'll see to both of them.' Spelton said: 'Thank you for sending me word about Eric. I came in haste. I was given an official errand to you at just the same time, anyway. I met Joseph at Hawkswood.'

'Come inside,' I said.

We went in. The crowd followed, to be met by Kate and

Bessie and shown into the parlour. I steered Christopher to the small room that Eric had used as an office and partial storeroom. He had kept records there, concerning stock and harvests and income, and also a couple of shelves of useful things such as candles, a tray of mixed nails, some balls of twine, some pigskin bags containing seed of various kinds. It was a gloomy little room but it was private. In answer to a glance from me, Brockley came with us.

'What is this errand?' I asked.

'I wish I could have got here for the funeral,' Christopher said. 'I must apologize because I could not. This is a terrible business! Eric was my cousin, and his mother is my Aunt Anne and I've heard from my Uncle Diccon that she was so shocked by the news that . . . well, she is in her bed, paralysed all down one side. She may never recover. Ursula, I came by way of Hawkswood. I went there partly to see if there had been another letter from Janus, which there had. Wilder had it safely and I took charge of it. I have it with me now. But I also went to Hawkswood to fetch you. You are needed by the queen.'

'Another summons to the court?'

'Yes. Ursula, tell me, while you've been on your travels, staying in various hostelries, no doubt, have you heard any talk about the queen and the Duke of Alençon?'

Brockley and I were both startled. Because we had.

We had been about fifty miles from West Leys, spending the night at an inn in the market town of Basingstoke. It was a market day and the inn was busy. We could only find one room and were lucky even to manage that. We all had to crowd into it together. We ladies shared the one big curtained bed while the innkeeper found a truckle bed for Brockley. Joseph slept over the stable along with other grooms, and our horses were turned into a paddock, since the stalls were all full. We had gone down to the public rooms for supper and there we had mixed with the crowd, a mixture of local people and folk from outside the district, who had come to the market. And yes, there had been talk of the queen and Alençon, and not pleasant talk, either.

I explained. 'There was lot of speculation,' I said, 'about

whether the queen would or wouldn't marry him, and would it be safe for her to have children at her age, and what would happen to the English religion, if she plighted herself to a prince who is a Catholic, even though he's supposed to be tolerant. Some were saying that once married, he would want the crown matrimonial – he would want to be king!'

'And,' Brockley elaborated, 'someone said that if anything were to happen to the queen, God forfend, well, if there were a baby, then would this French duke be the regent until his child grew up? And how safe would the Protestant religion of England be then?'

'Yes,' I said. 'And the same man said that tolerant or not, the pope would get at him; his own family in France would get at him . . . he's committed to a campaign in the Netherlands but wars cost money. Likely enough he'd need support from his kin and suppose they will only help him with finance, if he tries to make England Catholic?'

'All that?' said Christopher grimly. 'A lot of ordinary people seem to know a good deal about affairs of state!'

'Yes, apparently they do,' I said. 'It was a considerable crowd and some of them were indeed well informed. And there was more. There were some who said they'd take up arms to stop the marriage. There was a man who was drinking a tankard of ale and he banged it down on a table, so hard it spilt, and cried out that he'd take up arms too, and someone else shouted that the only good Catholic princes were dead ones!'

'And then?'

'We all edged away. We didn't want to get entangled. But I meant to report it. I was going to write to Walsingham or Cecil about it. Only, we had to get Eric home first. Anyway, I reckon that those things weren't just being said in one inn or one town. It's likely enough that Walsingham and Cecil already know.'

'They do,' said Spelton gravely. 'And that's partly why you're wanted. The queen is upset and longs for your support. Though it isn't just that. The duke and de Simier have returned to France now, but before they left, de Simier told her something she didn't want to hear. He told her about the secret marriage of her favourite, the Earl of Leicester.'

'Oh, dear,' I said. 'So he did find out, or else de Lacey did.'

'You knew of it?'

'Lord Burghley told me. It's Lettice Knollys, isn't it?'

'I knew, too,' Brockley said unexpectedly. 'It's common knowledge at court. De Simier and de Lacey were both bound to hear of it. Only it was being kept from the queen. Until now, evidently.'

'Yes. Her majesty is furious, and in addition, there's a rumour at court that before de Simier and the duke left England, Leicester attempted to get de Simier assassinated.'

'Did he?' I asked.

'I really don't think so,' said Christopher, 'but the rumour is there. De Simier himself started it, I think, in retaliation for Leicester's opposition to the marriage, which was quite passionate. Her majesty is distressed, Ursula, for several different reasons, all at once. When she heard of Leicester's marriage, she almost sent him to the Tower, except that the Earl of Sussex persuaded her not to. He said it would make the people of England even angrier than they already are. She sent him away from the court instead. But that appalling rumour is still circulating. I fancy the queen may want you to investigate it. Anyway, she is in a bad state of mind and needs you at her side. As soon as possible.'

'But . . .'

'But what?'

'I can't. I mean . . .' I began on the story of Thomas's disappearance and Eric's death and the suspicions which Brockley and I now harboured. Spelton listened, his eyes growing wider and wider as I spoke of the possibility that Eric had been murdered.

'I called this a terrible business, but it's worse than that!' He was clearly horrified. 'This is diabolical! My poor Aunt Anne! My poor uncle! These things are like stones flung into a pool; the ripples spread far and wide, and that anyone should deliberately set them going . . .! But what are you proposing to do? What can you do? How can you confirm your suspicions? And meanwhile, the queen has summoned you. That must come first. That concerns the whole realm – not just one family.'

'I see,' I said bitterly. I had been through all this before. It was not the first time that I had been bidden to put the good of the realm before the interests of private life.

Christopher, however, was thinking. 'You could reasonably take a day or two to prepare before travelling to Richmond – that is where the court is just now. Can you think of a way to make good use of such a short time?'

'I can't think how to investigate Eric's death,' I said despairingly. 'We're *here* now, and Rosmorwen is three hundred miles away! There was an inquest but it was no use.' I thought feverishly. 'If we only knew, if we could only find out, what really happened to Thomas, that might give us a start! Knowing that might point clearly to the person responsible for both his loss and Eric's. Only I can't see how to do it. The search was so thorough.'

'If he's alive, he has either run away or been got away and if so, there's not much chance of finding him,' Spelton said. 'But if he is dead, his body must be somewhere. Has every possibility been covered? How wide was the search?'

'It was very wide.' I went into details. 'But there are woods and heaths all over the county where a body might lie hidden for a long, long time.'

'Or be found by someone exercising a dog, or a gamekeeper patrolling his master's land. And the further that the killer or killers had to transport it, the greater the chance of attracting notice. If I were disposing of a corpse,' said Spelton thoughtfully, 'I would want to do it as quickly as possible and that would mean getting rid of it somewhere not too far from where I did the killing. You say his mother insists that if he is dead, the body must be in the pinewood belonging to the family?'

'Yes. But that was searched more than once. I took part in one of the searches myself.'

'You looked everywhere? You and all the others who helped? On the ground, to see if it had been disturbed, in hollow trees, in undergrowth?'

'There isn't much undergrowth in that wood. But yes, everywhere.'

'Did you,' said Spelton, 'think of looking *up*?'

SIXTEEN
Lapis and Silver

So now we knew. I looked at what lay in Brockley's palm and what had been suspicion hardened into certainty. We had done what Christopher said. We had searched the fir wood again, looking upwards. We had found Thomas. And we had identified his killer – or one of them.

We had decided that although I must go to Richmond with as little delay as possible, I should nevertheless call at Hawkswood, leave Dale, Sybil, Tessie and Harry there, and then, with Brockley and Joseph, go straight on to Firtrees to investigate the pinewood once again. Just one day would suffice, or perhaps two, if we found anything, Brockley said.

Spelton would ride straight to Richmond to deliver the latest Janus letter and announce that I was on my way, but had paused at home to settle my small son and his nurse there, before following him. That would be accepted, as long as I didn't prolong the delay.

And here we were. Whoever had got rid of Thomas had put him in a sack – in fact, in four sacks, making a thorough job of it – and then tied the whole horrible package up in stout twine and slung it high among the dense evergreen branches of a massive silver fir. The arrangement wasn't visible from the ground unless one was looking for it, peering intently upwards, searching for a place where the thick growth of fir needles seemed unnaturally dark, where there ought to be at least a few tiny chinks of light, and yet were not.

I didn't look towards the horrid heap that Joseph had brought to the ground, but stared instead at the object that Brockley was showing me.

'This could have been pulled off a jacket or doublet when . . . whoever it was, was disposing of him up in that tree, struggling with the twine and trying to wedge the whole nasty package into the branches,' Brockley said.

Joseph nodded. 'Wedged in a fork, it were, good and tight.'

'Or,' said Brockley, 'if Thomas fought for his life, it could have been wrenched loose then. His jacket and shirt have rents and bloodstains. He was stabbed from behind, more than once. He could have had a little time to struggle, reach backwards, claw at his assailant . . .'

'Brockley, don't!'

'I'm trying to imagine what happened. No one reported hearing cries for help; perhaps his attacker had a hand over his mouth. But if Thomas did fight, he could have grabbed at this and then the sacking and the branches did the rest.'

It was a button. A big button. It had a central stone of lapis lazuli, set in silver, and the stone had a little motif carved into it. I had seen buttons like that before.

'We thought it,' I said, 'but now we know it. Robert Harrison.'

'And his father as well,' said Brockley. 'George Harrison has charge of Edmund Harrison's papers, has he not? Master Meddick said he had written to Edmund about the tin mine. George Harrison must know about it, and he would be next in line to inherit it. I fancy he is after that mine, and poor Master Lake, under the terms of Edmund's will, was in the way. The son helped the father. They kept themselves informed of Master Lake's plans and laid their own accordingly. One of them went to Cornwall at the same time as we did, and arranged the note, and followed the messenger, ready to meet Master Lake at the mine. Perhaps he told Master Lake that he was there on Tremaine's behalf.'

'And then politely let Eric walk into the mine in front of him, knocked him out and then hitched his horse to the roof support and . . . we know the rest,' I said. 'Eric would have had no suspicions. He hadn't a suspicious nature. Two monsters, as you said.' I was shuddering.

We fetched the handcart, and between them Brockley and Joseph loaded the horror onto it, piling the sacks on top so that I need not glimpse what lay below.

'We can't just take this straight to Firtrees,' I said. 'Lisa mustn't see it! I think we'd better get the local vicar to help. We'll report our suspicions to him. I really do recognize that button. When we met Robert Harrison while we were sheltering from that storm, he had them on his doublet. One of them actually fell off! I noticed them because they were unusual.'

'So did I,' Brockley said. 'Also . . .'

'He offered to marry Jane, very soon after Thomas vanished. Almost as though he knew for sure that Thomas was dead.'

'And,' said Brockley, 'didn't he say he meant to go travelling to see his employer's English customers? Maybe he went to Cornwall instead. But I wonder why he wants to marry Jane. Conscience?'

We made our way out of the wood, pushing the cart. I tried to think things through.

'Possibly,' I said, 'he wants to make sure that Lisa doesn't start legal proceedings after all. I know she didn't seem to be considering it, but what if she changed her mind? Marrying Jane would be a wise move.'

'It would,' Brockley agreed. 'I'd reckon that father and son planned all that ahead like everything else. He made that offer only a few days after Thomas vanished.'

I said: 'We had better make haste to find that vicar!'

SEVENTEEN
Royal Fury: Royal Plea

When we got back to the horse-drawn cart we had left in the lane, I collected the gown that I had brought with me, retired among the trees, and changed into something more suitable for visiting a man of the cloth. I knew my part of Surrey well enough to know that Lisa's parish church was called St Andrew's and was at Priors Ford. We found the vicar, whose name turned out to be Dr Gideon West, practising the organ in the church, and presented ourselves.

I had not previously met Dr West and was thankful to learn that he knew all about Thomas's disappearance, had taken part in the first search, and well understood the fact that my summons to the royal court had to be obeyed. He was a sensible, middle-aged man, and to my relief, he took all responsibility from me. If I would prepare an account of how we found the body, and our suspicions about the murderers, he would see that they reached the right authorities, and that the necessary inquest was arranged. I would probably have to come from court to attend it, but would be informed about that in due course.

I wrote my deposition for him in the vicarage study, and after that, he came with us to Firtrees, to inform Lisa of our find. It was a painful business but at last we left him comforting her and explaining the formalities of inquest and funeral. For the moment, the matter was out of our hands.

We went home for one night and the next day, I rode to Richmond Palace. I took Brockley and Dale with me and also a groom. Brockley had seen to the horses last time, but it had been complicated for him, attending both on them and me. The newlywed Joseph would naturally want to stay with his bride, so I took the youngest Hawkswood groom, Eddie, to look after our horses.

We were halfway to Richmond when I discovered that the lapis and silver button, which I ought to have left with Dr West, was still in my purse, but it was too late then to do anything about it.

Richmond was one of Elizabeth's favourite palaces, and it was even more beautiful than Hampton Court, with its wind chimes and the grace of its slender windows and towers, which always looked as though they were stretching skywards in an attempt to touch the heavens. We crossed the Thames at Kingston Bridge and once at the palace I found that I was expected and that rooms were ready for me. I said to Dale that as soon as our unpacking was done, I must find out where the queen was and announce my arrival. Looking from the window, I glimpsed her in the grounds, unmistakeable even from a distance because wherever she went Elizabeth moved in a cloud of ladies and courtiers, with a page running ahead to clear a way for her.

'She's going to the bowling alley, I think,' I said, as Dale helped me out of my crushed riding dress and began dressing me in something suitable for the court. 'Let's go there.'

We made our way down two narrow flights of stairs and out into the open air. The bowling alley wasn't far away, but we were not destined to get there without interruption. In fact, we met with three.

Our first encounter was with Antoine de Lacey, who seemed delighted to see us. 'Mistress Stannard! You have returned! Her majesty will be overjoyed!'

'You are still here, M'sieu de Lacey? I thought you would have gone back to France with the duke and M'sieu de Simier.'

'I had a little business to complete – some investments that I made while we were in England. My master gave me leave. Have you heard the rumour concerning the Earl of Leicester, by the way?'

'About his marriage? Or the tale that he attempted the life of Jean de Simier?'

'Oh, please, keep your voice down. These palaces are full of prying ears and eyes!' De Lacey looked furtively round, as though he feared that a spy might be lurking among the bushes of a nearby shrubbery.

'My master fell ill after a dinner at which the Earl of Leicester was also present but I know nothing to suggest that the earl had anything to do with it,' he said. 'Or anyone else, for that matter. I am glad, though, that for the time being, my master has left the country. I feel responsible for him.' He paused and then added, in a low voice: 'I was presented to you as Jean de Simier's clerk, but my duties are a little more onerous than that. It was known, before ever he or the duke set foot on English soil, that there might be opposition to this marriage. My real function was that of, well, of a bodyguard. I was to watch for danger and give warning or protection as best I could. I have had training.'

'I see,' I said, thinking that anyone so nondescript in appearance did not look much like anyone's bodyguard. Though it was true that unobtrusiveness could be useful. He could watch for danger as a cat might watch from long grass – ready to pounce at the right moment. I said: 'I have only just arrived and I have not yet seen the queen. I must speak with her to find out how I can best serve her. Perhaps you could tell me one thing. Is the Earl of Leicester here?'

'No,' said de Lacey, and his smile was malicious. 'The queen dismissed him when she heard of his marriage.'

'And it was M'sieu de Simier who informed the queen.'

'Quite.' Clearly, de Lacey didn't feel apologetic about it. 'Leicester nearly found himself in the Tower, except that Thomas Radcliffe of Sussex spoke for him – a noble act, considering that Sussex and Leicester detest each other. In the end, the queen just sent Leicester away – told him to go home and rejoice the heart of his wife, since he could no longer rejoice that of his sovereign. He is at his house in Wanstead.'

'There have been some lively events since I was last at court,' I remarked.

'There have indeed,' said de Lacey. 'It has become a veritable hornets' nest.' Once more, I detected malice. He gave us a parting bow, and took himself off, somewhat abruptly.

'There's something odd about that man,' said Dale disapprovingly.

'Yes, there is, but I can't decide exactly what,' I said. 'I think he was trying, delicately, to warn me that all isn't well in the queen's household. Well, I shall soon find out. Now, come along.'

Once more, we started towards the bowling alley but again we were accosted, this time by Sir Thomas Radcliffe, Earl of Sussex, himself. He appeared suddenly round a bend in the path, stopped, swept his hat off in gracious welcome, and said: 'Mistress Stannard! So you have arrived! Welcome back.'

We both curtsied to him, smiling, for although I knew he was eager for the Alençon marriage, a point of view that I couldn't share, he was nevertheless a pleasant and honest man and known as a loyal friend to the queen. To look at, he resembled a large and very masculine faun. I had seen pictures of fauns in a book about the legends of Ancient Greece, shown to me and my cousins by the tutor who had told us so many tales of the ancient world. Sussex had a long, dark face, with a chin that stretched far enough to overlap his ruff, narrow dark eyes and pointed ears. His voice was deep and calm and I wondered how much that voice had helped him when he was dissuading Elizabeth from consigning Leicester to the Tower.

'I am pleased to be back,' I said. 'How is her majesty?'

Sussex jerked his head to indicate whatever might be happening somewhere behind him. 'She is practising her skills at bowls and slaughtering skittles.'

'Slaughtering . . .?'

'Her majesty,' he said gravely, 'is upset, has been for some time. You know about the Earl of Leicester?'

'And his marriage? Yes.'

'It's not a crime to marry,' Sussex said, sounding weary. 'And this is a perfectly respectable union between a widowed man and a widowed woman, in the presence of witnesses, including the bride's father. But I had to argue the point with her majesty. The trouble is that for many, many years she has relied on Leicester's devotion, and though in many ways she is perceptive and knows what goes in the minds of her councillors, well, in other ways – well, she does not understand men. Does not understand certain needs.'

'I am here to help her if I can.'

Sussex considered me. 'You know her as well as anyone

does, I think. She will tell you herself what she wants of you. She is missing Duke Francis and that isn't helping. He is quite remarkable, you know – the duke, I mean. He's hardly a fine figure of a man!' We all smiled, Sussex, Dale and me, remembering the duke's short stature and pockmarked face. 'But he has something,' Sussex said. 'Character, an atmosphere, something in those lively dark eyes of his and a great deal in his well-tutored mind! He is knowledgeable about modern sciences, he can speak several tongues and he can recite poetry by the furlong! He has moved the queen as no other man has, not even Leicester.'

'I certainly thought that he created an impression,' I said carefully.

'I regret that he has gone back to France,' said Sussex. 'The latest news is that he may well have to deal with a crisis in the Netherlands before he can return to England. It's true that there is much to be done to convince the people of England that the marriage is desirable, but it might be easier if he were here to promote himself! The queen needs him, anyway. She is angry, as much as anything, because she is miserable without him. Do your best for her, Ursula.'

'I'll try,' I said, and he bowed and took his leave, passing us and walking on, back towards the palace. Dale and I went thoughtfully on, and a few moments later had our third encounter, for we saw Lady Margaret Mollinder approaching. She, however, merely paused long enough to say: 'Mistress Stannard! The queen will be so glad to see you. She has been waiting for you to come,' and then smiled and went on her way.

She was wearing a gown of dusty pink, scattered with pale green leaves, in which she looked extremely pretty, and I noticed how beautiful her brown eyes were. They were that soft shade which recalls the petals of the heartsease flower. It was a shame that she couldn't be with her husband. Perhaps, I thought, that would be put right soon. There was surely no reason why she shouldn't, now, travel to join him, if an escort could be found.

Dale and I walked on again. Another moment, and we were at last in sight of the bowling alley, a grassy avenue between dark yew hedges. The wooden skittles, several feet tall and gaily painted, were at the far end and attendants were ready to pick them up as fast as Elizabeth knocked them down. Which was frequently, for Elizabeth was very clearly in a royal temper and taking it out on the skittles. In fact, slaughtering them. Sussex had chosen the word well.

Informally clad in kirtle and loose overgown, no doubt to give her freedom of movement, she was hurling the bowls again and again into the heart of a defenceless row of targets, flinging her victims over with such violence that they crashed into each other and fell into heaps, to be picked up by the alley attendants (who sometimes had to dodge her majesty's murderous onslaught themselves) and replaced so that they could be furiously assaulted again. Ladies, courtiers and a couple of pages were standing at a safe distance, effacing themselves for fear of attracting the royal rage in their direction. Dale and I stopped short but Elizabeth had glimpsed us from the corner of an eye, and swung round to look at us properly. 'Ursula Stannard! So you have deigned to answer my summons!'

Her voice was harsh and her golden-brown eyes bright with fury. Dale and I both sank into very deep curtsies indeed, bowing humble heads, and rising warily.

'I came as quickly as I could, your majesty,' I said. 'I am glad to be here and am ready to help you in any way that you wish.'

'Humph!'

Elizabeth in this mood was unpredictable and dangerous. We waited, meekly. 'We will speak in private,' she said to me. She was holding a ball, which she now tossed carelessly towards the skittles, but this time without intending to hit them. Ignoring her entourage, she beckoned to us, swung round with a vicious swish of her skirts, like an angry cat lashing its tail, and strode off towards the palace, taking it for granted that we would follow. Which, of course, we did.

Elizabeth walked swiftly. The usual breathless page rushed ahead to announce her coming at every stage, generally managing to do it a bare two seconds before she caught up with him. We went indoors, up a flight of stairs, through an antechamber where more courtiers were standing about, past a pair of gentleman pensioners in scarlet uniforms, who were standing guard on either side of a door to an inner chamber where some of her ladies were busy with tapestry work, and then past two more guards into a small room beyond, much the same arrangement as the one at Hampton Court. The page, panting, gave up at this point. There was no one in the small room to whom he could announce the queen, anyway.

Dale was still with me, but Elizabeth looked at her sharply, whereupon Dale curtsied again and retreated back into the company of the ladies with the tapestry frames. Elizabeth deposited herself in a chair like a small throne and sat there staring at me. I bent my head and waited.

'You know what has happened?' she said at last. 'The Earl of Leicester, Robert Dudley, my sweet Robin, on whose help and support I have so long relied, has . . . has . . .'

'Yes, ma'am. I have heard.'

'I wanted to send him to the Tower but Sussex, who has also served me so well and faithfully for so many years, advised against it and I do sometimes heed advice. So I sent my Robin back to the arms of my sly cousin Lettice. I was so angry. But I was growing calm, learning to accept, and then I received a letter from him, begging permission to return to court! As though we could be as we were, as though nothing of moment had happened, as though he could do as so many of my Council do, dividing their time between my court and going home to be with their wives and families! As though he were not *different* . . .! I was angry all over again. I still am!'

I arranged my features into an expression of sympathy and enquiry but still kept silent. There had been a time when I would have gone to her, perhaps even put an arm about her, but over the years Elizabeth had changed, grown more formal, more remote, more frightening. I dared not presume. This time, she hadn't even invited me to sit.

'I called you back to court because I need you to help me,' she said at last. 'Because it isn't just that my sweet Robin has . . . has taken a woman in wedlock – my own cousin and not a woman I can admire! Lettice Knollys has an eye for men! He will be lucky if she stands by him for long!'

She paused, needing breath, her eyes dangerous. I continued to wait.

'There has been an accusation against Robin,' she said. 'Nothing to do with his marriage. Before my dear Duke Francis and his man de Simier left for France, de Simier had an illness, with violent sickness and gripes. It was after a dinner attended by both him and Robin. A rumour arose – I believe myself that it was begun by de Simier – that Robin had tried to have him poisoned. Robin clearly regards the estate of matrimony as suitable for himself, but is opposed to it for me! The rumour is that Robin wanted to make the duke think my court an unhealthy place, to drive a wedge between him and me. The tale is all round the court and there are those who believe it! Disprove it, Ursula! That's what I want you to do. Use your talents to disprove it! I don't know how you can set about it, but do it, just the same! I implore you!'

Christopher Spelton had been right. I was to investigate. I wondered, rather wildly, how. But the golden-brown eyes were pleading with me, and the shield-shaped face was drawn as if in pain.

'I wish Duke Francis were still here,' said Elizabeth. 'I wish it so much. I am a woman as well as a queen. There are times when like other women, I need a man to lean on and Robin . . . Robin is no longer such a man. I long for the duke to come back. But meanwhile, Ursula, my sister, it is on sisterhood that I must rely instead. Help me, Ursula! I am so angry with Robin, and yet . . . and yet . . . I mind about his good name. I shall fall ill if it is not cleared. I storm and rage – and then I go to my chamber and weep in private. Prove Robin's innocence. Do that for me! It would comfort me so much and besides, what if my dear Francis should fear to return to England to marry me because he thinks he may be a victim too? Because he fears that he may be murdered? Take that dread away, Ursula. Please!'

EIGHTEEN
Blockage

I was to prove Leicester's innocence. Splendid. I hadn't the least idea how to set about it and suppose he wasn't innocent? What then?

Meanwhile, something else arose to command my attention. Word came that Sir Francis Walsingham wished to see me.

I climbed the steep staircase that led to his office, arrived in his antechamber, and was ushered into his presence.

Walsingham had offices in each of Elizabeth's palaces and they were all alike. If I had been brought blindfolded to any of them, and then had my eyes uncovered and been asked to identify which palace it was in, I probably couldn't have done so. He always had an anteroom for his clerks and another room for himself and his personal secretary and any visitors. In each palace, the rooms had panelled walls and diamond-paned windows. In one or two cases, the panelling was of the costly linen-fold style and might have been identified from that except that most of the panelling, linen-fold or otherwise, was obscured by charts, maps, blackboards covered with chalked letters, where coded missives from agents overseas were in process of being unravelled, and shelves piled high with documents, books, files and stationery.

The offices all smelt the same, too, of dust and ink. Walsingham did not go in for the pretty and the frivolous. I had never seen his home and sometimes wondered what it was like, and whether, when he was there, he ever discarded his austere black gown and skull cap and wore something more colourful.

He greeted me with his usual restrained enthusiasm, for though he and I had had frequent dealings in the past, he did not approve of women being involved in the kind of work I did for the queen.

I can't say I liked him. The queen didn't, either. She quarrelled with him often and had been known to throw things at him. His loyalty was unquestioned; he was utterly trustworthy; but he was so very stark and stern and though he was said to be a loving family man, in his professional capacity, he was ruthlessness personified.

However, he was courteous. He offered me a seat, gave me his grim idea of a smile and asked after a kitten he had once given me.

'She flourishes,' I said. 'And catches mice regularly. I have named her Artemis. A big name for a little cat, but Artemis was a huntress.'

'She comes from a long line of excellent mousers,' said Walsingham appreciatively. If he had been a cat, I thought, he would have been a good mouser, too. 'Now.' His tone changed, suddenly, to aggression. It was like a missile hurtling without warning from the mouth of a cannon. 'I believe that you have been much involved in investigating the disappearance of a youth called Thomas Harrison. I have read the report that you left with Dr West of St Andrew's in Priors Ford. I am aware of your suspicions of George and Robert Harrison. I believe there was a button found along with Thomas's body. Did you keep it in your possession?'

'I . . . yes. I meant to leave it with Dr West but I forgot. I have it here in my purse.'

'Your purse is on your girdle, I see. Show me the button.'

I took it out and handed it to him. 'I think,' I said, 'that George Harrison probably knew about the tin mine before Edmund's death. They were brothers, after all, and they met when George came back to his wife. I have an idea that the seeds of the crime – crimes – were sown as soon as George realized that Lisa had had an affair and that he could ruin her in the eyes of her husband. He'd always kept in touch with Robert. I believe that they wanted to push Lisa and her children right out of the line of inheritance.' ·

'You put most of that in your report,' said Walsingham coldly. 'No need to repeat it.' He bounced the button on his palm, looking at it thoughtfully.

'Robert Harrison has probably gone back to France by now,'

I said, feeling the need to persist, to drive my point home against what felt like a wall of obstruction. 'Nothing can be done about him until he returns to England, but when the grape harvest is over, he will come back to marry his cousin Jane Harrison. He and his father can be apprehended then.' A question occurred to me. 'How was it that you saw my report?'

'I am kept informed of what is happening in the lives of certain people,' said Walsingham. 'That report was most comprehensive, but I don't find your tale convincing. The tin mine gives the father and son a motive but the world is full of people with good reasons to murder other people, and yet they don't do it. George may have informed on Lisa Harrison, as it were, simply for moral reasons. After all, Edmund was still alive then. Or are you supposing that George and Robert disposed of Edmund as well?'

I hadn't considered that. But when Edmund died, Robert had been in France, and George was at Marjorie's house. The Firtrees servants had informed him and he had despatched a messenger to France.

'No,' I said. 'I don't think that.'

'I'm glad to hear it! You seem to be hurling accusations of murder about somewhat freely! Whatever the man Tremaine may say, it seems to me more likely that the death of Master Lake was an accident . . .'

'He was summoned by a mysterious note!'

'It may have been a message about anything. There could be a woman in the case. It could have been an invitation to an assignation . . .'

'Not Eric! He was in love with his wife and Kate is expecting their first child . . .'

'Are you really such an innocent, Mistress Stannard? That is a time when gentlemen often stray, for obvious reasons. The summons to the mine may mean nothing sinister but those concerned may be afraid to come forward, for fear that they will be accused of harming him. As for this button, what of it? Such buttons are a commonplace.'

It was still in his hand. He bounced it again. 'My own tailor in London once offered me buttons identical to this but I didn't care for the pattern. Mistress Stannard, you have been

summoned to court to carry out a task for the queen. I wish
she would leave such investigations to me. They are not suitable for a lady such as yourself. However, the queen will have
her way and you must obey her wishes; that I understand. I
think she also needs a kind of support from you, in what must
be a strange time for her, as she considers changing her estate.
It will be a serious step. Put your mind to her business and
leave this other affair alone. That is an order.'

'You are forbidding me to pursue the matter of two murders?
Thomas Harrison and Eric Lake are just to be . . . left?'

'For the time being, yes. It is a relief to me,' said Walsingham,
'that the inquest on Master Lake arrived at a sensible
conclusion . . .'

'But it didn't! The coroner was a dull little man who couldn't
believe in anything so dramatic as a murder. I doubt if he'd
ever been faced with such an idea before, and he couldn't take
it in. Nor could the jury. I told them about the note but they
dismissed it, said – as you did just now – that it could have
been about anything and perhaps did come from Tremaine,
only he was afraid to admit it. They wouldn't even believe
that the signature wasn't in his writing. The coroner said it
was impossible to be sure about such a thing. I believe half
of the jury couldn't write anyway! That coroner virtually told
them to return a verdict of accident and they obeyed him.' A
thought struck me. 'Did you somehow . . . arrange that?'

'No. I knew nothing about Master Lake's death until I saw
your report. The Cornish inquest verdict was pure good fortune
for me. I can only hope that the coroner who is in charge of
the inquest on Thomas Harrison is similarly obliging. I can't
control either him or the jury. But I can take certain steps.
From your report, it seems that you did not actually see
Thomas's body.'

'No, I didn't. Brockley wouldn't let me.'

'Very proper. Brockley, therefore, can attend the inquest and
testify to finding the body. Spelton can also attend, and testify
that it was his idea to look up into the trees. Neither of them
will advance any theories about who killed Thomas. I shall
see them personally and make sure of that. I want a verdict
of murder by an unknown person or persons and I hope to

get it. I have my reasons. You are to concentrate on her majesty's interests.'

'But . . .!'

For a moment, Walsingham looked as tired as Thomas Radcliffe but when he spoke, his face hardened. 'Leave Thomas Harrison and Eric Lake *alone*, Ursula! Now then. The queen. I am worried about her. The step she contemplates is huge. She will have to give up half her power. The Duke of Alençon will expect to rule jointly with her; that is the nature of a man. And there are other dangers.'

I was appalled by the idea of ignoring the deaths of Thomas Harrison and Eric Lake but Walsingham looked at me so sternly that I dared not pursue them now. I said nothing.

'For a woman of the queen's age,' Walsingham said, 'child-birth presents a considerable risk.'

This time, I was expected to comment. 'Am I to dissuade her?'

'If you can. Sussex will oppose you, of course. Well, the ultimate decision will be hers.' Again, there was that look of tiredness. 'Meanwhile,' he said, 'try to save Leicester's good name. For myself, I don't believe for a moment that he ever tried to injure de Simier. Leicester can be wrongheaded and even violent, but he is not one for knives in the dark – or potions in the wine, either. I know him. Well, mistress, that concludes our business, I think. Please, devote yourself to serving your royal sister.'

I said: 'You mentioned your tailor. I have often admired the excellence of your clothes.' This was true enough. Walsingham's taste in dress was sombre, but his doublets and hose were always cut to perfection, from costly materials. 'Does he supply women's gowns at all?'

'No. John Willingdale, master tailor, specializes in gentlemen's garments,' said Walsingham. 'You must get your fine gowns made elsewhere.'

'Very well,' I said humbly.

Which was a pretence, for I did not feel humble. I was seething. I was to leave the matter of Thomas and Eric, was I? How dared he dismiss them so casually! I couldn't.

'There is one matter which you might consider,' Walsingham

said, 'as it is part of serving her majesty. The last letter from
Janus – the one that Christopher Spelton brought here, just
ahead of you – speaks of rumours now current in France, that
some move may be made to prevent the marriage between the
queen and Alençon, either by discrediting her, or by discrediting him in *her* eyes. In France, there are ardent Catholics
who want to see Mary Stuart on the English throne. They
certainly don't want treaties – or marriages – between France
and England. You might keep your ears open for anything that
could bear upon that.'

'I will indeed,' I said, smoothly, concealing my feelings.

I was furious with him. Yes, I would do my best for the
queen, but I would not stop trying to bring George and Robert
Harrison to justice. Walsingham was blocking my path for no
discernible reason and I meant to overcome the blockage. I
made for my apartment, where I found Dale, stitching.
'Where's Brockley?' I asked her.

'In the stables, I think, ma'am. Giving Eddie a hand.'

'Please fetch him.'

When Brockley came, I said: 'I have a commission for you.
It may mean a visit to London . . .'

With Brockley on his way, I had for the moment done all I
could for Thomas and Eric. I turned my attention to Elizabeth's
requests, wondering hopelessly how to deal with them. Had
the rumour about Leicester attempting the life of de Simier
been started as part of a scheme to damage the chances of the
Alençon marriage? If de Simier had started it, it couldn't be,
for he was surely on his master's side and therefore in favour
of the marriage. He might resent Leicester's opposition, but
he had done Leicester enough harm already, by telling the
queen about Lettice Knollys. No – de Simier wasn't a likely
source for the rumour. So, where on earth was I to start? I
felt strongly inclined to run away, to go home and retire
to bed and bury my head under a pillow.

There was one thing I could do, I supposed. I could talk to
Leicester himself.

NINETEEN
Deceit in High Places

Leicester was said to be at his house in Wanstead, about sixteen miles away, if one were a crow; longer if one must follow roads and tracks, which had a habit of winding. Early next morning, I took Eddie, with Dale on his pillion, and set off on horseback.

The day was humid but at least it was dry and the roads were good. We were there by noon. In the front courtyard, servants came out to us and I announced myself, asking if the Earl of Leicester were at home and if he would see me. His butler, pointing to another archway, said that my lord was in the stable yard. Eddie was already leading the horses off to the stables so Dale and I followed him. We found Robert Dudley, Earl of Leicester, famed for being the elegantly dressed and powerful friend of her majesty, prosaically clad in old clothes, leaning over a tub of soapy water and washing a large wolfhound, which was yelping in protest and had splashed its master lavishly with water and soapsuds.

I knew Leicester, of course, had known him for years, ever since he appointed me to the household of his first wife because she feared that she was in danger and he wanted me to watch over her and try to reassure her. She had died, mysteriously, and he had been accused of her murder, but I knew him innocent of that. All the same, I had still, at first, neither liked nor trusted him and certainly I was never impressed by his looks, handsome though he was.

But over the years I had seen how Elizabeth depended on his steady devotion, which never seemed to falter despite his quick temper and imperious nature. For her he had been a rock on which she leant for support, and I was sure that once she had accustomed herself to the idea that like other men, he needed a wife for his bed and his home and perhaps a mother for lawful children (he had one natural son, but no tactful person ever mentioned that), then she would take him back into her favour. I hoped she would. I did not dislike him now.

Seeing me, he stepped back, shaking water from his hands. 'Ursula Stannard! What brings you here? *Jeff! Peter!*' Grooms came running. 'Help Mistress Stannard's groom with her horses and take this dog over for me! He just needs rinsing now; you'll want fresh water – stop yelping, Brutus, you're not hurt; you just don't like the smell of soap. Come into the house, mistress. My wife will be pleased to see you.'

He spoke with pride in his voice. No matter how angry Elizabeth might be, Leicester was obviously not ashamed of his marriage.

I also knew Lettice Knollys, now the Countess of Leicester, and like the queen, I was wary of her, for her long sloe-blue eyes always seemed predatory and she was unashamedly appreciative of good-looking men. Though it was true that her first husband had left her alone for years while he was on duty in Ireland and that must have borne hard on a woman as interested in sex as Lettice was said to be.

Leicester, brushing soap off his clothes and wiping his wet shoes on a mat, led me and Dale inside. We heard Lettice's voice somewhere in the distance, whereupon Leicester said: 'Ah. I know where she is,' and a moment later, we were at the door of her stillroom, where the new Countess of Leicester was being a busy housewife, instructing a maid to clean out some bottles including those with only a little left in them.

'Those odd inches won't be used. Throw them away and wash the bottles well, ready for the new season's preserves and . . . my lord? Mistress Stannard! You should have let us know that you were coming!'

The stillroom was abandoned to the maid, and we repaired to my lady's parlour, which was comfortable, domestic and not what I would have expected as a setting for Lettice, who at court had been fashionable and proud to an extreme degree, and wasn't known for her embroidery. Today, she was simply dressed with neither ruff nor farthingale, and there was an embroidery frame with some part-done work on it, lying on a window ledge. She smiled at Dudley and me and pulled a settle forward for me and I thought that she seemed different, gentler than I remembered, and clearly desirous of pleasing her new husband.

There were refreshments, an invitation to stay to dinner and small talk, just as one might expect, and at my request, Dale was allowed to sit with us. But at length, Leicester, who had been watching my face, said: 'I imagine that Mistress Stannard had some reason for this visit. Had you, Ursula?'

'Yes, my lord. I am on the queen's business.'

'Lettice . . .' said Leicester, and before he had reached the rest of the sentence, she had nodded, and smiled again and slipped tactfully out of the room. I could hardly believe that Lettice Knollys could be so biddable.

'So. What is it?' Leicester asked, as the door closed behind her. He glanced doubtfully at Dale.

'Dale knows my business,' I said. 'I often discuss things with her. My lord . . .'

I stopped, not sure how to say what I must. Leicester grinned. 'You have come to ask or to tell me something difficult. Well, speak your mind. The queen never hesitates to speak hers,' he added, and the grin vanished. I saw how her rage had pained him.

'I came to ask . . .'

I stopped again and Leicester groaned. 'Say it, whatever it is! Presumably you aren't going to tell me I am destined for the block. A squad of soldiers would have come for that! It must be something a trifle less terrible, but what?'

Frankness seemed the only way. 'The queen has asked me to find out whether you really did try to . . . try to . . .'

'Try to what?'

'Get rid of Jean de Simier.' I got it out at last.

'You mean did I try to poison him, or have him poisoned?'

'Yes.'

'The answer is no.' He looked irritated but took the question in good part. 'He had an attack of food poisoning, I think. Unless someone else wished to dispose of him, but I doubt that. Others of the Council besides myself are unhappy about this proposed marriage with Alençon, but – good God, if the Duke of Alençon's emissary were poisoned here in England, it would blacken the queen's name from end to end of Europe. None of us would deal in murder anyway. I have been accused of it, as you know. But I was innocent then and I am innocent now.'

Like Sussex and like Walsingham, he looked tired. 'Though how I can prove that, I don't know,' he said. 'I don't think it can be proved. I may have to live with the suspicion for the rest of my life. I can only say that if you wish me to swear my innocence upon a Bible, standing in a house of God with one hand on the altar, I will do so. I can do no more. There is a chapel here.'

'You would do that?' I asked. 'It wouldn't be proof – I don't see how we could produce proof – but it would be something to tell her majesty. I think she would find it close to proof. She knows you well, after all.'

'I will so swear,' Leicester said.

He did, too, and in a most dignified manner, changing first into good clothes and clean shoes, calling his chaplain, and investing the whole business with great formality. With one hand on a Bible and the other on the chapel altar, he swore his innocence. When it was done, I dined with him and Lettice, and across the meal we talked as civilized people should, of mutual acquaintances, of harvest prospects and a little – carefully – of the latest news, but avoiding sensitive subjects such as the Alençon marriage. Then I took my leave.

It was dusk by the time Dale and I returned to our rooms at the palace. It was too late that evening for a private audience with the queen. I would make my report to her in the morning. One duty had been discharged – at least as far as it possibly could be. Now I had only to worry about unknown schemes to dislodge the Duke of Alençon from his English plans (how on earth did Walsingham expect me to investigate that?) and also, the task which I had set Brockley.

Dale and I were both weary. We were resting and sharing a flagon of wine, when to our annoyance a page arrived at the outer door of our suite to announce that Antoine de Lacey wished to call upon me.

I would have liked to refuse him but thought I had better not. Therefore, I welcomed him politely and asked what had brought him to visit me.

'You can help me, I hope,' he said. 'I came earlier, twice, in fact, but no one was here. You have been away today, it seems.'

'I rode to Wanstead, to call on the Earl of Leicester.'

'Indeed? You are in touch with him and on friendly terms? Well, that could be convenient.'

'In what way?'

'I have an errand to the earl.'

'You mean to the Earl of Leicester?'

'To him and also to her majesty. Late yesterday evening, a courier arrived, bringing letters, one for myself, one for the queen and one for the Earl of Leicester. They all came from my master, Jean de Simier. This morning I was granted the favour of a short audience with the queen and I gave her letter to her. She was glad to receive it. It exonerates the Earl of Leicester. My master has thought matters over and concluded that his illness was accidental, and that his suspicions were unfounded. He apologizes.'

So de Simier really had been the source of the rumour, but perhaps genuinely, not mischievously. I was happy to hear it, though it made my journey to Wanstead seem irrelevant. 'The earl's letter, I have already sent on,' de Lacey said. 'However, my own, which gives me certain instructions, does I think repeat much of what my master has written to Leicester.' He reached inside his doublet and pulled out a scroll. 'This is mine. You are welcome to read it. I wish you to do so.'

He handed it to me. In it, de Simier explained that he had written an apology to Leicester for casting doubts on his character. It seemed a euphemistic way of referring to an accusation of attempted murder, but still, an apology it presumably was.

The text further explained that de Simier was now sure of his ground because he had recalled that at the dinner after which he had been taken so unpleasantly ill, there had been a dish consisting of small roundels of duck flesh on spikes, half a dozen or so to a spike, accompanied by a rosemary dipping sauce. The dish was not popular as the duck roundels seemed underdone. De Simier himself, however, being fond of duck, had taken three or four spikes. It had since been pointed out to him that duck was one of the meats that should always be thoroughly cooked; that if underdone, it could cause trouble. Thinking it over, he had remembered that the roundels had tasted slightly odd, metallic. He feared that he had been unjust. By way of expressing his regrets in a material fashion, he was sending the earl a small keg of exceptionally fine wine. It would be delivered to de Lacey, who was to invite the earl to dinner, entertain him well, and broach the wine on that occasion, thus making a little ceremony of it.

'But I can't invite him to dinner here,' said de Lacey. 'The queen herself told me, this morning, that he is still not welcome at court. However, I can invite him to dine with me at a good inn. I would leave it to him to choose a suitable one. I would invite my lord's countess as well, and perhaps, Mistress Stannard, you would join us? And perhaps another couple – so that the company is not too pointedly political. My own feeling is that it should be a little informal, merry and sociable, even though the reason behind it is serious. There is such a solemn feeling about the court, these days. I would like to lighten the air.' He gave me a broad smile that illuminated his otherwise uninteresting features.

'If I am to attend, I would have to ask the queen's permission,' I said.

'Will you do that?'

'Very well,' I said.

De Lacey left at last. Dale and I sat talking about this latest turn of events and she began to fret because Brockley was so long away, but he arrived half an hour later, to her obvious relief. I was very pleased to see him, too. 'So here you are!' I said. 'What news? You found Master Willingdale?'

'I did.' Brockley looked pleased with himself. 'It was easy. His Guild were only too pleased to give me his direction. I didn't wish to start scandalous rumours by mentioning that this was part of an enquiry into murder. I represented myself as the servant of a gentleman who had lately returned to England from a foreign posting, was looking for a good tailor and had been recommended to go to Master Willingdale. I was quite inventive,' said Brockley. 'I said that Willingdale's direction had been mislaid during the gentleman's very rough voyage across the English Channel and . . .'

'Never mind that! What did you learn?'

'When I found Master Willingdale, in his shop in a narrow little lane in the City, I didn't tell *him* any tarradiddles. I was frank about my purpose and I showed him the button.' He produced it, holding it up. 'I asked if he had ever seen such a button before, indeed, if he had ever offered this pattern to Sir Frances Walsingham. He said no, he had never seen it before and therefore had not offered such a thing to Sir Francis. He was intrigued by the pattern – wondered where he might obtain some. I couldn't help him there, of course. So, madam, it seems that Sir Francis Walsingham was – er – deceiving you.'

'Lying to me. Deceit in high places! And all to dissuade me from regarding it as good evidence against Robert Harrison. Well, well, well.'

TWENTY
A Merry and Informal Party

The queen did not object when I asked if I might attend what I had privately named de Lacey's Apologetic Dinner. I told her about that and it amused her, which was a good thing for when I entered her room, I was just in time to see her throwing a slipper at a lady in waiting who, apparently, had failed to starch a ruff properly.

The lady fled our presence and the queen, with a lightning change of mood, let herself laugh at my name for the dinner and was glad when I told her of Leicester's solemn oath. 'He is a man of piety in his fashion,' she said. 'He respects God and I think would not have taken such an oath unless he meant it. Even without de Simier's apology, that oath would convince me. I thank you, Ursula. You did well. You will be rewarded. Yes, go to the dinner. Have a pleasant time.'

I mentioned de Lacey's suggestion of asking another couple and she said: 'Oh, by all means. Take young Lady Margaret Mollinder. I will ask Sir Christopher Hatton to escort her. She is not very happy at court,' said Elizabeth. 'She says she misses her husband. Ah well; I can sympathize with that. I miss Alençon even though he is not yet my husband. You may approach both her and Hatton on the matter.'

'Will you soon let the Earl of Leicester come back to the court?' I ventured.

With another sudden change of mood, Elizabeth frowned and her eyes sparked with the anger that made people quail, including me. Then she relaxed. 'Not yet. Eventually, I will, but first he must learn that he cannot offend me with impunity. I would find it easier to forgive him for his marriage if he were not so opposed to mine! One thing I will not do, and that is allow his wife, my wretched cousin Lettice, to come to court with him. I have never liked or trusted her.

She had better not show her face again in my presence!
Ever.'

I bent my head and made no comment.

Leicester accepted the invitation and duly chose the venue for
the dinner, selecting the Castle Inn in Kingston, as being
convenient for the guests from court. A private dining room
on the first floor was bespoken for the occasion, which took
place a week after my visit to Wanstead.

We set out by river: myself, the Brockleys, Antoine de
Lacey, Lady Margaret Mollinder and her maid, a young woman
called Lucy who clearly had an affection for her mistress, and
Sir Christopher Hatton. Lean and dark and long-chinned, he
had a certain resemblance to Sussex, and was just as much of
a devoted servant to the queen. There were rumours that he
was secretly married but no one ever learned the truth of that
for sure and I doubt if Elizabeth ever knew that such a rumour
existed. To her, he was forever a bachelor, a gifted dancer, and
available, when she wished it, to act as an escort for her or
for any court lady in need of one.

Brockley came along so that he could help to trundle the
little handcart on which Antoine had placed the precious keg.
It had not been sent from France but had been ordered by
letter, from a London vintner. Antoine had stored it in his
room in the meantime and as he had no servant of his own
and was entitled to make only limited use of the royal servants, I lent him Brockley to assist in getting the keg from
palace to barge, and from barge to hostelry.

The barge we used belonged to Sir Christopher. It bore us
from Richmond to Kingston on a leaden, sluggish river. The
day was leaden and sluggish too, too thundery for October.
We had all eyed that sky doubtfully and brought cloaks in
case we needed them. The air on the river was a little fresher
than it was ashore, though, and the journey was agreeable.

So was our welcome at the inn, for the innkeeper, delighted
to cater for such a distinguished party, bowed himself nearly
double as he greeted us, handed Dale and Lucy (and the cloaks)
over to his wife, who promised that our attendants would be
looked after, and then showed us upstairs to the dining chamber,

where Leicester and Lettice already awaited us. Brockley and de Lacey carried the keg up between them. Then Brockley left us to join Dale and Lucy downstairs, while the rest of us settled ourselves at the dining table.

The arrangements seemed to be excellent. The table, which was round, was elaborately set and there were two side tables, one holding a silver platter, the other a tray with glasses and a tall jug. The keg was set down beside it. We, the guests, had of course dressed to do justice to the occasion. Hatton wore black, but in a rich material, and de Lacey was in amber, with big puffed sleeves, slashed with yellow silk. Leicester's sleeves were less spectacular but his crimson brocade doublet and hose were striking, while Lettice had a beautiful peach-coloured gown embroidered with flowers of all colours, and Lady Margaret had chosen a charming, youthful gown of interwoven white and silver.

The queen's reward to me for my efforts at Wanstead had not been in money, but in kind. She had sent me a fine rope of genuine pearls and a pair of matching earrings. I was wearing the pearl rope as a double necklace, teemed with an open-fronted gown in green brocade, over a lighter green kirtle embroidered with little white leaves. The overskirt did not have a hidden pouch stitched inside it. I was hardly likely to need picklocks or a dagger on this occasion, and though I had money with me, my green velvet purse was on my girdle.

Since the table was circular, there was no head to it, but the seats consisted of stools and one chair with carved arms. 'That's for the guest of honour,' said Antoine, gesturing to Leicester. The earl took his seat, with Lady Margaret on his right and myself on his left. Antoine sat on the other side of Margaret, Hatton on the other side of me, and Lettice was between them, opposite to her lord.

'I left it to Antoine here to choose the food,' Leicester said as we settled ourselves. 'He's our host, after all.' From the moment we were assembled, Leicester had taken charge of the conversation, avoiding any reference to the reason behind the dinner, complimenting Lady Margaret and me on our dresses, and talking of harmless matters: the sticky weather, the new horses he was buying for the queen's guard – he was still her Master of Horse and was managing to perform his duties in spite of being banished from court – and some alterations he was having made at the Wanstead house.

Hatton fitted smoothly in, adding comments here and there, and Lettice, gracious as never before, echoed Leicester's remarks, fanning herself when he spoke of the weather, observing that the new horses were all to be grey – 'and the same height; it is a challenging task to find them' – and approving the alterations which would give her husband more space for his books. 'He is such a great reader.'

Platters of bread were brought in, accompanied by chicken and pork soup with saffron and cumin, and with it, we had a cooled white wine. 'But this is not the special wine that my master Jean de Simier has sent,' Antoine told us. 'That will go best with meat. We'll have it presently.'

Over the soup, conversation continued to be courteous and general. Hatton recounted a comical anecdote about hunting, mainly addressing Lady Margaret; as her escort, he evidently thought he should try to entertain her. She responded with polite laughter, though I noticed that she often twisted her wedding ring. She was pining badly for her husband, I thought.

The soup was followed by a fish pie and our glasses were refilled with the white wine. But while we were eating the pie, two inn servants brought in a joint of roast beef on a carving dish. They set this down on the spare side table and one of them, after some histrionic sharpening of a knife, carved it into slices, which he laid tenderly on the silver platter. The other broached the keg, filled the jug, and from that filled the glasses. He brought the tray over to us and handed out the glasses.

'It has had time to settle,' Antoine said. 'And Brockley and I were most careful with it. It's a red wine, very full bodied and velvety. I have had it in France and I can speak for its excellence.'

Hatton, inhaling the fragrance from his glass, said: 'I recognize this. I think I could even name the vineyard it comes from. If I'm right, it's an excellent vintage.'

'I think you will find it so,' said Antoine. 'And now . . .' He rose to his feet, holding his glass high. 'Now let us acknowledge why we are here. We cannot avoid that. So let us drink a toast. To the clearing of my lord of Leicester's name – my master Jean de Simier begs forgiveness for his foolish accusation – and to the future union of your country, my lord, with my own, when the Duke of Alençon and your most noble queen Elizabeth stand before the altar and are made one in marriage.'

He drank, with a flourish. We all did the same and Hatton exclaimed: 'To the clearing of a name and the hope of a royal marriage,' which was generous of him, for I was well aware that he was among those who feared the outcome of marriage – any marriage – for the queen.

The dish of beef slices was brought over and a choice of sauces was offered. Side dishes of salad and savoury beans were set out and more bread was brought. I began to talk of a letter I had that morning received from Kate Lake. She had decided that she wished to sell Eric's dark-chestnut gelding and wondered if I would like to buy it.

'Only,' I said to Leicester, 'she isn't sure what it is worth. She wants advice. I don't know how old it is, but it's a good-looking animal and well-mannered and it must be nearly sixteen hands.'

Leicester was always ready to talk about horses. 'I might be interested in it myself! However, if Mistress Lake can have it brought to Wanstead, I could examine it and suggest a suitable price. I could . . . what the devil is happening to the light? M'sieu de Lacey . . .'

While we were eating, the air, hot and heavy to start with, had become even hotter and heavier and the sky had been steadily darkening. 'We're in for a storm,' Antoine remarked.

Lightning flickered and thunder rumbled. A moment later, it became so dark that we could hardly see each other's faces. 'Lights!' Antoine shouted at the two serving men.

They hurried away to return a moment later with two branched candlesticks. The thunder and lightning were now continuous and the wicks were kindled only after some nervous fumbling with a tinderbox. The candlesticks were brought to the table. Antoine, noticing that both Leicester and Hatton had almost emptied their glasses, shouted for the jug to be filled up and brought to the table as well. 'I'll top up the glasses,' he said, to the servant who brought it. 'It's only a storm, but look at the way your hands are shaking!'

His own weren't perfectly steady, for he slopped the wine a little and splashed one of his sleeves, muttering a fastidious oath and then saying, most unfairly, that he couldn't see why a commonplace thunderstorm should make all the servants go into a dither. Eating and drinking resumed.

'That's better,' said Leicester, folding a slice of beef into a piece of bread and engulfing it with obvious pleasure. 'We can all see what we're doing now. Never mind the dithering servants, de Lacey. The service is good enough and so is the food. I thought it would be – I know this inn. The cook knows his business.'

'The salad is beautifully arranged,' Lettice agreed. 'Almost a work of art. It seems a shame to break into it!'

She was interrupted by another flash of lightning, this time a giant one. For a startled moment we saw each other's faces lit up not by the soft candlelight, which had been completely overwhelmed, but by a hard, blue glare. Then came an immense crash of thunder. It sounded as though a landslide were falling out of the clouds. The whole building shook. Dishes rattled. The wine jug slopped. The serving men shied like frightened colts and Lady Margaret sprang to her feet with a shriek, jolting the table, which tilted. I too stood up, leaning across the table to stop the candlesticks and the dish of beef slices from sliding straight into Hatton's lap. Several wineglasses also started sliding towards me and I retrieved them too, pushing them back to their places. Outside, with a sudden swish, the rain began, a heavy downpour that drummed on the windows. There was another flash but a less alarming one and the next rumble of thunder sounded further away. The table settled back.

Lady Margaret sat down and said shakily: 'I'm so sorry. I was silly. I have never liked thunder.' Hatton said something kind to her, in a low voice. We resumed our dinner. Lettice asked me where I had bought the brocade for my gown, Hatton went on talking quietly to Lady Margaret while Leicester and Antoine entered into a discussion about some political matter.

The course finished. Hatton proposed a toast to our host, Antoine de Lacey, and our guest of honour, the Earl of Leicester, and we all drank. The dessert course arrived. A honey and saffron quiche was served, ready sliced and accompanied by jugs of cream. 'Really excellent,' Leicester declared, after one bite. 'I congratulate you, M'sieu de Lacey . . . M'sieu? What . . .?'

A strange expression had crossed Antoine's face. He half rose from his seat. 'I don't know . . . I feel . . . dear God, my stomach! I think I'm going to be . . .'

He turned aside just in time to avoid actually vomiting over the table. He threw up on to the floor instead. We stared at him in horror.

And then I became aware of three unpleasant things, all at the same time.

One was that Hatton and Lady Margaret were also looking ill and clutching at their stomachs. Another was that I too was about to vomit. The third was that I was also about to have diarrhoea.

It might be better not to describe the next half-hour or so in too much detail. We were all stricken. The serving men must have run for help because suddenly the room was full of people: the innkeeper, his wife, Dale, Brockley and Lucy. There was a terrible smell in the room. Basins were being offered. A ghastly salty drink was being thrust upon me, which made me vomit even more violently.

After that, memory becomes hazy. As if through a mist, I recall Dale and one of the inn's maids helping me into another room, and onto a bed. I felt myself being undressed and heard Dale exclaiming. There was a horrible stench. Someone gave me a drink of water. Someone seemed to be washing me. I was sick again.

After that, I vaguely recall Lady Margaret being carried in and laid on the bed beside me. I heard her crying. There were still a few lightning flashes and the sound of thunder in the distance and rain was still driving against the windows.

Then sleep came. When I woke, it was morning. Birds were singing. I was no longer ill, though I felt very weak and my stomach muscles ached. Dale was asleep on a truckle bed and Lady Margaret was lying next to me. She was on her side, quiet and pale and still. I lifted myself on an elbow and looked at her.

The horrible smell was there again, and on Lady Margaret's pillow, next to her face, was a revolting pile of mingled vomit and blood.

Lady Margaret Mollinder was dead.

TWENTY-ONE
One Careless Word

Except for poor Lady Margaret, we all recovered quickly. By the afternoon, though we were still weak, the rest of us had even begun to feel hungry again. A physician had been called, however, who recommended that we all rest for a time, so we stayed at the Castle Inn for three complete days more, though there was much sending of messages, for the queen had to be told what had happened and Lady Margaret had to be carried back to Richmond so that plans could be made for her funeral.

Brockley acted as the messenger and took Dale with him to collect night-gear, fresh linen and two dresses for me, with kirtles. I had only the dress and linen I had been wearing when the illness struck, and all of that was stained beyond hope.

On the third day, Hatton and Leicester, as the two senior men of the group, called us all to join them in Leicester's room.

'We shall have to report what has happened,' said Leicester. 'But we need to be careful what we say. We must all say the same, and stand by it.'

'Food poisoning,' said Hatton. 'That's the story that's been told in the messages we've sent to Richmond so far, and we must hold to that. Rumours of any other kind of poisoning must be quashed. They are absurd, of course, for who would want to harm that poor young lady? But rumour isn't logical. There was a keg of wine sent by Jean de Simier to my lord of Leicester here, and it is known that my lord is not in favour of the queen's marriage to the Duke of Alençon. It is also known that although de Simier has apologized for the earlier rumour, he resents my lord of Leicester's attitude. If scandalous talk arises, it will be quite as dangerous as the rumour about my lord trying to poison de Simier! There will be such a public outcry against de Simier and through him, against Alençon, that there would be no chance of the marriage proceeding. I don't favour the marriage any more than the earl here, but the decision belongs to the queen, not to anyone else, and in any case, I think I can say, my lord of Leicester, that neither you nor I would want it halted by scandal.'

'No, indeed we wouldn't,' said Leicester with feeling, and I knew that he was thinking of the mysterious death of his first wife, and the suspicions that had clustered round him then. 'It could even be said that it was a scheme on *our* part to discredit de Simier and Alençon! A scheme that went somehow wrong. Who knows what *they* will say – the *they* that is our nickname for the imaginative and talkative men and women of England! No. Food poisoning is probably what really happened and in any case, that's our story and there's nothing odd about it in such thundery weather.'

I said: 'But what do we really think?'

Leicester looked at me. 'We don't,' he said. 'Better not. Lady Margaret was unlucky in that she was more sensitive to whatever it was than the rest of us.'

'No one can be sure,' said de Lacey, 'where the venom, whatever it was, came from. If it really was food poisoning, it could have been in the food! There was pork in that soup and pork can be dangerous in sticky weather.'

'The innkeeper,' said Hatton, 'tried a little of the wine on a stray dog. The dog fell ill, though it hasn't died, and now seems to be recovering. It was the wine, for sure.'

A cold worm of suspicion coiled itself in my stomach. And as I looked Leicester in the eyes, I knew that he felt the same. The trouble had lain in the special keg of wine. And the provenance of that keg was . . . suggestive . . .

In the barge, on the way back to Richmond, Brockley came to sit at my side. 'Madam . . .'

'Yes, Brockley?'

'I managed, yesterday, to take a really close look at that keg,' he said. 'It had been emptied and taken down to a store-room to be cleaned. Such kegs are useful; the innkeeper isn't one to let a handy windfall slip past him.'

'Yes?'

'It had been tampered with,' said Brockley. 'In the lid, there was what, at a brief glance, looked like a knot mark in the wood. But when I looked closer, I could see that a hole had been drilled there. It had been filled in with something – clay, perhaps – and then the whole lid had been varnished. I looked hard enough to make sure. I have no doubt at all that there was tampering, madam.'

I thought about it. 'Well, de Simier can't have done it in person – the wine was ordered from a London vintner; he can never have set eyes on it. Though someone could have acted on his orders. Antoine? Only, why would de Simier give such orders? *He* wouldn't want to risk ruining the Duke of Alençon's marriage prospects! Marriage to the queen would make de Simier the close friend of a king! De Simier just can't have been responsible for this.'

'Madam, have you not told me and Fran that your mysterious correspondent Janus reported a plot that was said to be afoot in France, to scuttle the marriage?'

'You think that we may have been the victims of some scheme of that kind? But surely the aim wasn't to kill Lady Margaret!'

I shook my head, trying to clear my mind. It refused to clear. 'I'm getting confused. I'm muddling up what actually happened with what rumour may say. I *can't* see any thread of sense in this.'

We returned to Richmond, and our bland story of food poisoning – so convincing considering the thundery weather – was accepted. I did speak to Walsingham. I reminded him of the Janus report about a plot against the queen's marriage, and I told him of Brockley's discovery that the keg had been tampered with. He agreed and said that Lord Burghley shared my suspicions; indeed, that a quiet investigation was taking place.

'But where it will lead, how successful it will be, is another matter. For the moment, I advise reticence.' He repeated what Hatton had said. 'We *don't* want to start a scandal!'

Thereafter, life at Richmond seemed to go smoothly on. Brockley and Spelton duly rode off to Woking one day to attend the inquest on Thomas Harrison and came back to report, glumly, that the verdict had indeed been murder by a person or persons unknown. The queen was still temperamental and was said to be missing Alençon a good deal, but she followed her normal routine. She attended Council meetings, met ambassadors, held a dinner for a number of bishops, rode and danced. On one occasion, she called Antoine de Lacey to demonstrate his conjuring to her, and rewarded him lavishly for it.

Now that Leicester's reputation was restored, I wanted to go home, but the queen told me that a masque was being planned that she thought I would enjoy and I was invited – well, bidden – to stay on for that. With Elizabeth, invitations and orders were apt to be indistinguishable.

I took up the good-natured offer that Leicester had made, to help in arranging the sale of Eric Lake's horse. It turned out that after the inquest, Christopher Spelton had taken a little extra time off from his duties in order to pay yet another visit of condolence to his cousin Eric's widow. He took charge of bringing the horse to Wanstead. He told us that Lisa was also making a visit to West Leys as company for Kate for a while, now that her brother and sister-in-law had gone home, and that Lisa was full of news about the plans for Jane's wedding; it seemed that Robert was expected back from France very soon. Kate was well, Christopher said, and behaving sensibly, keeping calm and making preparations for her baby. She had begun to interview prospective nursemaids.

'I am being careful,' he said to me. 'I am taking my time. For the moment, I remain just her husband's cousin, concerned for her welfare and that of my future baby cousin. But you can imagine my hopes.'

'I wish you well,' I said, and I meant it. I had done right in choosing to remain at Hawkswood and remain Ursula Stannard, even though, at times, thinking of Christopher's friendly brown eyes and knowing what pleasant company he could be . . .

Well, well. Never mind all that. I put such ideas resolutely aside and concentrated on the matter of Eric's horse.

Its name was Firefly and Leicester was impressed with it.

He proposed a good price for it and he would clearly have liked to buy it himself, but gave way with grace when I reminded him that Kate had actually offered it to me and that I was interested.

I had chosen to go to Wanstead, taking the Brockleys with me, to see Leicester inspect the horse, because I had had an idea.

'If the horse is sound, and if you like it, Brockley,' I told him, 'I want to buy it for you. You are a fine horseman and worthy of a really good mount of your own. Your Mealy is a nice, sturdy cob but . . .'

'I'm very fond of Mealy, madam,' said Brockley mildly. 'And he is a good sturdy animal, as you say. If he's to be sold, I don't want him to go to just anyone.'

'You're always fond of your horses, Brockley, and quite right too. But I wasn't suggesting that we sell Mealy. He could be very useful!'

He could indeed. My chief cook, John Hawthorn, was a large and heavy man but I reckoned that Mealy would be capable of carrying him if necessary. 'There are always errands at Hawkswood,' I said, 'and though we now have a number of horses, it's amazing how often there isn't one available just when a horse is wanted. Is Mealy harness-broken, by the way?'

'No, madam, he is not.'

'Well, you can train him to the shafts. You'll enjoy working with him and he'll be extra-useful once he can pull a cart. Anyway, see what you think of Eric Lake's horse.'

'I already know,' said Brockley. 'I've seen the animal, after all – I had plenty of time to observe him when we went to Cornwall. He is a fine-looking horse.'

And in his voice, there was definitely a note of longing. When we rode back to Richmond, he was leading Firefly.

Back at Richmond, I had made some arrangements. I had been granted stabling for only three horses – for me, Eddie, and the Brockleys. Dale always preferred to ride pillion, when she had to ride at all. But I had persuaded an amused Leicester to give me a note for the head groom, instructing him to make an extra stall available for just one night, so that if we did come back with Firefly, he could be accommodated. The next day, Eddie would lead Mealy back to Hawkswood and Firefly would have his stall.

'Mealy will stay at Hawkswood. I promise,' I said, when Brockley, even though he had thanked me for buying Firefly, looked at me as though I had asked him to betray his country. 'Really, Brockley! You haven't married him!'

'I know. I'm sorry, madam. It's just that this feels like saying goodbye to him.'

'He'll be there at home when we get back,' I said firmly.

We saw Firefly bestowed and then went indoors, to be at once caught up in a strange new atmosphere. The palace seemed to be full of people chatting in corners and looking secretive, and we could hear musicians rehearsing; the sound of musical instruments, often repeating phrases over and over, seemed to penetrate everywhere.

Then, looking out of a window, I saw the Master of the Revels alighting from a barge, and a number of porters carrying oddly shaped packages from it, and realized that all this to-do was concerned with the masque that the queen had mentioned to me. The Master of the Revels was bringing props from where they were stored at the Tower.

I accosted a page and discovered that the promised masque was to take place that very evening, after an early supper. Apparently, the queen had had a couple of ambassadors to dine and wished them to share the entertainment. One of them was due to set out for home leave the following day, so the event had been brought forward.

When everyone entered the hall where the performance was to take place, dusk was falling, though there was light in plenty, just as there had been at Alençon's reception. Banks of candles and tall candle stands were everywhere, and more stands encircled the space that the actors would use. The audience would have a clear view.

The ladies, including the women servants, who were allowed to watch from one end of the hall, had all dressed in their best for the occasion and so had Elizabeth, who was a glittering figure in peach and gold, seated on a dais with steps up to it, on which chosen ladies and courtiers could sit. The dais was draped in blue velvet which made sitting on the steps reasonably comfortable.

The two ambassadors, and also Walsingham and Cecil, all in long, formal gowns, were on the dais itself, two on each side of Elizabeth, and various other people had lesser seats set on the floor of the hall, to either side of the dais. An usher showed me to one of these, and directed the Brockleys to a bench just behind.

I found myself beside Antoine de Lacey, who was wearing a beautiful blue outfit, the doublet shoulders dramatically puffed, the sleeves slashed with silver silk. De Simier must pay him very well, I thought, judging by the way he dressed. He greeted me courteously, expressing pleasure that I had fully recovered from the food poisoning. I thanked him politely.

The masque took the form of a highly moral drama, mostly played by men and boys of the court, though there were some hired musicians and singers and also some professional performers such as tumblers, conjurors and clowns. Virtue, played by a fair-haired young page, who made quite a convincing maiden (and would no doubt be mercilessly teased by his fellow pages later on), was pursued by the Seven Deadly Sins, one after the other. Sometimes, she saved herself, sometimes she was rescued from danger by a character called (according to the Master of the Revels, who had a powerful voice and acted as a Greek chorus), an Honest Farmhand, who wore a leather jerkin and short hose and was armed with a pitchfork.

At the start of the performance, the Sins paraded together, wrangling over which of them was most likely to overcome Virtue's resistance, and then agreeing that each should try his luck in turn.

Pride was a tall, swaggering fellow with a sword too big for him, which he drew and brandished, before tripping over it. I hoped for his sake that it was blunt. Greed was skinny and prowled about, grabbing purses from the rest. Lust was large and handsome, stripped to the waist and given to rippling his muscles, Envy small and skulking, staring hungrily at the others. Gluttony was fat – I think with the help of cushions – and was seated behind a table where there was food which he kept pretending to guzzle. Wrath was enormous and flourished a great big club; Sloth was flopped on a bed and said his lines languidly from a supine position.

Then the Honest Farmhand stepped forward and promised to protect Virtue with his life and his pitchfork, and after that, he and the Sins withdrew behind a curtain and Virtue, sweet and innocent, took the stage and to an accompaniment from a lute-player, sang a suitably sweet and innocent song about gathering flowers.

One by one, the Sins appeared and attempted to seduce the maiden, and Virtue, with witty lines and coquettish retreats behind some bushes and statues, which had been set round the stage in between the candle stands, routed them all, helped by the Farmhand. The musicians had a tune and a song to go with each of them, and at suitable moments the hired entertainers did their turns. The clowns, for instance, followed Pride, making fun of him and his antics with his sword.

By that time, the performance had begun to spread off the stage area and spill into the body of the hall. Lust's courtship followed Pride's and he, amid much laughter (and from some young gallants, regrettable cries of encouragement), energetically chased Virtue all over the hall. The Farmhand saw him off with the aid of the pitchfork, and in the process bounced round the hall so vigorously that a number of people got up and retreated in genuine alarm.

As the Farmhand finally chased Lust away, he stuck his pitchfork enthusiastically into Lust's rear end. This was startlingly realistic and I hoped that the apparent blood was only red ink. Lust turned a somersault on his way out, whereupon the tumblers ran on and did their turn, while Virtue gratefully thanked her rescuer, who gave her a chaste kiss on the cheek and then withdrew. This part of the proceedings gave rise to more whistles and cries of encouragement from some parts of the audience, and then to loud booings as the Farmhand failed to seize the opportunity to go further.

The whole performance was becoming more and more lively. Wrath danced a war dance, which also carried him out into the hall and caused several ladies to shriek and shrink back. He threatened the trembling Virtue with his club, and was routed, not this time by the Farmhand, but by Virtue herself, kneeling humbly in an attitude of prayer.

'The soft answer turneth away Wrath,' declared the Master of the Revels, but as soon as Wrath, head bowed and club drooping, had gone, on came a conjuror, accompanied by a young assistant.

The conjuror began with some remarkable tricks with a length of rope, causing de Lacey, who was watching intently, to wonder aloud how he did them. 'I dabble in conjuring tricks but I've never learned that one!'

'How did you come to dabble in conjuring?' I asked him. The conjuror was now performing some less exciting card tricks and for a moment I let myself be distracted.

'Oh, my grandfather was a travelling entertainer – singing, juggling, conjuring. He was eventually taken on as a permanent entertainer at a chateau. While he was there, he helped the bailiff, as you would call him, with the estate management; he had a flair for it. He married the bailiff's daughter and their first son was brought up to take over from his father one day. I was not the first son, however,' said de Lacey, wryly. 'I was the fourth! I had to find my own path. I was given an education. I made myself into a secretary, got into the employ of Jean de Simier. But juggling and tricks were a family tradition, you see, though I am not so very skilled in them. My brothers are all more gifted than I. So is this fellow. He's a real magician.'

The card tricks were followed by some amusing japes, during which the magician took a jewelled brooch from under a lady's hood – the lady squealed and then squealed even louder when she discovered that the brooch was one that had been on her shoulder a moment before but was there no longer – and then the assistant handed his master a flambeau, which the conjuror lit from a bank of candles. He then gave a demonstration of fire-eating. At this point, the increasing rumbustiousness of the masque caused an accident.

The magician made a great drama of the business, prancing round the hall, scaring the audience by now and then thrusting the torch at them, declaring that he must prove that the fire was real. On his third circuit, he came close to where Antoine and

I were sitting, and he thrust too hard. The tip of the flame caught the puffed shoulder of Antoine's blue doublet and for one horrible moment, a flame leapt up beside his ear. He sprang up with a yell, and Brockley leapt forward, snatching up a fold of the velvet that draped the dais beside him, and clamping it over Antoine's shoulder.

The fire-eater reeled backwards, looking appalled and babbling apologies. The moment passed. Antoine sank down again, clutching at his ear and the side of his face, where he had been momentarily scorched, and spluttering terrified exclamations in a foreign language.

An usher pushed through the shouting, gesticulating crowd, took him by the arm and led him away, declaring over his shoulder that the scorch would be treated and please would the ladies and gentlemen sit down again: all would be well. Meanwhile, the fire-eater had prostrated himself before the royal dais, begging for forgiveness, pleading that it was an accident, just an accident. He hoped with all his heart that the gentleman was not much hurt. His poor heart, indeed, was broken and . . .'

A page appeared and murmured into Elizabeth's ear. The queen announced, in clear, ringing tones, that happily, the gentleman's injury was not grave. 'Those around him were quick to come to his aid.' She held out a hand to the fire-eater. 'You are forgiven.' Her voice was sharp; these days, Elizabeth was so often sharp. But she said the right things. 'Come, rise, and kiss my hand.'

The unfortunate magician got shakily up from his knees, stepped up on to the dais and kissed the slender white hand. Then he ran from the hall. The queen signalled to the Master of Revels to proceed once more and the drama went on, more soberly, until the end, when Virtue thanked the Honest Farmhand for the help he had given her and accepted his offer of marriage, whereupon he revealed himself as not a farmhand at all, but a prince in disguise, who had long desired to marry, but wished for a bride who did not covet wealth and power.

Amid the cheering and applause that followed all this, I sat silent. For the foreign language in which Antoine de Lacey had expressed his terror should by rights have been French, but it was not. It had been a frantic babble but one word had emerged from it very clearly, for he had cried it out twice. *Quemar!* I knew that word. I knew what it meant and I knew what language it belonged to. I had been in Spain and while I was there, I had heard *that* word a number of times. It meant *to burn.*

Antoine, under the stimulus of great fear, had let out one very careless word. In Spanish.

TWENTY-TWO
Glass and Keg

That Spanish word gnawed at me. It went on gnawing throughout the rest of the masque; throughout the dancing that followed; as I retired for the night. It still gnawed after I had blown out my bedside candle and tried to compose myself for sleep.

It was not reasonable that Antoine de Lacey, in a moment of panic, should exclaim in Spanish. It just wasn't. He was a Frenchman. If he reverted to Spanish under frightening circumstances . . . what was I thinking! *Reverted?* That word had sprung into my head unbidden, but now, so to speak, I took it out and inspected it. It implied that Spanish had been a former language of his, a childhood language – a first language. Fear and shock had called it out of him. So was Antoine, then, really a Spaniard? If so, what was he doing in the household of the Duke of Alençon, and if that was somehow in order, acceptable to the duke, then why did Antoine conceal it? He *had* concealed it – at least, he had let it be thought that he was French. In which case . . .

I turned over restlessly, pushing my coverlet back. I never closed my bedcurtains anyway and hadn't closed my window shutters either, but even with all these left open, the night was stuffy. We were into November, yet the weather was still mild and even muggy. I was not surprised, a few moments later, to hear a rumble of thunder and to see a flicker of lightning beyond the window.

Then, stirred by the thunder, came the memory of the storm during the dinner at the Castle Inn.

According to Brockley, the very special keg of wine that was a gift and an apology to the Earl of Leicester had been tampered with. That had made no sense, since the only fatality was the unfortunate Lady Margaret. But now, the

thunder was bringing back the events at the Castle Inn, as
fresh as new.

The party seated round the circular table. Leicester in the
seat of honour with Lady Margaret on his right and his wife
Lettice opposite him. A vivid flash of lightning, Lady Margaret
springing up with a cry of fright, jolting the table. Things
sliding about. I had stopped a candlestick and a dish of meat
from hurtling off the table on to Hatton's knees and I had
grabbed some slithering wineglasses, thrusting them back
where they belonged.

Or had I? They had been the glasses used by Lettice, by
Lady Margaret and by Leicester himself. Stopping them had
been awkward, as I had only one hand. The other had just
dealt with the candlestick and was still keeping the dish of
meat under control. In pushing the glasses back and allocating
them to their owners . . . I saw it now, as clearly as though it
were happening before my eyes. Leicester's glass had been,
as it were, first in the race. As I thrust it back, it had bumped
into Lady Margaret's and then slid past it *on the other side.*
Suddenly, I was certain. It had come from Leicester's place
and when the glasses first began to slide, it was the one furthest
to my right. But in replacing them, I had accidentally let it
become the centre one, with Lady Margaret's glass to my
right. And that was the glass I had unintentionally given to
Leicester. His glass had gone to her and hers to him. Only
Lettice had had her proper glass restored.

I sat up in bed, confused. Was I correct? Why had I never
thought of it before? But yes, I *did* have it right. I knew I did.
Now, work it out, Ursula. Think. Assume that Antoine tampered
in some way with that keg. But whatever he put in it wasn't
lethal. It had made the rest of us just ill. Including Antoine
himself. He perhaps hadn't drunk much of his wine and he
could have exaggerated his symptoms. He knew that whatever
he had done to the wine wouldn't kill him, anyway, or us,
either. What had it been? Something to induce sickness and
some kind of laxative? At home, Gladys had such things in
her repertoire of herbal remedies. There were children about
– Harry, the three-year-old toddler Johnny who was the son
of Simon, one of my grooms, and his wife, Netta. They also

had a two-year-old daughter, Rosie. Where there were children, there was always the chance that however earnestly you warned them never to eat berries from bushes unless an adult were there to say it was safe, one of them would forget, be attracted by a pretty, colourful berry and eat poison. Potions to clear poisons out of the system were kept in most households where there were children. Something of the sort had been in that wine, I thought.

Only, somehow or other, something else, something really lethal had been put into *Leicester's* glass, and only his – except that his had ended up at Lady Margaret's place.

Leicester, then, had been the intended victim.

Well, what would have happened if Leicester had died, poisoned after drinking wine sent to him as a supposed gift from de Simier? It was well known that Leicester was opposed to the marriage. He had influence with the queen and though de Simier had discredited him with Elizabeth by revealing his secret marriage, he would probably creep back into favour. Could that after all point a finger at de Simier? Had he tried to dispose of Leicester, not out of revenge, but in order to remove a man he and perhaps Alençon too, saw as an enemy?

No, impossible. If it were found that Leicester had been the victim of a murderous plot by either the duke or his man, that would assuredly turn Elizabeth against the marriage. If Leicester had died, Elizabeth would have grieved bitterly and she would not forgive anyone who was even suspected of having a hand in his demise. I thought that both the duke and de Simier would have the intelligence to realize that. Murdering Leicester wouldn't help the marriage along, but the opposite.

Who else, then, might want the marriage stopped? The answer to that was no mystery. Janus had reported that there were people who were scheming against it, and it wasn't hard to name some of the factions. Spain certainly wouldn't like it. An alliance between her hereditary enemy France and her Protestant rival, England? Perish the thought!

And Antoine, in a moment of panic, had cried out in Spanish.

I lay back, heart pounding.

Antoine could have tampered with the keg easily enough.

It had been stored in his room. But how had he poisoned Leicester's glass?

Yes, how? After the jug had been brought to the table, Antoine had filled our glasses himself, yes. But he had done it in front of us, in full view. If he had put anything into Leicester's glass other than wine from that jug, I – and the others – would have seen him do it.

That Antoine was responsible for poisoning the wine seemed all too likely, but how he had done it remained unanswered.

'Stop!' barked Elizabeth. The two ladies who were playing the spinet and lute for the pavane we were practising hastily snatched their hands off their instruments and the one at the spinet said: 'I am sorry, ma'am, it was my fault . . .'

'Yes, Lady Frances, it was,' said Elizabeth belligerently. 'You went straight on into the next phrase, while Mary, on her lute, did as I told *both of you* and repeated the three bars before, and a fine jangle of discords you produced. We are practising a *variant* of the dance, to allow couples to revolve on the spot a second time before proceeding further round the floor. The same variant is repeated ten bars later. Why do you not listen to my instructions?'

'I am sorry, ma'am! But I am so accustomed . . . my fingers know the melody by heart . . .

'You are supposed to keep control of both your fingers and your heart! Now, again, from the beginning!'

It was Elizabeth's habit, unless business matters such as Council meetings or audiences for ambassadors, delegations or sometimes private people should intervene, to spend part of the morning in dancing practice. Being skilled in music as well as in dancing, Elizabeth was quite capable of inventing her own variations to any given dance, and sometimes confused her own ladies sadly in the process. This was one such time, and Elizabeth, clearly, was once more in a bad temper. Some people put this down to the fact that she was missing Alençon; some thought she might be missing Leicester more. Privately, I had a different theory.

It was the day after the masque. Brockley had gone to see Mealy off to Hawkswood and then intended to take Firefly out. I had been bidden to attend the dancing practice. I was getting a clear view of Elizabeth's frame of mind and after all, I knew her well. If my guess was right, I pitied her.

The music started again, with one or two wrong notes. Elizabeth swore and Lady Frances said unhappily that the sun was in her eyes and she couldn't see her music properly. 'You complain because after last night's storm, we now have sunshine?' said Elizabeth dangerously.

I sympathized with Lady Frances, for the sunlight streaming through the tall, slender windows into the small hall where we were dancing was very bright, as though the rain a few hours ago had washed the face of the sun. Elizabeth caught my eye and said: 'Ursula, take over the spinet. You know the melody, I think. See if you can put in the changes.'

Lady Frances rose from her stool, looking thankful, and I took her place. The practice went on.

I succeeded in following the new instructions without disaster, perhaps because I wasn't nervous. Unlike Lady Frances, I wouldn't really mind if Elizabeth were to lose her temper with me and order me out of the court. I had a home and a life of my own; I was not one of her paid attendants.

Indeed, I longed to return to Hawkswood and Elizabeth would probably let me go, now that Leicester was no longer suspected of trying to murder de Simier. I was only staying because . . .

Because I wanted to unearth the end of the mysterious attempt to poison Leicester, and I couldn't, not until I could see *how*.

Back in my apartment, Dale was repairing the embroidered hem of the gown I had worn at the masque. In the disturbance over de Lacey's accident, I had trodden on it. I tried to settle to a little sewing as well but I was restless. We took a small midday meal in the common dining chamber, and then, leaving Dale to go on repairing embroidery, I went out to take Jewel for a ride in the nearby deer park.

The storm had cleared the air and the wind was fresh. I cantered through the park, glad to be away from the palace, and indifferent to the fact that court ladies weren't supposed to ride alone. I was tired of court protocol and proprieties, weary of a world infested by plots and people who said one thing while they were thinking of something quite different. I wanted to go home so very, very much.

In the park, though the mating season for the fallow deer was over, the spotted stags were still in full antler and some were still restless. I hadn't heard of anyone being attacked by a fallow stag – though red stags sometimes chased people during the rut – but Dale would have been nervous if she had been with me. I felt safe enough on horseback. On Jewel, I was merely an excrescence on the back of an animal belonging to another species. It struck me suddenly that much of the trouble surrounding the queen and the future of England sprang from human equivalents of competing stags. The desire for power was so universal, and so dangerous. I wished even more strongly that I could get away to Hawkswood.

I found the ride soothing, however, and returned from it eased, though still homesick. I had come to a decision. There had been others beside myself at that dinner. I was as sure as I could be that Antoine had been responsible for poisoning Leicester's glass. I couldn't imagine how, but perhaps one of the others had noticed something. I must ask them. I went in search of Sir Christopher Hatton.

TWENTY-THREE
Wooden Spoon

Sir Christopher was attending on the queen, and it was near the end of the afternoon before he left her and I managed to accost him in one of the wide galleries between her quarters and his. It was not a successful meeting. He was courteous, because he was always so; Hatton was a gentleman. But even when I had given him all my reasons for suspecting Antoine de Lacey, he refused to be helpful.

'Look, Ursula, the food-poisoning story has been accepted and may well be the truth. And . . .'

'The keg was tampered with,' I insisted. 'And de Lacey, in that moment of panic, called out in Spanish. And the glass of wine that Lady Margaret drank was originally Leicester's.'

'You can't be sure of that. You could be wrong about which glass was pushed back to which place. The keg may have been tampered with, or may not. There could be other reasons for making a hole in the lid and then sealing it again . . .'

'Such as?'

'To check on the contents; to make sure the vintners hadn't cheated, something like that. As for de Lacey's exclamation; are you sure you heard it correctly?'

'Yes, I am!' I looked at him in exasperation. 'You mean, there's to be no scandal! But what if a further attempt is made on Leicester's life? What if it succeeds?'

'Leicester is no fool. What you are suggesting has occurred to him already – even though he doesn't know how it was done, and knows nothing of these pieces of evidence you describe. He is taking precautions.'

'How much does the queen know?'

'Everything that Leicester and I have thought of. But she of all people wants to avoid scandal! If the people of England came to suspect that Alençon or his henchman de Simier were trying to dispose of the Earl of Leicester because he objects to Alençon's suit, there would be a terrible outcry against them and therefore against the marriage. Dear Mistress Stannard, leave it alone.'

It was useless to argue with him. 'Very well,' I said, and turned resentfully away. It was too late to do any more that day, but tomorrow, I told myself, I would go to Wanstead.

I left early, mainly so as to be out of Richmond Palace and therefore out of reach before, as was quite likely, the queen could send for me to play the spinet for her dancing practice again. I took Brockley as my escort but not Dale, who was tired and complained that she couldn't abide all this disturbance and didn't feel up to travelling to Wanstead again. For once, she was willing for me to go alone with Brockley.

I really would have to take more care of Dale, I thought. Life with me had never been easy for her and she wasn't getting any younger.

The Earl of Leicester was at home and as hospitable as ever, summoning someone to take my cloak, ushering me into a parlour, asking for news of the court and the queen, sending for refreshments, calling to Lettice to join us. But when I broached the reason for my visit and asked if he had seen de Lacey do anything suspicious, his face darkened.

'Mistress Stannard, you were present when Hatton and I put it to all of you that the best thing we could do was to accept that we had been the accidental victims of food poisoning. Because it is very important that—'

'There should be no scandal.' I interrupted him in a peremptory fashion, which sent his eyebrows up, but I was so very weary of that phrase. The whole subject of that dreadful dinner was becoming like an old song, with a repeated refrain that jarred more whenever it was repeated.

'Quite,' said Leicester. 'Scandal must be avoided at all costs. You must not think, Mistress Stannard, that it hasn't occurred to me that I could have been the target, and that the scheme somehow went amiss . . . yes?'

I had opened my mouth again and with an air of gracious consideration towards someone who was being a nuisance, he paused to let me speak. 'I am quite sure,' I said, 'that when

Lady Margaret jolted the table and sent wineglasses sliding and I pushed them, I accidentally exchanged two of them. You got Lady Margaret's glass and she received yours.'

'You may be right. I am not saying that you aren't. But I *am* saying that it would be wiser to keep silence, to stop public feeling from developing. In France there are those who don't want the marriage to take place, but there is also a strong faction here who object to the idea of the queen wedding a Catholic prince.'

I thought of the things we had heard on the journey back from Cornwall, and was silent.

'Believe me,' said Leicester, with feeling, 'I realize that I could be in danger. I am safeguarding myself. I have men here; there is someone on watch all the time, including all through the night. I am not attending functions or accepting invitations; nor am I now angling for a summons back to court. When I ride out, I take an escort and I never go in the same direction twice running, or return by the same route as I used when setting out. My kitchen staff have all been with me for years and Lettice herself oversees their work, anyway. Do you not, Lettice, my love?'

'Yes.' His countess had been sitting quietly, bestirring herself only to pour wine for us and offer us cinnamon cakes. 'I am constantly in and out of the kitchen,' she said now. 'And the cooks are all obliged to taste the food they prepare, before serving it.'

'As for your question about *how* de Lacey could have contaminated the wine that day,' said Leicester, 'I certainly didn't see him do anything even remotely suspicious.'

It was no use. I thanked him for his time and his hospitality, declined an invitation to dine and prepared to leave. 'Your cloak is hanging up in the entrance vestibule,' Lettice said, very much the gracious hostess. 'We will fetch it on the way out. I will see Mistress Stannard to her horse,' she added smilingly to Leicester. 'You haven't finished your wine. At least *our* wine supplies are safe! Come, Mistress Stannard.'

Once we were in the vestibule, she lifted my cloak from the hook where it was hanging, and said: 'I think I know how de Lacey could have poisoned one of the wineglasses and now that we know how my lord's glass was exchanged for Lady Margaret's, it all hangs together. My husband wouldn't want me to tell you what I think. *He* knows, of course, from me. Only I think you *should* know. I am not so disturbed by the thought of scandal as my lord is. In my view, anything that could stop the Alençon marriage is a good thing. It's not safe for the queen or for the country. My husband can talk solemnly about the queen being the only one who can decide, but the rest of us would have to live with the results.'

She scanned my face anxiously, as if seeking permission to go on. Her eyes, which were indeed the matt blue of sloe berries and so often looked both sleepy and come-hither, were now sharp with intelligence instead.

'Tell me quickly,' I said. 'Before we're interrupted. Your husband might wonder what we're lingering to gossip about!'

'At that awful dinner,' said Lettice, dropping her voice, 'I was sitting opposite Robin. You were beside him. When the wine flagon was brought to the table and de Lacey refilled everyone's glasses, he didn't walk round the table to do it, or even reach round him. He leant forward from his place, which was roughly opposite you and Sir Christopher and sideways on to me, and he filled the glasses one at a time, drawing them towards him, each in turn. He was quite quick about it, but I thought at the time that he'd positioned himself rather oddly, though I didn't then attach much importance to it. Do you remember?'

'No, I can't say that I do. How do you mean?'

'I mean that I don't think any of us could see exactly what he was doing. He had those big sleeves, puffed from shoulder to elbow, if you recall. His right sleeve completely blocked my view. He was also slightly turned, so that my husband and Lady Margaret must have been looking at his left shoulder. And neither you nor Sir Christopher could have seen exactly what he was doing either because somehow, he curved his left arm round and the sleeve of that one hid the glasses from you as well. It *did* look awkward. But since then, I've wondered if it was deliberate, so that no one could see his hands. Well, could you?'

'I . . . I can't remember.' I thought about it, casting my mind back. 'No, perhaps not.'

'And do you recall,' said Lettice, 'that de Lacey spilt some of the wine when he was pouring it, and swore?'

'Yes, I remember that! I thought he was being a little unjust when he complained that he couldn't see why the servants should be upset by the storm.'

Lettice smiled. 'Well, I think that when he spilt that wine – it was on to the wrist of his left sleeve – it may have been on purpose. He put the jug down, and pulled out a handkerchief to mop his wrist with. I saw that much though not clearly, because he was so very quick about it. Then he put the hand-kerchief away and pulled another glass towards him to attend to it, and I think that one was my husband's. He filled it but I couldn't see him do it because then, his right sleeve was completely in the way. I am wondering if he could have palmed something that he had picked from his sleeve – from inside his cuff – when he mopped it. Something he could have dropped into my lord's glass.'

'But what?' I said. I tried to think it out. 'It must have been powder or liquid and it would need a container. Paper or glass.'

'It need only have been small,' Lettice said. 'A little paper packet or a tiny phial with a stopper, I should think, and powder inside. That would be the easiest. He would have opened it and used it while his hands were hidden. It would all need some sleight of hand. But, Mistress Stannard, M'sieu de Lacey is clever with conjuring tricks.'

'God's teeth! Yes, he is! He calls it dabbling but I've seen him give a display and I would say that he was quite skilled though he claims that he isn't. Have you told your husband all this?'

'Yes, but until now, we couldn't see how Lady Margaret could have got the wrong glass. I thought perhaps de Lacey had somehow confused the glasses, but my lord kept on saying nonsense, and I am not to start foolish rumours.'

'Or cause scandal,' I said bitterly.

'Yes. But what you say explains it. Only de Lacey could have contaminated the keg and whoever doctored the keg must also have doctored that glass. It *was* doctored. Poor Lady Margaret died! The rest of us recovered quite quickly. I don't believe for a moment that it was all an accident. And the real target must have been my husband. No one else is likely.'

'No,' I said. 'I agree!'

'I see,' said Cecil. 'You have certainly found out a great deal, Ursula. We have wondered, as you have, if Leicester was the target of a plot but thundery weather and the accidental contamination of food did seem a reasonable explanation. I suppose we should congratulate you.' But he looked grave. Even stern, I thought.

'Accident was a very reasonable explanation. But now,' said Walsingham, none too pleasantly, 'along comes Mistress Stannard with what sounds like genuine evidence.' He didn't sound delighted.

I had requested an interview with Walsingham and been granted it, but when the page brought me to his office, I found Cecil there as well. I was pleased at first, since I felt that both of them ought to know of the information that I was bringing. Except that now it was clear that neither I nor the information were welcome.

'I am sorry,' I said, 'if you would have preferred this whole miserable affair just to sink into oblivion, but I was a victim too. Of course it is for you to say what shall be done with any discoveries I have made. But I felt it right to make them if I could and to inform you of the result.'

'You say,' said Walsingham, 'that when the glasses started sliding about, you think you pushed them back to the wrong places and that the glass Lady Margaret drank from thereafter was really Leicester's?'

'Yes.'

'And if that idea were to get about,' said Cecil, 'so that the public came to think the Duke of Alençon and de Simier attempted the life of an English earl, it would probably mean a mob in the street on the wedding day, wanting to assassinate the bridegroom!'

'We don't like this marriage any more than Leicester does,' Walsingham said. 'But we cannot have it said that the queen is involved with – even in love with – a man who sends his minions to murder her servants. You should trust us, Ursula.

At the moment, the situation in the Netherlands, which demands Alençon's attention, is working for us. It will delay the ceremony and a sufficient delay could protect her majesty's safety, by reducing or even cutting out the hope of an heir. Every birthday that she has brings that moment nearer.'

He smiled. Walsingham's smile could be, and on this occasion was, sinister enough to frighten a demon, or any legendary hero. Julius Caesar, Alexander the Great, might both have quailed before it.

Cecil said: 'All the same, I agree that we can't simply ignore your news, Ursula. As you know, there are factions in France, and assuredly in Spain as well, who wish to prevent the marriage and may be scheming to do so. If de Lacey does have Spanish origins, then he may be part of such a scheme and not a dutiful servant of Alençon and de Simier after all.'

He ruminated. 'Janus is investigating those rumours and will report to us. Meanwhile, in the light of what you have told us, we will enquire into de Lacey's background, if we can. I think we must.' He sounded exasperated. 'We will go that far.'

'My department already has,' said Walsingham. Both Cecil and I looked at him in surprise.

'I do have the backgrounds of foreign visitors investigated,' said Walsingham. 'Ambassadors, envoys, their secretaries, grooms and valets. My department is thorough, believe me. De Lacey's father was French but his mother was Spanish and as a child, he made occasional visits to Spain, staying with his maternal grandmother and playing with Spanish cousins.'

'But . . .' I said.

Cecil said: 'I could wish your department were less discreet, Walsingham. That piece of information should have been shared with me.'

'It proved nothing,' said Walsingham. 'The man had been accepted by the Duke of Alençon and Jean de Simier, had apparently behaved as a loyal and competent employee, was in fact pursuing a well-paid and successful career in his father's country. Now, after all, it seems that all may not be as it seems. His outburst at the masque suggests that there could have been more Spanish influence in his childhood than anyone has realized.

Even Alençon may not realize it. But still . . .' he frowned, obviously thinking '. . . we *must* keep the matter from spreading round the country in the form of garbled theories.'

'So, what do you recommend?' enquired Cecil. 'Ursula's evidence is disquieting. We must avoid scandal but nor can things be left as they are. If the man is guilty, he may try again.'

'The Earl of Leicester is taking precautions,' I said.

'There is still one thing that I want to get clear.' Walsingham stopped suddenly, grunted, and sank down onto a stool. I remembered that he suffered from a bowel complaint that caused him to have gripes and sometimes attacks of diarrhoea. After my own recent experience, I could sympathize. For a moment, I pitied him. He worked loyally and competently for an exacting mistress, who trusted him but didn't like him, and he had to toil on, and deal with crises, while suffering poor health. His couldn't be an easy furrow to plough.

'I am all right,' he said, after a moment. 'Just a twinge. I want to be sure that I have the details right. Your idea, I think, Ursula, is that the venom in the wine was intended not to kill but to cause illness in everyone at that dinner, and therefore act as a cloak, under which more serious poison could be introduced into just one glass, and take the life of just one person. It would presumably be hoped that he was just unlucky – that there was bad food or wine at the table and that he had ingested more of it than the rest of you, or was more sensitive to it.'

'Yes,' I said. 'It would have needed craftiness but de Lacey is a clever conjuror. He might well have managed to doctor Leicester's wine undetected.'

'I think,' said Walsingham, 'that in view of your information, Ursula, and in the interests of protecting my lord of Leicester *and* the good name of her majesty, we must get de Lacey out of England. I recommend that he be unobtrusively removed under escort, taken to the coast and put aboard a ship bound for France – accompanied by a very watchful escort. Meanwhile, we must send a messenger ahead, to tell the Duke of Alençon when to expect de Lacey and why he is being sent home. What the French do about him when he lands will be very instructive. Meanwhile, as far as the public in England know, the guests at the Castle Inn all still had a most unfortunate and quite accidental experience of food poisoning.'

I let out my breath in a long sigh of relief. It was out of my hands now. I had done my duty. The rest was up to Cecil and Walsingham. I could go to the queen and ask permission to go home. Only, there was one thing still on my mind.

'I hope to return to Hawkswood soon,' I said. 'With her majesty's consent, of course. But whether I am here or there, there is still this unhappy business of the murders of Thomas Harrison and Eric Lake. I am almost sure that Robert and George Harrison were responsible and . . .'

'Ursula . . .' said Cecil.

I stopped. Cecil smiled and his smile was not sinister but kindly and also patient. 'Christmas is not so very far away,' he said gently. 'We are into autumn now. Not too soon, perhaps to think of Christmas gifts. Mine to you, dear Ursula, will I think take the form of a very large wooden spoon.'

'A . . . a what?'

'You really do enjoy stirring events up,' said Cecil. 'Like a cook with a mixing bowl full of eggs and sugar, or a witch with a cauldron full of newts' eyes and chopped-up snakes and deadly nightshade. But we must ask you – no, command you – not to stir this particular cauldron.'

'But *why not?*'

'Leave it!' said Walsingham. 'We mean it, Mistress Stannard. You don't know as much as you think you know. You are trying to meddle in things you don't understand. *Leave it alone!*'

TWENTY-FOUR
The Queen's Fiat

stopped feeling sorry for Walsingham. I went away seething and still utterly unable to understand why a simple matter of law and order should be treated in such an extraordinary way. Murder had been done. Twice. Yet both Walsingham and Cecil seemed to think that it didn't matter; that the miscreants should not be pursued even though we knew who they were. Just what, I wondered, would the queen think about that?

Did she know of this strange decision, which in a way touched the safety of every soul in her realm? I had been given to understand that Cecil and Walsingham kept her well informed, but had they told her about this? Suddenly I doubted it. Dear God! If one – two – murders of harmless citizens, one of them a mere boy at that – were to be ignored, what kind of precedent did that set? Whose life, thereafter, would be safe? Would Elizabeth ever consent to such a state of affairs?

Back in my rooms, I sat by the window, which overlooked an orchard, and puzzled and frowned, until Dale begged me to tell her what was wrong. Finally, I explained. She at once fetched Brockley, my dear, reliable Brockley, who was so much more (at one time very nearly far too much more) than just a manservant, and Brockley was decisive.

'Madam, you should go to the queen. You are her sister – and she *is* the queen. The care of this land is her charge. She would want to be told.'

'Poor Elizabeth,' I said. 'I wouldn't want to live her life! Such a weight of responsibility – and all the time in fear of plots and surrounded by men with ambitions . . .'

'Go to her, madam. That's my advice.'

I wanted to see Elizabeth, anyway, to ask permission to go home. I sought a private audience and it was granted.

Elizabeth's private chamber had a view of the river and the ripples cast reflections on the ceiling. In sunny weather, they were flickers of golden light but today was overcast and both the water and its reflections were steely and dour. So was Elizabeth's face, as she sat there, formally dressed, on her throne-like chair. She greeted me with a smile, however, an austere one but still a smile.

'We welcome your company, Ursula. We have just spent an hour with my ladies and a merchant who had brought samples of material suitable for new gowns, for them and for me. My ladies argued interminably, chirping like sparrows, over whether to choose peach or cinnamon or apple-green. Anyone would have thought, listening to them, that they were discussing things to eat! It was absurd. We will ask the Master of the Revels to work it somehow into the next masque; it should produce much laughter. So!' Her tone sharpened. 'You wished to speak with us, Ursula. We take it that you want to go home. We have been expecting this.'

Then she sighed and dropping the royal *we*, said: 'I have never been able to blend you into my world, have I, my sister? You have never truly liked the life of the court. Well, I shall not refuse you. The Duke of Alençon cannot return to England yet; he has a campaign ahead of him, in the Netherlands. But he will come back eventually and then . . . then I must marry him. My country needs it. When he comes back, then I may call on you again, to stiffen my resolve. Until then, you are free to go back to Hawkswood.'

'I do want to go home,' I said. 'That is part of the reason why I am here. But there is something else. It's a complicated story, but there is something I think you should know. May I tell you?'

'You may.'

I set out for her, as simply and plainly as I could, the whole tale of Thomas Harrison's disappearance and the discovery of his body, the death of Eric Lake and its probable reason, and the suspicions I harboured concerning George and Robert Harrison. She listened without interrupting, her pale, triangular face more like a shield than ever, her golden-brown eyes intent.

'I did not know,' she said at the end. 'And I am shocked

that I did not know. What are Walsingham and Cecil about, I wonder? They are honest men; I have never had cause, for a moment, to doubt either their loyalty or their wisdom. I don't understand this, Ursula. But I am appalled. I do not take lightly the idea that my subjects can be murdered and justice denied to their memories or to their kin. I shall pursue this matter, have no fear. And I will let you know the outcome.'

'I would be grateful, ma'am.'

'I will see to it. I said, you are free to go to your home. Go today if you will, as long as you come back when I want you, when the duke returns to England.'

I ventured to say: 'The thought of marriage still worries you, then, ma'am?'

'Can you ask that?' She looked weary. 'I have worried and worried and shouted at my ladies and even slapped them because I am so *very* worried.'

I had guessed right. If Elizabeth's irritable temper of late had been partly due to the absence of her lover, it had also been due to fear of him.

'You know my feelings,' she said. 'Childbirth itself is a sufficiently alarming prospect, but before that comes a surrender that for all your reassurances, and the reassurances of others, I sometimes think I cannot endure. I miss the duke, I want to be with him, to talk to him, dance with him, even . . . even flirt with him. But to lie there and let a man *invade* . . .'

'Ma'am, it isn't like that, or it shouldn't be . . .'

'Ah! So you admit that it can be and sometimes is!'

'If the duke knows his business,' I said carefully, 'and from what I have seen of him, I would say that he is a man of sensitivity and also – knowledge . . .'

'Experience, you mean. You may as well say it.'

'Experience, then. In that case, he will know how to stir, to inspire you, so that you *want* him, in . . . in that special way, and then there will be no question of invasion; you will be welcoming a guest into your being, a guest you want to welcome, long to welcome, with all your heart.'

'And body?'

'Yes.'

'I hope you're right. Some of my ladies have said much the same thing. I still . . . oh, let it be. I shall recall you when I need you. And you will come!'

'Yes, ma'am. I will come,' I said.

'As for the other matter,' said Elizabeth, her eyes hardening, 'I will indeed look into it. Murder shall not go unregarded in *my* realm!'

Many times, after long journeys and sometimes after terrifying experiences, I had been thankful beyond words to see Hawkswood again. This time my journey hadn't been long and I hadn't been in danger – at least not much though being half poisoned might count as danger, I supposed. But when I glimpsed the chimneys of home in the distance this time, I was as grateful as though I had been to Cathay and back and fought dragons along the way.

As we neared the gate-arch, Dale, from her perch behind Brockley (fortunately, Firefly had accepted a pillion rider without more than a disapproving snort or two), put it all into words.

'I'm that glad to be back, ma'am. I can't abide the court these days and that's the truth. It was always stiff and formal in a lot of ways but now it's become a thousand times worse. The queen's so distant, not like a human figure at all! Whenever you see her, she's just like a . . . a gown, all brocade and silk and ropes of pearls . . . with . . . with a sort of walking statue inside it and she's surrounded by her ladies and hordes of guards, and there's a page running ahead to announce that she's coming through this doorway or that and everyone's to get out of the way . . . it's not a natural way for a woman to be!'

'She's not like that all the time,' I said. 'She dances, and talks to guests; she's not always surrounded, as you put it.'

'You see her in ways most of us don't,' said Dale. 'But, ma'am, do *you* like being at court?'

'No,' I said truthfully. 'In fact, I agree with you. The court has grown very stiff.' And with that, we rode into our own courtyard, and my household came out to greet us with smiles and happy exclamations and Harry was there, and home enclosed us all in its cloak of comfort.

Ten days later, Christopher Spelton arrived. I was in the east room, studying the household accounts for the time of my absence, and making out a list of stores to be purchased. I had at one time used Hugh's old study for these tasks, but the east room, with its three cushioned settles and its floor strewn with rugs, was more comfortable and had better light as well as being quiet, and my habits had changed. I used the study now mostly for seeing visitors who came on business. I didn't hear Christopher arrive, and didn't know he was in the house until Sybil brought him to me, with Adam Wilder on her heels, carrying the usual welcome to a guest in the form of a tray of refreshments.

They left us to talk in private, and having motioned Christopher to a seat, I took one opposite him rather than seating myself next to him. With Christopher, I was careful, always, to offer friendly hospitality but nothing more intimate. 'Have you been calling on Mistress Kate again?' I asked.

'I have. How did you guess?' said Spelton dryly. 'I visit West Leys when I can and offer any help or advice the lady might require, since her family are far away in Dover, and you, her former guardian, have also been away, at court. I am biding my time. Kate is young. She can't mourn for ever, and the child, when it is born, will turn her mind towards the future. Then – I think – I hope – she will consider that future, consider the advantages of having a man to help her run her farm and be a father to her little one. Meanwhile, I make sure she doesn't forget my existence.'

His brown eyes were bright with his hopes and they were probably justified. He would win his Kate before too long and I could only wish him well. 'How is she?' I asked.

'She is in good health. She is a sensible young woman and knows that she must eat and sleep properly for the sake of her baby, and that surrendering too much to her grief would be bad for both of them.'

'I will find time to visit her soon. Have you called on me to bring me news of her, or have you some other purpose?'

'Yes, I have. I have news for you, apart from Kate's welfare. I was charged with a message for you, from the queen; it gave me a good opportunity to see Kate. The message is that there is a warrant out for the arrest of George and Robert Harrison, for the murders of Thomas Harrison and Eric Lake. Robert is out of the country at the moment but is expected back shortly, to fulfil his promise to marry his cousin Jane. That marriage will not take place now, of course, but he won't find that out until he gets back to England. He will probably be picked up as soon as he lands.'

'So, the queen has acted,' I said.

'The queen?'

I explained the curious embargo that Walsingham and Cecil had placed on my search for the killers of Thomas and Eric, and my subsequent interview with Elizabeth. He nodded.

'Yes. I see. Her fiat trumps the decisions of Cecil and Walsingham. I didn't realize that you had inspired it. Well done, if I may say so. I can't understand why Lord Burghley and Sir Francis were against taking action.'

'Nor can I. Thank you for the news, Christopher.'

'Cousin marriages are bad things, anyway,' he said, sipping wine. 'They breed sickly children, as often as not, and in my opinion, the old church was right to forbid them. Jane is well out of it.'

'She is indeed!' I said with fervour. 'And not just because of that! To think she might have married one of her brother's murderers! Tell me, is there any news of Antoine de Lacey? Moves against him were also being planned; Cecil and Walsingham didn't try to block *those*. Did you know that he is suspected of attempting to ruin the queen's marriage plans? Have you heard about the dinner he arranged for Leicester?'

I explained about the accidental exchange of Lady Margaret's glass for Leicester's. He was interested. 'So that is how it happened that young Lady Mollinder died! Your mistake saved the earl's life, by the sound of it, though it was the worse for her, poor wench. Did you know that de Lacey has disappeared?'

'He's probably been quietly removed from the country, put on a ship for France and sent off under guard,' I said. 'I think that was the plan.'

'Yes, I know about *that*, but the plan was never put into action. He vanished too soon. I am not on close terms with either Lord Burghley or Sir Francis Walsingham, but I have cultivated some of their employees. Both Cecil and Walsingham are furious. De Lacey slipped out of Richmond Palace one afternoon and didn't return and no one knows where he is. They don't want to issue a warrant for him – he's a foreign national and part of Alençon's entourage; it could be politically damaging. But he is being quietly sought.'

'So I should hope,' I said. 'I think he might be a dangerous man. Will you stay to dine?'

TWENTY-FIVE
The Rage of Spain

After dinner, when Christopher Spelton had left, I went to my chamber and looked into my mirror. I was forty-five years old now, and although the mirror showed me that my hair was still dark, that I had few lines and my eyes were still an undimmed greenish hazel with clear whites, nevertheless, within myself, I was aware of my age. I was no young girl, but a mother of two and a grandmother by one of them and I had seen the world.

Christopher was about the same age as I was, but it was natural enough for him to prefer Kate, who was still young, with no lines at all in her face, as yet, even though she had seen trouble during her short life. That very trouble probably made him feel protective, and that she had borne it all with considerable courage, would only have enhanced his wish to look after her. I knew Christopher Spelton well enough to know that.

On her side, once Kate had recovered from her first grief, and had Eric's child safely in her arms, she would need a man and before long she would realize it. While I had no need of a husband. I had had three and that was quite enough for anyone. I had my home – two homes, Hawkswood and Withysham. I had my household. I had my dear Dale and my trusted Brockley, and if he and I had never been lovers, there was all the same a close if unspoken bond between us that I did not wish to break. Nor, I knew, did he, although he had at times pushed his feelings aside and encouraged me towards a new marriage, out of a sense of duty and a wish for my well-being. Brockley was a most honest man.

No, I did not need Christopher, but before long, Kate probably would, and I must be glad for them both.

I lingered in my room for a while, thinking about the queen.

She was forty-six, older than me by several months. She was right to fear the dangers of childbirth. She had asked me to soothe her fears of marriage, but she hadn't asked for reassurance about childbirth and I couldn't have given her that anyway. I feared it myself. I tried to imagine what would happen in England if Elizabeth attempted to give it an heir and failed to come through. I tried to imagine how she herself would feel, if once a child were conceived and the ultimate business of giving birth, with all its dangers, became inevitable.

Perhaps it was my duty – was still my duty – while there was still time, to discourage her. Walsingham and Leicester would approve and so would Cecil, even if they didn't do so openly. We couldn't rely on the Netherlands situation to solve the problem; it might come to an end quite quickly. Meanwhile, the Earl of Sussex was anxious for the queen to marry and have an heir, but it seemed to me that he was shutting his eyes to the risks. Perhaps I should go back to court forthwith, and set about scuppering his hopes.

I went downstairs again, turning my thoughts elsewhere. I really must make plans about Harry. He was fast approaching the age of eight. I had myself made a good start in his education but when we were in Cornwall I had realized that he needed a proper tutor and I must get on with it. Between my court contacts and the social circle to which Hugh had introduced me, I had a wide acquaintance. I could think of a few names. I would go to the study now and write some letters.

Five days later, I sat by the fire in the east room, perusing three replies. The weather had now turned cold and I was glad of the fire. Its soft crackling was the only sound, for the house was quiet.

Brockley, I knew, was in the stable yard, trying to teach a reluctant Mealy to back between the shafts of a cart. Cooking was under way in the kitchen, the maids were cleaning the great hall, and Harry was upstairs, doing a Latin exercise which I had told him he must finish before he could go out. Sybil and Dale were also upstairs, engaged on some mysterious task which they wouldn't show me; I suspected that they were making me a Christmas present, probably embroidered sleeves or gloves or slippers.

The first of the letters was written in such a small, cramped hand that I had brought a magnifying lens from the study so as to read it more easily. I would need eyeglasses soon, I said to myself, as I examined the credentials of a Master John Hewitt. He had tutored the two daughters of one of the queen's ladies and was now seeking another position, since the elder daughter had just married and the younger one, though she was only fourteen, was betrothed.

I read with care, seeking answers to the questions I had asked about his teaching methods. The mother of his previous pupils had never said whether or not he was kind to them, but I did not want Harry to be roughly treated. Learning, in my opinion, should be a pleasure, not a matter of fear, and a great many tutors did make it frightening.

I was immersed when I heard feet and voices approaching, and the door was opened to reveal Adam Wilder, looking harassed, which he never did as a rule, and with him . . .

'M'sieu de Lacey!' I said faintly.

'The same.' Antoine pushed past Adam and came straight on into the room. He glanced over his shoulder at my affronted steward and said: 'Thank you. That will be all. I have a private matter to discuss with your mistress and must insist that we are left undisturbed. No one is to come to this room until they are sent for; is that clear?'

'Perfectly, sir,' said Adam and then looked at me, eyebrows questioningly lifted.

'As the gentleman says, but please remain within call,' I said.

'Not too close,' said Antoine and his voice had an unmistakably nasty edge. 'I want no eavesdroppers. Return, if you please, to the servants' quarters.'

Adam bristled, but I gave him a nod, and he went. I hoped he would be sensible enough *not* to go to the servants' quarters but to stay within earshot as I had requested, but the situation was uncomfortable for him and I didn't want to prolong it. He left the door open but Antoine kicked it shut. Then he stood with his back to it, staring at me. He looked as unremarkable as ever, but he was carrying both sword and dagger and his eyes were dangerous. I saw that I was in the presence of a very angry man. I was still holding the letter and the magnifying lens. I put them down, quietly. 'This is an unexpected visit, M'sieu de Lacey.'

'I'm sure it is. I was meant to be in France by now, if you and the Council had had your way. Taken there under guard and handed over to the henchmen of the Duke of Alençon, unmasked as a traitor to France and a servant of Spain. Isn't that what you expected?'

'And wanted,' I said. I must not show fear, I thought. Why should I, anyway? I was the mistress of the house, here in my own parlour; if I were to shout loudly enough, Adam would *surely* be near enough to hear. This man was an enemy, to me, to the queen, to England. And I was sister to that queen, and daughter, however illegally, of a famous king.

'You escaped from the court before you were taken,' I said. 'But you will be found. You realize that?'

'Very possibly, though I do have friends. I have one or two at court; one of them warned me of the plans that were being made for me.'

I made a secret vow to let Cecil and Walsingham know that somewhere among their employees was a traitor.

'I also have friends in London,' de Lacey said. 'A family of Spanish sympathizers have been sheltering me and making plans on my behalf. I hope to get away to Spain safely. But I very much wanted to deal with you first. Your interference, your nosing into matters unsuitable for a lady, your tattling to Sir Francis Walsingham and Lord Burghley, have spoiled my future plans, spoiled Spain's hopes. In Spain, we avenge wrongs. I am here to avenge mine.'

It struck me suddenly that if this angry intruder were to seize my throat, and did it quickly enough, I would not be able to call for help and he could then murder me quite easily. I felt the blood draining from my face and he saw it and laughed.

'Oh, I am not going to kill you, dear Mistress Stannard. It is a tempting thought but after consideration, I decided against it.

I would be sorry to wipe you out of the world, for you are still quite beautiful; in fact most attractive, and that would be a waste. Beauty and attraction should be given homage, not destroyed. This room isn't quite warm enough for a son of the south,' he added, with apparent inconsequence. He moved to the hearth and poked the fire. 'That will improve things, I think,' he said.

Then he lunged. In one smooth, fierce incredibly swift movement, he threw a powerful arm round me, clamped the other hand over my mouth and pushed me backwards, down on the settle from which I had just risen. I tried to bite, but failed. He was on top of me, weighing me down. And leaning to the right, reaching out towards the hearth, grabbing the poker. Its tip was red-hot.

'One sound from you,' he said, 'and I use this. Then your beauty *will* be spoiled, for ever, and you will lose an eye, and I shall both regret that and rejoice, even if I find myself in a dungeon, or worse. Though I will probably be able to fight my way out through your servants; with luck, I shall escape. But be quiet, be amiable, and you will escape unhurt. I will allow it. I really *don't* want to do permanent harm to such a charming lady, but I do want to make it plain to her that she cannot, with impunity, arouse the rage of Spain. Meanwhile, I'll make sure that this stays – nice and warm.'

He pushed the poker back into the fire and looked at me. 'You will be quiet?'

I managed to nod and he took his hand from my mouth. Then he removed his sword and laid it on a small table close at hand. After that . . .

I had known three husbands and also experienced one, enforced love affair. But I had never been raped, never been so utterly unready for congress as I was now. So this, I thought, as he scraped and rasped his way into me, tearing dry and unwilling tissues on the way, was what the queen feared. This invasion, this assault on one's deepest privacy, this ugly pain. I almost did scream, but he saw my mouth open and clamped a hand over it again. The tears poured out of my eyes, down my temples, into my hair. The horror went on and on. When it finally ceased and he withdrew, I was a ruin, a shaking, agonized shell. He stood up and put on his sword again.

'Very satisfactory,' he said. 'You'll never forget that, will you? You have learned now that for a lady, wisdom lies in minding her needlework and her household and leaving men's business alone. Leaving Spain's business alone . . .'

Behind him, the door was flung open. I half sat up, stared in amazement at the man who burst through it, and then collapsed back because I had no strength and every movement hurt.

'And perhaps you will now learn something,' said the voice, most improbably, of Robert Harrison. 'That you cannot attack an English lady in her own home and not pay for it. You had better draw that sword.'

TWENTY-SIX
Settles and Swords

Through a haze of pain and shock and also embarrassment, for my clothes were disarranged and I wasn't too far gone to realize it, through all this, I peered bewilderedly at Robert Harrison. He had cast off his doublet and thrown it into a corner, drawn his sword, and was advancing on de Lacey with what looked like murderous intent. Well, if the pair of them were going to slaughter *each other* . . . I wouldn't object to that.

De Lacey also threw off his doublet but he didn't go for his sword. Instead, he went for the poker, which was still sticking out of the fire. Robert promptly kicked it out of his grasp. 'Draw, damn you, or I'll run you through where you stand!'

Then, all in a moment, the room was full of people. On his way through the house, Robert must have created a stir, for the entire household seemed to be crowding in after him. Adam was first through the door, but behind him came Sybil and Dale, who must have rushed downstairs when they heard the commotion below, and from somewhere or other, Gladys had appeared, and Brockley came last, at a run, breathless and horrified, exclaiming that he had seen Master Harrison arrive and dismount and rush into the house and what in heaven's name was going on here . . .?

'He's trying to fight a duel! Are you out of your mind, man!' Adam shouted at Robert. 'You can't fight in here, it's a parlour, the mistress is present!' He seemed to become suddenly aware of the women at his heels. 'You women, take care of Mistress Stannard! Look at her; she's been attacked!'

They ran to me, crying out.

'Ma'am, what has happened to you . . .?'

'Dale, she's been . . . oh no, oh, Ursula, surely he didn't . . .!'

'Clear enough what the rotten bugger did, look you!'

'De Lacey there raped me,' I said furiously. Anger had come to my rescue. The pain was lessening and the feeling of helpless collapse was passing too. My hammering heart was quietening. I pulled myself upright. Dale was tugging my skirts into decency. 'Ma'am, let us get you to your bed! Can you stand?'

'I want to see this!' I said. 'I want to see that whatever happens, that damned servant of Spain doesn't get away! Don't pull at me like that! Let me stay and see!'

'You let her be.' That was Gladys. 'She wants to see him dead and so would I, if it were me he'd gone for!'

'Who'd go for you, you fanged witch!' De Lacey rounded on Gladys. 'I know who you are; there're those at court who've met you. Been tried for sorcery, haven't you? Witches are heretics. The stake, that's where you'd go if this were Spain, for that's the sort you are, it's plain to see!'

'Here, don't you call me a witch . . .!'

'I'm waiting! I'll count to five!' shouted Robert. He made a threatening movement and all but tripped over a rug. 'Someone get these damned rugs away from our feet; they'll have us skating all over the room!'

Brockley thrust his way past Adam, snatched up the rugs and threw them into the corner on top of the two discarded doublets. Meanwhile, in the interests of self-protection, I heaved myself off the settle and retired to the comparative safety of a window seat. Dale again begged me to come away but I would not, and after a moment, she and Sybil followed me and the three of us sat there, wedged together. Gladys, defiantly, planted herself on the settle and over her shoulder, said: 'You leave her be!' to Dale. 'Time for soothing potions later. She wants to see that man's blood and so do I! Don't you?'

We couldn't have got to the door anyway, because the fight had already begun. Brockley withdrew to the door and there he and Adam stood, side by side, while other people peered from behind them, shocked and agog. The only sounds in the room now were the clash of blades, the shuffle and stamp of the contestants' feet and their snatched breaths as they circled and struck, feinted and struck again.

De Lacey, I thought, was still hoping to get hold of the poker, but Robert knew it and was blocking his way. Leaning forward, I whispered to Gladys: 'Get that poker if you can and put it where de Lacey can't reach it.'

It was a long poker and its handle was always cool enough to touch. Gladys scrambled forward and grabbed it. She handed it back to me. De Lacey swore – in Spanish – but had to attend to his swordplay, for Robert was pressing him hard. He fought back, however, with vigour and skill. He was highly skilled, I could see it, as good at swordsmanship as he was at conjuring tricks. It was an even match. I found myself desperately praying for Robert, even though Robert himself . . . what in God's name was the murderer of Thomas and Eric doing here in my parlour, avenging my honour, and where *had* he come from, all of a sudden, and how?

There was a noise, almost a snarl, from Robert. De Lacey's sword had cut him; blood had flowered on his left upper arm. He shook the arm as though he were trying to shake the pain away, and blood flew, splashing onto the floor. A moment later, he skidded on it, bouncing off the wall behind him.

'Aha!' De Lacey emitted a sound of triumph and his next onslaught drove Robert back to bounce off the wall again. He recovered and lunged forward but he was off balance and lurched sideways. I heard myself whisper: 'Oh, no!' and Gladys muttered something in Welsh that sounded like a curse, and with that, left her seat, hobbled swiftly to the corner where the rugs and the discarded doublets lay, dragged out one of the doublets and threw it at de Lacey's ankles. It entangled his feet and he stumbled, lurching sideways. 'Get him!' Gladys shouted at Robert.

Robert stepped back, lifting his blade aside and waited for his opponent to recover. Helpfully, he kicked the doublet out of the way.

Gladys emitted – or rather, shrieked – a veritable torrent of outrage, mostly in her native Welsh, but the last few words came out in English. 'You fool, you could have had him then!'

Robert, however, merely gave her a quick smile, and then returned to the attack as de Lacey regained his feet. But the incident had disturbed de Lacey's concentration. I was no expert in such matters but I could see that he was fighting now with less assurance, and Robert, who had no doubt used the brief hiatus to draw breath and steady himself, was in the ascendant. I found myself crossing my fingers in the ancient gesture of well-wishing. I was strongly inclined to sympathize with Gladys. I understood the laws of chivalry which had made Robert forgo his advantage, but after the thing that de Lacey had done to me, I didn't feel he was entitled to such consideration. Besides, many years ago, I had myself fixed the outcome of a duel and if I had ever felt any guilt about it, it wasn't for long.

Not that any of this mattered now. De Lacey was tiring. He was losing his nerve. Then came a final slash from Robert's blade and blood was spouting from de Lacey's side, and he was falling, dropping to his knees on the floor and tilting sideways. He drew his knees up towards his chest as though to protect his stomach or to seek comfort from his own warmth. He made a sound like a groan, which rose into a howl, perhaps of pain, but I heard fear and despair in it too, and then it died away and it was all over.

Robert knelt beside him to feel his neck for a pulse and his chest for a heartbeat, and then rose, shaking his head. 'He's gone.' He looked reprovingly at Gladys. 'You shouldn't have done that,' he said.

'Done what?' demanded Gladys belligerently.

'Thrown something at his feet. You distracted him, disturbed his mind and gave me an unfair advantage. That wasn't in accordance with the laws of duelling.'

'Laws of duelling my arse!' said Gladys. 'He'd raped Mistress Stannard, and he was one of they murdering Spanish that want to drag old England back to the days of Bloody Mary and burn everyone that don't agree with them. *Men!*'

Adam said something to Brockley and the two of them stepped forward and heaved de Lacey's body up. 'Best put him in the attic room,' Brockley said. 'We'll have to report this and keep him here till then.'

'I suppose,' I agreed.

I watched them go. Robert was cleaning his sword on the fallen doublet. It was de Lacey's. He looked up from the task and met my eyes. 'You are wondering how I come to be here and why I should come so eagerly to your defence as though I were a hero instead of a monster who murdered a young boy and then a young husband, so as to get my hands on a tin mine?'

'Ma'am,' said Dale anxiously, 'you're hurt. Let us take you to your room.'

'Not yet, Dale. I want to hear what Master Harrison has to say.' I was still badly shaken but because, in fear of the poker, I hadn't struggled, I was not seriously bruised. What had happened to me was not very different from what happened, all too often, to innocent, unprepared young brides at the hands of clumsy and inexperienced young bridegrooms. Mentally, emotionally, the circumstances were not the same – dear God, no! – but the physical results were. It struck me suddenly, that when Harry reached the right age, I would have to find an older man – Brockley, perhaps – to instruct him, perhaps to arrange some kind of initiation for him. I jerked my mind back to Robert and noticed that his arm was still bleeding.

'Gladys, see to Master Harrison's arm!'

My senior maid, Phoebe, who was among the crowd in the doorway, said: 'I'll get warm water,' and vanished towards the kitchen, followed by Gladys. They were back within moments, Phoebe with a steaming basin, Gladys with a jar of ointment. Robert let them attend to him, putting his sword aside and helpfully rolling up his shirtsleeve. While Gladys mopped the cut, which wasn't deep, I said: 'Why were you not seized the moment you stepped ashore in England? There's a warrant out for your arrest!'

'I didn't land where I usually do,' he said. Gladys patted his wound dry, and applied ointment. 'I usually come in to Dover or Southampton. Only this time, I had the chance of a passage on a ship bound from Normandy to Cardiff, and intending to call at the port of Dunster, on the Somerset coast. I took the opportunity. I wanted to get back so as to keep my word and marry my cousin Jane. It was the least I could do for her. When I landed at Dunster, I hired a horse and reached Firtrees in two days. When I got there, I heard all about the warrant, from Mistress Lisa . . .'

'She was willing to see you?'

'Yes. Mother was there at Firtrees. Mistress Lisa and Jane weren't alarmed to see me because she had told them the truth. There were proclamations about the warrant in several places, including Guildford here in Surrey, but not in the West Country, because no one expected me to appear there. That's how I got through unrecognized. But anyway, my father had heard of the Guildford proclamation and he's given himself up and confessed. My mother brought the news to Firtrees. Before Father left,' said Robert, 'he made over Rosmorwen to me, a kind of payment for the trouble he had caused me. Mother had the deeds with her and gave them to me. And before I left Firtrees . . .'

Gladys, having bandaged his arm and pulled his sleeve down, turned her attention to me. 'Maybe Dale's right, you did ought to let us take you upstairs . . .'

'Gladys, be quiet! Phoebe, take that stained water away.'

'Before I left Firtrees,' Robert said doggedly, 'I in turn made Rosmorwen over to Jane. It will make a fine dowry for her; she will be able to pick and choose among prospective husbands. Poor little Jane. She made me a prim, serious speech of thanks, and formal regrets that she could not now proceed with our marriage. In fact, I think she's relieved! After all, she's very young. I'm over twenty years older than she is, as well as actually being her cousin!'

'Your father has confessed?' I said stupidly. Gladys, grumbling, had gone after Phoebe but Dale was still hovering and muttering. I shook my head at her. 'Please explain,' I said. 'Because the warrant was . . . is . . . for you as well as for your father and . . . I don't understand.'

TWENTY-SEVEN
The Haunted Wood

'**M**istress Stannard,' said Robert Harrison, 'I did not murder Jane's brother Thomas, nor did I kill my Uncle Eric. My father did both, and saying that hurts me, more than I can say. At the time when Thomas vanished, my father and I were at the Leatherhead house. After we met when you took shelter there, I had been absent briefly, visiting a couple of customers, but I had returned. The day that Thomas vanished, and for two days before it, Father went out each morning early and returned in the afternoon without telling me where he'd been. Well, why should he? He has his own life and his own purposes; I don't interfere.'

He emitted a short bark of laughter, with a disconcerting flash of those feral molars. 'His own purposes! On the day Thomas went missing, Father was back for dinner and towards evening, a messenger arrived from Aunt Lisa, begging us to come to Firtrees, explaining what had happened. Father and I rushed off at once. Mother was too tired to go riding off anywhere, so she stayed behind, but told us to send news as soon as we could. Father and I helped with the first search and stayed at Firtrees that night. We shared a room. In the night, my father woke me and told me . . . told me . . .'

His voice faltered. I said nothing. I had been injured by one killer and was having to be grateful to – was even being invited to commiserate with – a man who if not a killer had certainly been a killer's assistant. I waited.

'He said,' said Robert, 'that he had killed Thomas. He'd been planning it for days. For three mornings running, he'd been hiding himself and his horse in the fir wood, waiting for a chance to catch Thomas alone. When he saw him come out into the forecourt of the house, he called to him. When Thomas came out into the lane, my father stepped behind him and used his dagger. After that, he carried Thomas' body into the wood as far as he could, but it was heavy work for a man getting on in life . . . Those were his words; that's the way he put it, almost making a joke!'

He paused and swallowed before going on again. 'He put the body down somewhere and found a fallen branch and put that over it. He said he had an instinct to hide it. But he knew it would be found. The wood hadn't been searched immediately as there hadn't been time before nightfall. Everyone had been running about, questioning the villagers and cottagers and the Badgers people and looking in outhouses and so on. But the wood was to be searched next morning. Well, Father said he'd been thinking, and it would be best if Thomas wasn't found at all; if people at least thought it possible that he'd run away. It would be safer for him, he said. But he couldn't think how to get rid of the body and he wanted me to help him. *What could I do?*'

I knew the anguish in his voice was real. It was still there as he said: 'When he first told me, I thought I would have a seizure! I was appalled! I . . . it loosened my bowels; I had to relieve myself in a hurry, before anything else. But all the time, I was thinking, he's my father! I can't let Father hang! He will now, of course – oh, dear God, yes, he will hang! But at least not because I've let him down. I came back to him and sat just staring at him, in the light of a candle. He stared back at me, pleading with me, with his eyes. Then he begged me again to help him. And I remembered the shed where Thomas sometimes hid from his schoolbooks. Ladders were kept there. And when I was stabling my horse, I'd seen a pile of sacks in the grain store. All that gave me an idea. You know what it was. You found the body. Aunt Lisa told me.'

'Yes. You thought of hiding Thomas among high branches,' I said soberly.

'We crept out of the house,' said Robert. 'We took lanterns. Aunt Lisa keeps some on a shelf near the back door. We went to the shed for the ladder. We found a coil of good long rope there and some balls of twine. We took the rope and some of the twine. Then we collected some sacks and went into the wood.'

'But wouldn't some of those these things be missed?' I interrupted. 'And then people would start thinking . . .'

'We took the ladder and the rope back afterwards,' said Robert impatiently, 'and who is going to notice if a ball of twine is missing from a shelf of half a dozen? As for the sacks, does anyone ever count how many sacks there are in a pile?'

'That makes sense,' I admitted.

'Well, we plodded into the wood, carrying it all. God's teeth, what a business that was. I had the sacks and the rope slung across my shoulders and Father had the ball of twine pushed inside his shirt and we carried the ladder between us, him leading the way and me following. That bloody ladder! It was as though it was alive, and wanted to make trouble. It was so heavy and it kept on banging into trees; twice, in the dark, we got confused, tried to pass a tree on different sides and it crashed into the trunk and brought us up short!'

He paused for breath, shaking his head at his memories.

'That wood!' he said. 'I'm not a timid man. In France, I have seen . . . a thing or two. I was in Paris when the Massacre of St Bartholomew's Eve happened. I was supposed to be negotiating a deal with a wealthy customer there, who wanted to arrange regular deliveries of wine. That deal was never made. The customer was a Huguenot. He didn't survive. I saw horrors then that I shall never forget. But after dark, that wood . . .'

Sybil and Dale again interrupted, begging me to come with them and once more, I silenced them. I think that Robert hardly heard them.

'That wood,' he said, 'at night, was terrifying. It felt . . . it felt haunted! There was a full moon, and there were occasional glints of moonlight and it felt as if . . . one of the glints might suddenly turn into Thomas' wraith and advance on us, dripping blood. We wanted to avoid lighting our lanterns but in the end we had to, only they didn't give much light so we still couldn't properly see where we were going. But we did find Thomas's body. We got it into a sack and then into another sack and another and then a fourth.

'If you want to hide a body,' said Robert, with a sudden outburst of grim humour, 'a flock of hungry squawking crows might ruin all your efforts! We just hoped that the four layers of sacking and the clothes the corpse was wearing would be enough to protect it from crows and pine martens and the like. We tied the whole thing round with twine and then fixed the rope round it, leaving one long end; then we put up the ladder, and I took the long end of the rope up the tree and threw it over a high branch and then dragged on it . . . it was just barely long enough. Somehow I hauled the . . . the load up there. I'm strong. It kept banging on branches and knocking bits off them. We cleared the fallen twigs and cones afterwards, as best we could, by lantern light.'

He stopped, looking at me earnestly, seeking signs of comprehension. I said: 'You didn't clear them all. We found some still there.'

'I daresay. As far as I knew, the tree wasn't one likely to be cut down; it was the kind that's tapped for resin. I got the bundle fixed and I got the rope off, and climbed down and eventually we came back and put the ladder and rope back in the shed where we found them. That's when Father admitted to me that he was planning to get rid of Uncle Eric too! You see, he had told me that what he was trying to do was to get hold of the Cornish tin mine and after we got back from . . . from the wood . . . I said to him, what was the point, when it's been left to my uncle! Then he explained. I couldn't believe my ears! I said he mustn't, he just mustn't, Uncle Eric was *his brother*, for the love of God, and anyway, hadn't he frightened himself enough already? And he said that I was now very closely involved with Thomas's death and surely I wouldn't dare to change my mind and betray him!

'*You're planning all this just for a tin mine?* I said to him. *How did all this start?* Well, he answered that. It grew from small beginnings. He knew about the tin mine before he saw Uncle Edmund's papers – Uncle Edmund told him when they met at the Leatherhead house. And that, of course, is when he met Aunt Lisa. You were there, weren't you? That's when he realized about her affair in Cornwall and first got the idea of discrediting her and the twins, in the hope that Edmund would disinherit them. He meant to encourage that! Then everything would come to him eventually, tin mine and all.

Only then Edmund died and Rosmorwen was left to Uncle Eric, and there was talk of going to law to get the twins re-instated, and that's when my father really began to plan.'

'To plan murder,' I said flatly.

'Yes. He defended himself to me. He said that with Thomas gone, there would be no chance of getting Jane reinstated as heiress; Thomas was the one who so resembled Edmund. Anyway, I could marry Jane and make her property mine if need be. Marrying Jane was his idea. And he said I had no idea what poverty meant, but he knew and he'd bitterly resented it; the world owed him recompense. I have always known that he felt like that. He has let things out to me at times – how angry it made him, that other men could make money when he could not, no matter how he tried. The tin mine would make Rosmorwen really valuable, it could be sold for a very good price, but as things stood, though it would eventually revert to us, Uncle Eric was young; he'd outlive my father, and probably me as well.'

'Your father is obsessed!' I said blankly.

'Yes. He's not normal,' said Robert, and his voice now was full of misery. 'You should have heard him, talking about that tin mine and how much Rosmorwen could be sold for. He was excited, waving his arms. He'd never be a poor man again, he said, never, but he wanted, he needed, he *must* lay hands on Rosmorwen; Eric couldn't have it, he mustn't, *he'd* never known what poverty was. *Fate owes me something!* That's what he said. He was . . . he was almost . . . no, not almost, he *was* hysterical! He'd prospered fairly well in Sheffield but all the time it was Mistress Devine's money that was helping him. By the time she died, he'd run right through it and age was telling on him, and his tendency to chest colds; he couldn't work as hard as he used to do and he could see poverty closing in on him again. He said he felt that he'd crawled out of a swamp, only to have Fate put a foot in his face and shove him back. It seemed that those early years of poverty had eaten into him, eaten into his mind, destroyed every vestige of common sense, of . . . of proportion . . .' He stopped, breathless.

'What did you say in answer?' I asked.

'I insisted that he must stop! Of course I did! The idea of doing away with Uncle Eric was intolerable. Finally, he calmed himself, promised that he wouldn't harm Uncle Eric after all. I didn't trust him, though. I wanted to warn Uncle Eric but how could I do that without arousing suspicion against my father, and indeed myself? I worried and worried and in the end I held my peace and decided I would have to trust my father and I soothed my conscience by saying yes, I would marry Jane.'

'So you let your uncle take his chance.'

'Yes, frankly, I did. And prayed Father *would* keep his word. Only he didn't. He went off on what he called a little holiday at sea, for his health, and got himself to Penzance.'

'He had enough money for that, evidently,' I remarked.

'He did have some of his own,' said Robert. 'From his savings and the sale of his stock. But he demanded some from my mother. Said that it was legally his. He battened on her.'

His voice was angry. 'I advised him to go home when he wrote to tell me the straits he was in, but I never thought he would just snatch money from her the way he did! Well, when he decided to confess, for my sake – he's not quite without some human feelings – he told my mother everything and she repeated it all to me when we met at Aunt Lisa's. She was horrified, crying.

'He'd told her that he reached Cornwall before Uncle Eric, and did some reconnoitring. He'd had it in mind from the start, that he might use the mine itself as a trap. He visited the place after dark, twice, and prowled round it with a lantern. He said that straightaway he found a support that would obviously cause a rockfall if it were pulled away. Then he went back to Penzance but kept himself informed by making stealthy visits to Rosmorwen – seeing without being seen, that's how he put it. When he knew that Uncle Eric had arrived, he went back to Penzance again and set to work. He told my mother he'd had good luck, in finding a boy who belonged to a Rosmorwen miner, to take his note to Uncle Eric. He apparently hoped that Uncle's death would be taken for an accident.'

'Only it wasn't,' I said.

Harry had seen the note delivered, and Eric had not destroyed it. Except for those two facts, I thought, the deception just might have worked. Shuddering, I said: 'Your father is a very ruthless man, and so are you, if not quite in the same way.'

'Perhaps. But I am more inclined that he is, to be on . . . didn't I once make a little joke about being on the side of the angels? I am not by nature a criminal. When I speak of being on the side of the angels, I mean celestial beings with wings. My father is on the side of the ones that men made with gold. Perhaps the poverty of his early life isn't the only thing that drives him. He has a hunger for wealth that is apart from that, a natural greed.'

Angrily, I said: 'I don't believe anyone could do what he has done, even if he was . . . was . . . sick in mind . . . unless his nature had in it a strong streak of sheer wickedness!'

'You may be right. But he *is* my father.'

'You love him,' I said.

'No, I don't,' said Robert surprisingly. 'I don't even like him. But as I said, he *is* my father. It matters. Can you not understand, Mistress Stannard? How would you like to think of your father being hanged? Whatever he'd done.'

Such a feat of imagination was beyond me. After all, my father had been Henry the Eighth and he was one to take the lives of others, including two of his own wives. Queen Anne Boleyn had died at his orders; so had poor little Catherine Howard, who had been faithless, yes – which Queen Anne probably hadn't – but was hardly more than a child, a young girl who should never have been sought in marriage by a gross, diseased, ageing man. Everyone at court knew her story and many outside the court, too. Had I ever known King Henry, I think I would have feared rather than loved him. Had he, too, had a streak of wickedness in his nature? Or had he just been pitiful, deluded, still believing himself capable of holding the love of a young girl; still able to provide England with further princes, since the one he had was not strong? I didn't know. The thought of him sometimes made me shudder.

And yet, he *was* my father. I had had reason, once or twice, to remember that I was a king's daughter, so as to stiffen my backbone in times of danger. I suspected that Elizabeth sometimes did the same thing. Both of us knew the bond of father and daughter. I could partly understand Robert Harrison, though not entirely. A quality that should have been there in his tale seemed to be absent. He had suffered from shock, that was clear enough, but real horror, genuine recoil, genuine loathing, were oddly missing. He had been willing to . . . to *touch*, to involve himself directly, physically, with the monstrous thing his father had done. I didn't know what to make of that.

I wrenched my wandering thoughts back to Robert, who was still talking.

'I have tried to protect him. Now I too will give myself up; I may as well, for I shall be arrested anyway. As for why I am here, well, before I surrender myself, I wanted you to know the truth. From the first time we met, I have . . . liked you. I wish to stand well in your eyes. I didn't like thinking that you believed me to be a heartless killer. I was appalled when I rode into your courtyard and one of the grooms told me that Antoine de Lacey was with you! I am happy that I arrived in time to avenge you, though sorry that I was not here just a little sooner.'

I said: 'Brockley and I found Thomas's body. There was a button from your doublet, caught in the sacking. I recognized it.'

'I lost the button while I was up that tree,' said Robert. 'All the result of my mother's excellent cooking.'

Perhaps, then, the hateful image of Thomas, in terror, fighting for his life, was wrong. Perhaps he had died at once. I hoped so.

'I was suspicious of you before that,' I said. 'The button only confirmed – appeared to confirm – what I already thought.'

'Oh? What made you suspicious?'

'Your offer to marry Jane. It was as though you were already certain that Thomas was dead. But you couldn't have been, unless . . .'

'I see. Sharp of you, Mistress Stannard! Well, Jane can forget me now, but she has Rosmorwen and with me and Father out of the way, Aunt Lisa may be able to get the rest of Edmund's estate for her after all. There must be plenty of people willing to swear that her twin brother was the image of Edmund and was therefore presumably his lawful son – which would make Jane his lawful daughter. Anyway, she should find a good husband easily, and he won't be a cousin. Cousins shouldn't wed. I'll go now, Mistress Stannard. Your women are longing to take care of you.'

He gave the fretting Sybil, the indignant Dale and the glowering Gladys a smile that embraced all three of them.

'And so they should,' he said, 'for you have had a night-mare experience. When I give myself up, I will explain how the corpse that has just been removed from this room to your attic came to die at my hands. It will clear you of any guilt. Have no fear. Now, I shall leave your house, and leave you to be cared for as you need to be. Goodbye.'

He kissed my hand before he went. Then Dale and Sybil took me away and before long I had been put into a warm bath, my skin lovingly and kindly washed free of the contamin-ation of de Lacey's body, and then I was dried and helped to my bed and Gladys came with one of her potions, to help me to sleep. By the next day, I was not much the worse, except for the horror of the memory. That would haunt me for the rest of my life and I would have to teach myself not to think about it. It had happened, I said to myself, but it was now in the past.

Or so I thought.

TWENTY-EIGHT
The Coveted Gift

It wasn't fair. It wasn't *reasonable.* After just one, enforced union, I surely couldn't be . . . sheer arithmetic was against it. It was so unlikely. It couldn't be. It couldn't . . . It couldn't!

It was seventeen days since de Lacey's attack on me. Three days ago, I should have begun a course. I had not. Dale had noticed. 'Ma'am, I'm worried about you.' She stood in my bedchamber, her arms full of items for the washtub, looking at me anxiously. 'You're three days late, aren't you? You've not taken any of the clean cloths that were in the drawer ready for you. You're never late as a rule. It might be just shock, I suppose, I mean, you're not . . . not a young girl . . .'

'No, I'm in my forties and when women are in their forties, their systems do sometimes become disturbed. Let's hope it's just that and I'll get over it and go back to normal quite soon.'

'But if it isn't, ma'am . . .'

'I don't know what I'll do, Dale. I really don't know.'

I did, though. Improbable though this whole situation was, it was still *possible* and I had decided what to do if necessary. I despatched Dale to attend to the laundry, and then, once she was busy down in the stone-floored room we used on washing day, working with Phoebe and Tessie, who dealt with Harry's things, in a welter of steam and splashing water, I fetched Gladys to my bedchamber and said shortly: 'I'm overdue, Gladys. By about three days. It may be no more than shock but if it isn't . . . I will not bear a child to that man de Lacey. I *will not.* Can you help?'

'Look you, I wouldn't recommend any woman past forty to bear a child to anyone,' said Gladys. 'Not you, not the queen. Oh yes, I know all about what's going on at court; got it from Dale. Clean crazy, that's what it is, risking her life at her age. Should of got an heir ten years back if she wanted one that much. Nice state of affairs it'll be if we end up burying a queen what's been good to us, and go sticking a crown on the head of an infant in a cradle. It'll fall down over its ears and it'll squall and burp – a pretty coronation *that'll* be . . .!'

'Gladys, please! We're not talking about the queen. We're talking about me.'

'Yes, I know and yes, I'll help but we'd best make sure first. You been sick at all? Felt funny?'

'No. I haven't.'

'Could be just that what he did's made you shut down, as if you was a business that's stopped trading. There's a bit of time in hand. See how it goes for another week or whatever. Meanwhile, I'll get the right things together. Pennyroyal . . . I got some dried leaves in store. Girls from the village come asking now and then . . .'

'Gladys, if you've been breaking the law, I don't want to know. Isn't pennyroyal dangerous?'

'Can be, but I know how much to use. I ain't killed no one yet. And you're a fine one to talk about breaking the law, seein' you've just asked me to!'

'I know. And it doesn't matter even if it is dangerous,' I said wearily. 'I'd rather die than have de Lacey's bastard. But no one is to know. If we have to use it, then you get rid of your supplies, do you hear me? If anything happens to me, it's nothing to do with *you*. Understand?'

'Aye, aye. I understand. I ain't a fool. Meanwhile, you'd best go riding. Nothing like a bounce on a horse for outwitting nature.'

As it happened, the prescribed bounce became obligatory the very next day, when a messenger from Walsingham arrived at Hawkswood. I was commanded to present myself in his office at Richmond, forthwith. I left the next morning.

As before, I took Brockley, with Dale behind him, and Eddie as the groom. The messenger, who was a stranger to me, had orders to escort me and therefore rode with us as well. He was a stern, unsmiling man and not very agreeable company, and was visibly irritated by the presence of Dale, because a pillion rider always slows a party down. However, we went as fast as we could and reached Richmond in the early afternoon.

I was to have my usual rooms, the messenger said, but there was no time for me to go to them and wash and change before seeing Sir Francis; I was to attend on him immediately. He made this announcement while we were all getting off our horses, and I had to leave the Brockleys and Eddie to their own devices, while I followed our unfriendly escort into the palace, through the maze of passages and galleries and narrow stairs, to Walsingham's office.

There, the messenger handed me over to a clerk and disappeared, his duty done. The clerk too was solemn of face, and so was Walsingham's secretary, who came out of the main office as soon as the clerk announced me and walked past me without even glancing at me. I went in and the clerk closed the door after me, leaving me alone with his master.

It was like being alone with a thunderstorm. He was seated at his desk, apparently calm, but when he looked up at me, his dark eyes were so angry that they resembled glowing coals. Angry men had been my portion lately, I thought. First de Lacey and now Walsingham. Well, Walsingham could be relied on not to attack me physically. I stood where I was and said: 'You wished to see me, Sir Francis?'

'No,' said Walsingham grimly. 'As a matter of fact, I would like never to see you again, except perhaps with your head on a block.'

'What?' I blurted it out but he didn't reply. He just stared at me with those angry eyes and I wondered wildly if he meant what he said. Panic ran through me. Was I about to be arrested? But if so, why? 'What have I done?' I asked tremulously.

This time he did answer. 'You ignored my express orders. I told you to leave the matter of the Harrisons alone. But did you? No, you did not. Full of self-righteousness and believing that you know best, you went straight from me to the queen, and told her everything. Things I and Lord Burghley had most carefully kept from her, so that we could retain the services of the best agent this court has ever known. Have you had any letters from Janus recently?'

'From Janus?' I was wrong-footed by the apparent non sequitur. 'No, I haven't, but . . .'

'Well, you wouldn't. Because Janus is in the Tower. Robert

Harrison is in the Tower. Robert Harrison is Janus, you stupid woman. His wine-growing employer in France was well paid, by me, to provide him with a position that looked respectable, but also required him to travel, ostensibly to see customers, in reality, to carry out his secret duties.'

'But Robert Harrison can't be Janus!' I protested. 'One of the letters I had from Janus arrived while Harrison was in England! It was just after Thomas disappeared. Janus was supposed to be in France!'

'Robert Harrison is usually in France,' Walsingham agreed. 'He was however in England when his nephew vanished, and while he was here he did a little travelling, apparently to call on some of his employer's English customers. In fact, he was following up a lead connected with the scheme he had got wind of – to damage the queen in some way and put a stop to the Alençon marriage plans.'

'So he sent the letter from somewhere in England?'

'From London. He was actually looking for the family of Spanish sympathizers who later on sheltered Antoine de Lacey after he escaped from us. We have picked up the family now – two half-Spanish brothers and the wife of one of them. They are in the Tower as well.'

'I see,' I said, bemusedly.

'George Harrison is the man who murdered the boy Thomas and also Master Lake,' Walsingham said, 'but Robert helped his father to conceal what he had done. He seems to have done that because Robert Harrison is a good son. He is also a *brilliant* agent. He has a network of contacts, some of whom don't know how they are being used; and he doesn't flinch from doing whatever may need to be done, for the protection of England.'

'Indeed!' I said. *Whatever may need to be done.* Now I could understand why a natural level of horror and recoil had been absent from his account of his father's iniquities. As an agent, he must have gambled with his own life and that of others; from the sound of it, he was prepared if necessary to take lives directly. He was inured to killing.

'He has done more,' Walsingham was saying, 'than any other agent I have ever known to outwit the queen's enemies, thwart their plans, *learn* their plans, and report his findings to us. Before he came back to England this last time, he had uncovered the fact that de Lacey was Spain's agent here, entrusted with the task of wrecking the chances of the queen's marriage by creating a scandal. There seems little doubt that the sorry events at the dinner in the Castle Inn were de Lacey's doing. Probably Jean de Simier's illness was his doing as well, and he no doubt encouraged the rumours that my lord of Leicester was responsible.'

'I see,' I said.

'When you came and told me that you had evidence that Robert Harrison had been involved in a murder, yes, I was shocked. But for the sake of keeping Janus in the field, I would have let it go. Even if it meant letting George Harrison go as well. Janus is – was – *that* valuable. Now that I know that in fact Robert was *not* personally responsible for murdering anyone, I feel that even more strongly. The queen, however, doesn't agree! She says we are never to employ Janus again. He is an accessory to a crime, a heinous crime, she says. I pointed out to her that he was but an accessory and that out of loyalty to a parent. But there is no reasoning with her! She can be very obstinate.'

It was known that on occasion the queen had thrown things at Walsingham. It occurred to me that at times he probably yearned to throw things at the queen.

He had paused, visibly fuming, but now he burst out: '*Why* couldn't you do as you were bid? You just *had* to go and reveal his – Robert's – guilt to her majesty, and this is what comes of it. She will not wink at the murder of her subjects, she says, not for any reason. That, she says, is the sort of thing her cousin Mary of Scotland might do – almost certainly did do, over the murder of her husband Lord Darnley – but Elizabeth will have no part of it.'

I steadied myself. However furious Walsingham might be, he would be hard put to it to claim that I had committed a crime of any kind. I was not really likely to find myself faced with the block. 'I agree with the queen, Sir Francis.'

'I daresay. I expected nothing different from you.'

He had been holding a quill pen in his fingers. Now he

threw it down on the desk and pushed his chair back, violently. 'Many of us on the Council are uneasy about the queen's marriage plans but as well you know, we don't want them disturbed by the ruin of her reputation. Janus was her protector; one of the best we have ever had. And now! Well, George Harrison will be tried soon and he will assuredly hang, unless he dies first. He seems to have a lung complaint. He is in a common prison. Robert Harrison, by the queen's orders and because I pleaded for him – she did listen to me to that extent – is in the Tower, though in reasonably comfortable conditions. He will appear at the trial alongside his father but the queen has already decided that finally he will be returned to the Tower for as long as it pleases her, and privately she has said to me and my lord Burghley that she will release him after a year or so. But she will never agree to his reinstatement as one of her agents. You, my dear Ursula, have blindfolded England, put plugs of wax in her ears, tied her hands. Are you pleased with yourself?'

'I am sorry,' I said.

'It's too late for that. Please go away now. The queen does not know that I have sent for you, and I don't wish you to see her. You may stay at Richmond overnight. You will remain in your rooms and your meals will be brought to you. Tomorrow morning, you will return home and stay there and henceforth keep out of affairs of state.'

'And if the queen should summon me herself, at any time?'

'Then you will have to obey, of course.' Walsingham snorted with exasperation. 'That is another matter.'

I said slowly: 'She may do so – if and when the Duke of Alençon returns. She will probably ask me to . . . to stiffen her resolve to proceed with the marriage. I don't want to anger you again, sir. What would you wish me to say to her, if she does call on me?'

The fury faded from his eyes at last. 'Dissuade her if you can. It is possible for treaties to be ratified and kept, without the help of marriages. Without hazarding the lives of queens. Only, the scheme must be ended *without scandal.*' He leant back, and his face sank into lines of tiredness and, I thought, of pain. He was probably having an attack of the gripes.

'She is half in love with Alençon,' he said. 'Such things have no place in affairs of state, but they still happen, especially when a woman is concerned. If she summons you, try, as I said, to dissuade her. Otherwise, be good enough to *stay out* of the business of government, and spare us all your simple-minded womanly ideas of morality. The queen is the queen and that must be accepted but I find your presence in affairs of state decidedly annoying.

'I have no doubt,' he added, in a sudden echo of the Harrisons, 'that you see yourself as being on the side of the angels. No doubt the queen thinks the same about herself. Real statesmen have to be a little more subtle. Lord Burghley feels as I do. You disobeyed him as well as me. Now go away. I wish never to see or hear from you again.'

He picked up a small gavel from his desk and rapped loudly with it. His secretary at once reappeared. 'See Mistress Stannard to her suite,' said Walsingham. He picked up his quill again and seemed to immerse himself in his work at once. Silently, chastened, I followed the secretary out of the room.

Something odd was happening to me. My legs felt shaky and a dull pain had started in my lower abdomen. The secretary left me at the door of my suite and once inside, I went straight to my bedchamber and examined myself. Then I called Dale.

'Dale, I've come on.'

'Oh, what a relief if you have, ma'am! Thank God!'

I have never known whether I was only suffering from the shock of what de Lacey had done to me, or whether I had really conceived by him. I am inclined to think that I had. The course that I had started was unnaturally heavy, was accompanied by extremely violent cramps and made me unwell for days, which never happened as a rule. But the danger of pregnancy was over now, without the help of Gladys' illegal and possibly dangerous potions after all.

I was too unwell to leave the court the following morning, but three days later, feeling better, I set out for home. Walsingham might be furious with me, but if that meant that I would henceforth be left alone and not repeatedly dragged from my home to undertake alarming tasks for the state, it wasn't such a bad thing. Walsingham's outrage, I thought with wry amusement, had done well by me. I could go back to Hawkswood and take up my life there and be happy. Before being called back to court, I had made some enquiries and decided that Master John Hewitt, who had tutored the daughters of a lady I knew, would be suitable as a tutor for Harry, and the first thing I would do once I was home would be to write to him. After that . . .

I spent much of the ride mulling over the pleasant times to come.

On the way, we once more had an escort in the shape of a Queen's Messenger, but this was pleasant, too, because it was Christopher Spelton, bound on one of his regular journeys to deliver and collect correspondence from somewhere in Kent. And, of course intending to call on Mistress Kate Lake on the way.

'Another visit of condolence?' I asked him.

'Yes. Offering advice and help if she needs them, and to get her used to me,' said Spelton, grinning. 'To train her, if you like, to *rely* on me.'

'Good luck to you both,' I said. 'I mean that with all my heart.'

I meant what I said. A quiet life at Hawkswood was what I desired most of all. Yes, I had received a gift that I had coveted for a long, long time and hoped to keep.

Unless, of course, the queen had need, once again, of my support. She was in love, yet she was still afraid of love and she had her reasons.

I understood them. I too was afraid, and for her.

9 781780 295800